# CRIME AT HOME

A fiercely addictive crime thriller

CATHERINE MOLONEY

*Detective Markham Mystery Book 8*

JOFFE BOOKS

First published in Great Britain 2020
Joffe Books, London
www.joffebooks.com





**Join our mailing list for free Kindle books and new releases.**

ISBN 978-1-78931-396-3

*For Ma and Percy.*

# PROLOGUE

Shona Townley had to admit she quite enjoyed the build-up to Christmas even though, at sixteen and a half, she affected profound indifference. Seriously uncool to look like you bought into all the cheesiness. But she liked seeing gaudy decorations appear in the town centre and little market stalls pop up in the unlikeliest places. And things were more chilled at school. It was obvious the teachers switched off the nearer it got to breaking up for the holidays. Out came the 'fun' quizzes and DVDs, though officially they were supposed to be hard at it right up until the end of term. Well, bollocks to that . . .

The only cloud on Shona's horizon was her volunteering, or 'community service' as they called it at Hope Academy. She'd skived last week and felt bad about it. Mrs Bussell was a nice old biddy who'd taught history at Hope. Whenever Shona came visiting, she always got the tea and bickies out. Sometimes there was cake as well. And it was a laugh hearing her talk about what Hope was like in the olden days. All the staff wore batman gowns (come to think of it, Doctor Abernathy still did), and it was dead formal with prayers every morning. Nowadays there was just one assembly a week — usually Mindfulness or some rubbish like that — and most sixth formers didn't bother with it. Apparently, the teachers smoked like chimneys back then and went down the pub at dinnertime — not like the current lot, always banging on about 'healthy living' and 'emotional housekeeping'. It gave Shona a headache.

But community service was okay. Better than camping and shivering in fields like they did in other schools. She got to sit indoors and have a chat with the old folk. She quite enjoyed it, though it wouldn't do to say so.

Which brought her back to Mrs Marian Bussell. Shona had skipped their session last Monday afternoon in favour of Costa and a catch-up with the gang from Medway High. Told herself she'd swing by later in the week but somehow never got round to it.

Shona bit her lip. The old lady would have been looking forward to that cuppa and a natter. She had the feeling Mrs Bussell was lonely. There weren't any pictures of family in her ground-floor flat and she never mentioned her husband so he must be dead . . .

The sensation of guilt intensified. Mrs Bussell wouldn't snitch on her to school, but that only made it worse. She vowed to stay twice as long this time round, make it up to her somehow. And next week she'd bring some of her mum's mince pies and a prezzie. Maybe she could even lend a hand decorating the flat . . . there was that much tinsel at Hope, they were drowning in the stuff.

Slightly out of breath (*too many Quality Streets*, she told herself grimly), Shona rounded the corner into New College Close, a mixture of three-storey stone-fronted terraced flats and townhouses, which curved round a communal garden. Alright if you liked that sort of thing, she supposed, but not exactly cutting edge. Mind you, it looked picture-postcard in the snow — everything white and fleecy and perfect. There were no tracks other than hers this quiet Sunday afternoon and nothing stirred save for a little robin redbreast hopping in front of the frosted bushes. The sight of him made her feel quite poetical. Her spirits rose. Mum always said it was lucky to see one of them.

It would be okay, she told herself. Mrs B was bound to appreciate her coming round in her free time (on a weekend!). Maybe there'd be some more stories about Hope. She'd mentioned keeping a scrapbook or album. Perhaps there'd be something in there she could use for that social history project she was supposed to be doing in general studies.

It was getting a bit nippy now the sun was going in, gilding the white landscape with vermilion shafts. Shona took a last appreciative survey of the garden. Much nicer than the undercroft car park and bins round the back with the lonely playing fields behind them (the college to which the development owed its name being long gone).

New College Close was much posher than Shona's estate in Medway on the other side of Bromgrove. No ghetto blasters blaring. No kids skateboarding, smoking and squabbling. No doors banging off their hinges while adults bickered and bellyached. No druggies and smackheads. But she knew which she preferred. The Close was somehow too quiet, and she'd never clapped eyes on any of the neighbours — apart from once in the garden when she saw a man in a wheelchair talking to some bloke who looked like a vicar (any road, he was wearing one of those white collar thingies). It was the kind of place where folk most likely kept themselves to themselves and didn't go butting in. They were retired people and professional types . . . genteel — yes, that was the word for it. But somehow not very friendly.

Mrs Bussell lived in number seven, a ground-floor flat in the corner terrace. Number eight, on the other side of the communal hallway, was for sale and currently empty. The door into the building was generally propped open during the daytime for deliveries and visitors. Otherwise it was left on the snib. Apparently, some residents had complained about the lack of security, but the management company didn't want to know. 'We could be murdered in our beds before they'd get off their backsides,' was her elderly friend's frequent complaint.

The entrance lobby had a dank, musty kind of smell which made Shona wrinkle her nose disdainfully. Wouldn't hurt to give it a spritz with some air freshener, she thought. As it was, you half expected to see mushrooms growing out of the walls. With the price of these flats, you'd think they'd want to give a better impression.

To her surprise, she noticed that the door to number seven was slightly ajar and, for the first time, felt a stirring of unease.

That wasn't like Mrs Bussell. She was paranoid about security. Always said you couldn't be too careful these days. Even when she knew it was Shona, there was the click of the deadbolt and her eye at the spyhole.

Now that Shona thought about it, she remembered that Mrs Bussell had seemed twitchy the last time she visited — nervous — as though something was bugging her, the watery gaze skittering from side to side, as if she suspected someone might be hiding in the walls. Losing her marbles, poor old thing, Shona had thought at the time. But now she wondered, had the old lady been *afraid* . . . ?

Shona felt an overpowering reluctance to go into the flat on her own.

Perhaps she should have telephoned before coming. What if now wasn't a good time?

But she couldn't just slope off — Mrs Bussell might be in there sick or injured for all she knew.

'Mrs B,' she called in a voice quite unlike her usual chirpy tones. 'Mrs B, it's Shona. Y'know, Shona from Hope . . .'

Silence.

She licked lips that were suddenly dry. 'Er, I'm sorry I didn't come last week. Something came up . . . but I c'n stay for my tea today.'

Still no response.

Nervously, she pushed the door open and went in.

It was a compact apartment. Two bedrooms — one a box room really, which Mrs Bussell used as a study — living room, galley kitchen and minuscule bathroom. Laminated wooden flooring throughout gave the flat a modern, streamlined feel that was somewhat counteracted by all the knick-knacks and ornaments clustered on every available surface. A nightmare to dust, as her mum would have said. There was no separate dining room, but Mrs Bussell generally took her meals on a tray in front of the large flat-screen TV, an arrangement of which her youthful visitor thoroughly approved.

The living room's heavy damask curtains were drawn back, but white lace nets beneath screened the interior from the rear courtyard. Pity she didn't have a garden view, thought Shona inconsequentially before padding softly through the flat.

Everything seemed pretty much as usual.

Except for the smell.

She'd noticed it even at the front door. Really knocked you back. Sweet and almost *fishy*.

Shona was used to number seven being fusty. The central heating was usually on full blast. Could give Center Parcs a run for their money, as she told her mum. But today the radiators were stone cold.

No, this was something else. Something that made the chips from lunchtime roil and churn uneasily inside her. Taking shallow breaths through her mouth, she went into the master bedroom whose main window also overlooked the rear of the close. A funny little porthole on one side of the room offered a view of Bromgrove Old Road, along which she had just trudged.

Here, too, nothing looked out of place. Simple oak chest and dresser. Pine wardrobe. The ottoman sleigh bed, of which Mrs Bussell was so proud, dominated the room, mattress raised high on its wooden storage plinth. Shona couldn't see that it was anything to write home about. Personally, she'd have preferred a waterbed for comfort. That vast box reminded her of a coffin.

A coffin.

The smell seemed to be getting stronger. Like when she'd found two dead cats on the estate. God, it was putrid.

The girl suddenly became aware that her hands were slick with sweat. She felt as though the walls were closing in on her.

She lurched to the casement window and, after some mad fumbling, wrenched it open. Cold, clear air poured into the room and she gulped it down gratefully.

Afterwards, she told her mum it was as if everything happened in slow motion and she was looking down on the bedroom from above. 'I had to see inside that wooden box,' she said, 'but it didn't feel real — like I went somewhere else in my mind.'

Instinctively, she reached for the gas-lift lever which raised the neatly upholstered mattress away from its wooden platform. As though in a trance, she heard Mrs Bussell's confiding tones. 'You get so much more storage with one of these.'

*Oh God. So much more storage.*

Lying on their backs, hand in hand in the base of the bed in an obscene parody of romantic bliss, were Marian Bussell and another woman she had never seen before. She would never forget those shrivelled semi-mummified remains — the half-open eyes, opaque and filmy in death, and mouths slightly agape as though stopped up mid-scream.

The stench of death was now overpowering, blocking her throat and nostrils.

Shona knew only that she had to get out and stumbled blindly back through the living room towards the door. Once outside, she had an insane desire to lie down in the freezing snow, as though to decontaminate herself.

And then suddenly the spell was broken and she began to cry.

# 1. BAD OMEN

Like Shona Townley, DI Gilbert 'Gil' Markham had a bit of a thing for snow.

At 6 a.m. on the morning of Monday, 9 December, he sat on 'his' bench round the back of Bromgrove Police Station, heedless of the damp seeping through his overcoat, lost in wonder at the sight of the filmy skeins which had turned St Chad's cemetery and the neighbouring Hollingrove Park into a filigree wonderland. For entirely different reasons than Shona, he too had a sudden urge to lie down in that inviting powdery whiteness and make snow angels as though he was a child once more. He could just imagine the reaction of DCI Sidney (or 'Slimy Sid' as his boss had been christened by the rank and file) were he to be caught in that particular act. The DCI would be only too happy to file away such symptoms of galloping eccentricity with a view to exploiting them at Markham's next appraisal.

The DI, too, saw a robin redbreast, the little creature contemplating him shyly from behind the cemetery railings. 'They symbolize the souls of the dead,' his girlfriend Olivia Mullen was wont to tell him — as if Markham could ever forget them! Sometimes it felt as though wherever he went he was stalked by a legion of shadowy figures, dense as the carpet of leaves that covered the park at the first frosts of winter. He could imagine them pleading with him for justice in sibilant whispers.

And now two more were added to that ghostly roster.

Despite the cold of the morning, his forehead prickled with sweat as he recalled the appalling discovery at New College Close.

Even the pathologist Doug 'Dimples' Davidson had struggled for composure at the sight of those two figures entombed in the base of Marian Bussell's ottoman bed. It was one of the few times Markham had seen him lost for words.

'Mother of God,' he breathed finally. 'What kind of sick bastard does this?'

'How long have they been in there, doc?' As ever, DS George Noakes had cut to the chase, swallowing hard as he peered down at the ghastly leathery faces fixed in their rictuses of terror.

'Possibly some days.'

'An' they died of suffocation — is that it?'

'Asphyxiation seems the most likely bet. Though they were probably slipped a sedative or something of that kind to make them . . . more pliable.'

Noakes looked as though he was going to be sick and Markham didn't feel much better. Despite the freezing air pouring into the flat from the open bedroom window, waves of nausea swept over him.

The DI had a phobia about confined spaces, the legacy of an abusive stepfather who used to lock him and his brother in the cupboard under the stairs. He offered up a wordless prayer for the sibling he'd long since lost to drink and drugs. At least Jon had been spared the sexual predations that Gil himself had been unable to escape.

'What's the white-haired one got in her hand?' Noakes wanted clues.

Using tweezers, the pathologist's gloved hands prised a small object from the claw-like grasp.

It was a cheap enamel school badge.

'That's Hope Academy.' The DS squinted at the trinket. 'Yeah . . . my Natalie had one like that — tole me the bird on the front's meant to be a phoenix, summat about rising up an' renewing yourself — used to be the school motto until they started with them trendy slogans . . . like polishing a turd's gonna make any difference.'

'They call it "aspirational branding" these days, Sergeant,' Davidson observed mildly. He could tell Noakes was badly shaken and the rant was his safety valve.

'D'you think when they came round they held hands to . . . well . . . comfort each other?' Noakes's voice was hoarse. 'Christ . . . d'you think they were lying there all that time jus' whispering to each other in the dark, knowing no one was gonna come an' get them out . . . ?'

It was a terrible thought. One that had also occurred to the hysterical teenager who greeted them at the scene.

'I was supposed to come last week,' she sobbed, her pert little face swollen and distorted with grief. 'If I'd come when I was supposed to, maybe they wouldn't have died.'

The pathologist was what they called a 'dry old stick' down at the station, but even he had softened in the face of Shona's overwhelming distress.

'Don't take on so, m' dear,' he said gruffly. 'We don't know exactly what happened here. Whoever did this wanted them to be found.' *Eventually*.

'Took a chance though, didn't he?' Noakes observed after the distraught girl had been escorted away by a family liaison officer. 'I mean, he couldn't be sure someone wouldn't turn up, wouldn't clock the stench an' raise the alarm.'

'Oh, I'd say he was fairly confident about that, Sergeant. Knew Mrs Bussell's routine, had likely watched these flats for some time . . . Didn't you say the one across the hall's unoccupied — for sale?'

'Yeah.' The DS was thoughtful. 'That flash git from the management company said on the second floor it's a couple of PhD students an' a lecturer. They've broken up for holidays so likely gone home for Christmas.' Noakes's tone made it abundantly clear what he thought of the 'dossy' set-up that prevailed at Bromgrove University.

'Well, there you go: ideal from the killer's point of view.' The pathologist contemplated the two bodies in their improvised coffin. 'Mark my words, he had it all figured out.'

'What about on the third floor?' As ever, Noakes was stubbornly determined to have the last word. 'I mean, they must've noticed summat was up . . . the freaking awful smell for one thing . . .'

Markham consulted a piece of paper. 'Retirees on both sides. Don't get out much according to the management. Wouldn't necessarily have been alerted.'

'So this block's coffin-dodger central, right?' groused the DS.

'We'll have less of that thank you, Sergeant.' But Markham spoke mildly. Like Dimples, he could see his subordinate was thoroughly unnerved. And indeed, this whole scenario was unlike anything in his experience.

*Two bodies immured in an air-tight tomb behind the net curtains of a perfectly ordinary flat in a perfectly ordinary housing complex.*

As though the shadow of Edgar Allan Poe had suddenly fallen across this quiet corner of Bromgrove.

Even after the pitiful remains — rigid as carvings on a medieval catafalque — had been stretchered away under the pathologist's supervision, leaving a team of SOCOs to commence their silent rituals, a pall hung over the apartment.

'Who's the second vic?' Noakes enquired as they stood awkwardly in the living room.

'Her name's Dawn MacAlinden. Nurse at the Newman.' The DI referred to the psychiatric facility, situated in the quiet suburb of Medway, that had featured in previous investigations.

The DS's pug-like features were a picture of dismay.

'*Uh-oh*, here we chuffing well go . . . That means Sidney'll be mad keen to pin this on a nutter.'

There was no denying it, the DCI being legendarily predisposed to lay all social ills at the door of the 'mentally deranged'. Not least because this made it considerably less likely that any civic institution (including the local constabulary) would be tainted by association.

'Mrs Bussell was a retired teacher from Hope.'

'*Not again!*' Noakes scowled ferociously. Like the Newman Hospital, the local comprehensive had featured heavily in earlier cases.

'Ms MacAlinden was one of her former students.' The DS's gloom deepened at Markham's words. 'She lived at number twenty-seven — same kind of flat as this one — on the other side of the garden.'

'Fuck.' The DS looked alarmed. 'D'you reckon we'd better get over there and check the place out?' He forced a nervous laugh. 'See there ain't anything lurking under her bed . . . as in one of the neighbours!'

'Take it easy, Noakes,' the DI chaffed him. 'I've got uniforms on it. But I don't think there's some Crippen lookalike marauding round the close.' He looked round him. 'No. This was a one-off . . . very deliberately planned and executed.' He shivered. 'There's real evil here.'

'But . . . I mean . . . what could them two women have done that was so bad?' Noakes's bewilderment was palpable. 'You heard that lass Sheila—'

'Shona.'

'Whatever.' The DS ploughed on. 'You could tell she really liked the old woman . . . "Mrs B wouldn't hurt a fly," that's what she said.'

'Well *someone* bore her a grudge, Sergeant.'

'Mebbe it was really the other one he was after . . . Dawn Wasserface . . .'

'How do you mean?'

'Well, mebbe *she* was the target an' Mrs B got in the way so the killer had to finish her off while he was at it . . . collateral damage, like.'

Markham shook his head. 'Far easier to dispatch Ms MacAlinden in her own flat or some time when she was on her own. Anything else would involve unnecessary . . . mess.'

He shivered again. 'And this killer is the opposite of messy.' His voice softened. 'I know it's hard to take in, Noakes, but whoever it was wanted to kill them *both*.'

The DI's thoughts strayed again to those recumbent figures on the stretcher as they began their supine voyage to the mortuary. Suddenly, he found he could hardly bear to think of the pathologist probing that desiccated flesh. The ultimate indignity.

'This was all so calculated . . . so *deliberate*,' he said slowly. 'It may even be that he purposely posed them hand in hand like that.'

Noakes's normally beefy complexion looked almost green in the winter light.

'*Jesus*,' he muttered, looking at Markham with a kind of desperation in his eyes. 'It was bad enough imagining them lying in the dark clutching at each other so they wouldn't . . . die alone.' He loosened his shirt collar with a vicious wrench. 'But the idea of some sicko *arranging* 'em like that . . . *Jesus*.'

Normally Markham loathed profanity, but on this occasion he decided to cut the DS some slack. 'Yes,' he replied quietly, 'we're dealing with someone peculiarly wicked here.' He glanced at the other's stricken face. 'Try not to dwell on it, Noakesy.' Futile advice. 'All of this is just my theory. For all we know, it could have happened like you said and they reached for each other at the end.'

They moved into the hallway.

Noakes screwed up his face, much like Shona had done a short time earlier.

'Bit manky out here,' he grunted, sniffing the air. 'Kind of a fertilizer smell . . .'

'I believe the residents and management are somewhat at loggerheads over exorbitant service charges. Laneside — they're the facilities people — plan to spruce up the communal areas.'

'Well, they need to get a chuffing move on . . . folk don' want *eau de compost* when they come to visit.' The DS looked rather pleased with himself for this sally.

'Helped mask the odour of decomposition, though,' Markham mused. 'From our killer's point of view, it was very useful.'

On that sobering note, they left the building.

* * *

The DI shook himself. He couldn't lurk on this bench forever but felt curiously reluctant to stir despite the cold. The pristine snowy landscape looked newly baptized, which somehow made the discovery at New College Close even uglier.

As he emerged from the lift into CID, he heard a familiar voice uplifted in complaint.

'You'd think they could do better'n that poxy tree. We oughta have a decent one . . . proper deccies an' all . . . like them chocolate Santas.'

'You know you'd only scoff them, sarge,' came the reply followed by a gale of laughter.

Markham grinned, his spirits lifting.

The Christmas season, or 'Crimbo' as the DS called it, was Noakes's favourite time of year, during which he always offered ample testimony to the 'eternal child in every man'. Having come through a health scare earlier in the year, he was clearly anticipating the annual blow-out with bacchanalian relish.

The DI knew only too well that the mere presence of George Noakes at his side brought Sidney and the gold-braid mob out in hives. 'Uncouth', 'ignorant', 'insubordinate', 'slobbish' and 'walking time bomb' were some of the kinder epithets that he had heard bandied about. What was said behind closed doors or committed to those 'confidential reports' in HR didn't bear thinking about. Certainly his refusal to cut Noakes loose was bound to count against him when his appraisal came round. He could hear Sidney's nasal honk now. 'Holding you back, Markham . . . creates an unfortunate impression . . . out of step with modern policing

. . . diversity . . . minorities . . . time for a new broom.' Yadda yadda yadda.

But the DS was one of Markham's non-negotiables. The handsome, hawkish DI with his seemingly impenetrable reserve repelled many of those in CID. But he and Noakes shared a subterranean understanding that existed at a level beyond words. They rarely shared personal confidences, but he knew the grizzled warhorse had somehow intuited the trauma of his early years and understood the scars this had left . . . And that was the thing about Noakes. The slobbish exterior and tactlessness concealed an unexpected wellspring of sensitivity which meant he instinctively knew how to handle *people*, be they hardened villains, inarticulate teenagers or traumatized victims. However deficient he might be in those attributes so prized by Sidney and the CID honchos — silver-tongued diplomacy and adroit politically correct antennae — he had a humanity that meant he never dropped a clanger with those in crisis, somehow making them feel that the muddle of their lives was safe with him.

Markham's girlfriend twitted him about his 'bromance' with Noakes, but he knew she, too, had a soft spot for the big lumbering DS. And despite Noakes's much-vaunted contempt for 'arty-farty types', he had fallen hook, line and sinker for flame-haired Olivia's willowy charms and happily listened to her witty repartee with an attentive devotion to match any medieval troubadour. 'A voice like music,' he'd say when his bossy wife Muriel taxed him with this misty-eyed reverence. 'Like when they sing in the cathedral.' To which 'the missus' responded with a brittle laugh. Noakes was fiercely loyal to his overbearing other half, but on some issues he would not be budged and she had learned to tread carefully where Olivia Mullen was concerned. 'She's bewitched my husband,' Mrs Noakes pronounced to members of the Women's Guild, with a long-suffering air calculated to convey the impression that charity precluded any confidences on the subject of conniving hussies. Privately, she consoled herself with the reflection that her husband's boss — whose cultivation and handsome looks caused something of a flutter in the redoubtable lady's breast — was being cruelly imposed upon but would no doubt come to his senses in time.

Outside work, Noakes was a keen ballroom dancer, being surprisingly light on his feet for all his bulk. To watch him cha-chaing and fishtailing as if his life depended on it was to realize he possessed hidden depths. Not that his pursuit of the county glitterball was likely to raise him in DCI Sidney's esteem.

As he listened to the DS holding forth to his captive audience in the outer office, Markham resolved anew to resist any defenestration of his team at all costs. George Noakes was his wingman and that was that. Having been in many tight corners with him, he knew he could trust the other with his life. The man was family.

Lingering in the corridor, the DI's thoughts turned to the other two members of his team, or 'Markham's gang' as they had been resentfully dubbed.

DS Kate Burton should have taken her Inspector's exams by now but showed no inclination to leave him. 'Joined at the hip,' as Sidney put it in his unpleasantly insinuating way. 'Looks like you're a habit the lady just can't break.'

Burton was Noakes's polar opposite. Smart as a new pin where the other was a sartorial disaster, she had faced a struggle to join the force due to parental resistance ('no job for a woman' had been her father's initial response), eventually joining CID by way of a degree in psychology. Earnest, diligent and decidedly right-on (or 'tree hugger' as Noakes put it), the combination of Burton and her fellow DS had got off to a distinctly rocky start. Over time, however, a wary truce had broken out, with Burton learning to give as good as she got and exhibiting a certain dry humour in the process. Gradually too, Noakes came to appreciate her tenacity, doggedness and loyalty to their DI, whose meteoric rise in CID and natural hauteur meant he was by no means beloved by all. Markham's bagman had long since guessed that Burton carried a torch for her boss but never betrayed her secret, watching compassionately as she wrestled with her feelings before finally getting engaged to a stolid and unexciting DS in Fraud. The DI had no idea of Burton's ever having looked in his direction. The possibility simply never crossed his mind, though Olivia had intuited the hopeless infatuation. Like Noakes, she said nothing.

Though he might not have picked up on any romantic signals, Markham valued Burton's professionalism and physical courage — neither of which had been found wanting. He sensed also that Kate Burton was wistfully envious of the easy rapport that existed between himself and Noakes and yearned to gate-crash the party. With the start of this new investigation, he silently vowed to ensure she had her full share of the action.

The final member of the unit was DC Doyle, or the 'ginger ninja' as he was affectionately known on account of being a gangling carrot-top. Keen to get ahead, he was currently midway through a distance-learning degree in criminal law. Where his sessions down the pub with Noakes had once revolved around football and matters of the heart, he was now quite as likely to ask the latter to quiz him on PACE or other esoterica from the law enforcement training manual. 'Worse than bleeding *Mastermind*,' the older man grumbled, but Markham could tell he was secretly pluming himself on his newly acquired role of academic mentor.

Yes, he and his team — the 'Four Musketeers' as Olivia called them — would crack this case, though it promised to be more daunting than any they had yet encountered.

*Two bodies. Two women: one middle-aged, one elderly. Two neighbours.*

In the case of Mrs Marian Bussell there was no next of kin to be notified. Dawn MacAlinden's husband, a customer service manager at Bestway Cash and Carry, had collapsed when Markham and Noakes broke the news of his wife's death and had to be sedated. At least there were no children to compound the misery.

'Poor bugger jus' didn't take it in,' said the DS afterwards, looking badly in need of a stiff drink. 'Seemed to think it must've been some kind of accident.'

Better by far the bereaved husband should believe the entombment was random happenstance than have to confront a refinement of cruelty that had left seasoned detectives speechless.

The DI squared his shoulders and took a deep, steadying breath.

Time to get the briefing underway.

The hunt for a killer had begun.

## 2. THE CAST ASSEMBLED

'There you go, folks.' DC Doyle was characteristically upbeat. 'An espresso for you, sir. Then we've got a soy caramel macchiato plus a gingerbread and cream hot chocolate. And a decaf cappuccino for me.'

The DI shot Noakes a quizzical look.

'Gingerbread and cream hot chocolate, Sergeant. Correct me if I'm wrong, but aren't you meant to be on a health kick?'

'Cutting out treats jus' encourages cravings.' The other's response was suspiciously glib. 'Anyway, I've got quinine an' salad . . . the missus does me a packed lunch, see.'

Markham's lips twitched. 'I believe that's *quinoa*, Noakes. Foodies go wild for it.'

'Whatever,' the other said gloomily. 'Looks like a pile of bird droppings to me.'

DS Kate Burton made a strangled sound, as though her macchiato had gone down the wrong way, while Doyle grinned at her discomfort.

As ever, Burton and Doyle looked dapper — suited and booted as behoved ambitious young detectives keen to make their mark in CID. Noakes, by contrast, would not have been out of place in a remake of *Moby-Dick*, sporting some sort of fisherman's gansey topped by a mustard wind-slicker that finished halfway up his back. A truly hideous bobble hat decorated with capering reindeer completed the ensemble, though he now rolled this into a ball and stuffed it into the back pocket of a pair of baggy oatmeal cords that had clearly seen better days.

Mercifully there was no risk of the DCI joining them, since he was sequestered in a breakfast meeting with Superintendent Bretherton. Markham shuddered to think how he would react to Noakes's Captain Ahab look . . . but with any luck the team would be safely out of the station before Slimy Sid came prowling.

Burton smoothed her brunette bob into place, took a pristine pocketbook from her leather satchel and whipped on a pair of rimless reading glasses which magnified her eyes, transforming them into huge brown lollipops. Her button-nosed face turned towards the DI with an air of alert intelligence.

Doyle and Noakes exchanged wry glances.

*Scary.*

'Right,' the DI said. 'Let's get on with it.'

Carefully and succinctly, he talked Burton and Doyle through the events of the previous day.

'*Two bodies.*' Doyle was having difficulty taking it in. '*Under a bed* . . . I mean,' he struggled to visualize it, 'where would they *fit*?'

Markham came to his rescue. 'I believe they call them sleigh beds, Constable. Old-fashioned and ornate . . . often come with large bases . . . wooden and very heavy.'

'There was a case of some woman in America who was kidnapped and kept locked under a bed for years,' said Burton, her tone preoccupied. 'It was a husband and wife who took her. They were in it together — sort of brainwashed her, so when they let her out from time to time she was too frightened to run away.'

'Wow.' Doyle was intrigued. 'She got away in the end, right?'

'Oh, it went on for years. Sometimes she was locked in the box under the bed for twenty-three hours at a time. But eventually the wife cracked and turned her husband in.' She blinked owlishly. 'The point is, it's perfectly possible to imprison someone under a bed.'

'Dimples thinks they were most likely put there some time on Thursday evening—'

'After the killer slipped 'em a Mickey Finn or summat.'

'Correct, Sergeant.'

'When did they come round, then?' Doyle was pale beneath his freckles.

'The doc thinks a few hours later.'

'*Christ.*' The young DC's complexion was milk-bottle white. 'And they weren't found till Sunday . . .'

'Dimples is doing the PM this morning, but unofficially he thinks Mrs Bussell — the older lady — suffered a cardiac arrest soon after she came round.'

'What about the other one?' Burton's voice sounded small and lost.

'Asphyxiation and shock, but he can't be sure about the time frame till later.'

'So she lay next to her friend's corpse and suffocated.'

'That's the most likely scenario, Constable.'

'Too frightened to cry out in case she used up oxygen. *Fucking hell—*' The DC suddenly realized what he'd said and flushed to the roots of his hair. 'Sorry, sir.'

'That's alright, Doyle.' The DI's face was grim. 'An unimaginably horrible way to die . . . Self-locking steel hasps made it impossible to escape. Though, from the condition of the younger lady's fingernails, it would appear that she tried.'

'And no one had a clue?' Doyle's voice was the merest thread, and he looked like he had lost all enthusiasm for his frothy cappuccino.

'It sounds almost incredible, but in that block of flats it's just retirees — pretty much housebound — and some university people who'd already broken up for the holidays.'

'Plus the hallway was all scruffy an' smelly cos the management company couldn't be arsed to look after the place,' put in Noakes. 'The walls were rank . . . like they had fungus growing on 'em. With it being like that, folk likely wouldn't have noticed any extra stink for a while.'

Burton wanted to get off the subject of decomposition. 'Were there any signs of a struggle, sir?'

'No, Kate. I'd say Mrs Bussell knew the killer. There was no indication the place had been turned over.'

'He'd put a school badge in her hand.' Noakes prepared to enjoy the effect of this revelation on the other two.

'*What! A badge! Which school?*' they burst out, practically in unison.

'Hope Academy,' the DS told them with lugubrious relish. 'You might know that place'd turn up again like a bad penny.'

'Mrs Bussell taught history there,' Markham clarified. 'And Dawn MacAlinden was one of her former pupils as well as being a neighbour.'

'Guess where MacAlinden worked?' Noakes's triumphant expression alerted the other two to the fact that the coincidences were not yet at an end. 'Yeah, that's right . . . the pigging *Newman Hospital*. Like we haven't seen enough of that shithole to last a lifetime!'

Burton could be quite prissy about language, but when she recollected the history of the team's association with the Bromgrove psychiatric facility, she was obliged to concede that 'shithole' pretty well summed it up. Lightning couldn't strike twice in the same place, could it?

'You said they were found holding hands, sir?'

'That's right, Kate.'

'As in *posed* . . . ?'

'It's possible the murderer was making a point, yes.' Markham's keen grey eyes were steady on her face. 'Or it could be that they reached out for each other.'

Silence fell on the little group. From the outer office came sounds of boisterous whooping and cheering. *Prob'ly one of the lads messing about with that mistletoe*, Noakes thought, brightening momentarily. DI Chris Carstairs hoping to strike lucky with the blonde bird from Vice . . .

Burton's voice jerked him back to reality.

'Any likely suspects yet, sir?'

'I've drawn up a list of residents we need to interview as soon as possible,' the DI said, handing each of them a photocopied sheet.

'On the side nearest to Bromgrove Old Road the close has two blocks of flats, with six apartments in each spread over three floors,' he continued. 'Then there are six town houses and, facing towards Chapel Street, a further two blocks with five flats on two floors.'

'That's a lot of people.' Doyle was dismayed.

'I've narrowed it down.'

Noakes looked sharply at the boss. So Markham had gone door-to-door with the woodentops last night after sending him home, which explained the violet shadows under his eyes. *Typical*, the DS thought, with reluctant admiration.

'There are twenty-eight addresses,' the DI said. 'But a significant number are rented to postgrads and staff from the university — the majority of whom are away from Bromgrove for Christmas. Then there are several retired couples where serious health issues would appear to preclude any murderous enterprise. Of course, this is not to say we won't be checking out *all* the residents, but thanks to the university and social services, we can rule out a fair number.' He paused, raking his thick dark hair impatiently, a characteristic mannerism at times of extreme fatigue. '*These* are the names I want to focus on,' he continued, gesturing to the list he had given them.

'Did they know the victims, sir?'

'They were members of the Residents' Association along with Mrs Bussell and Ms MacAlinden, which strikes me as a useful starting point, Kate.' He smiled at her kindly. 'Also, I believe they all had contact with the victims in varying degrees.'

His team scrutinized the list.

'So, first up we've got Brian and Eileen Ledwidge. Retired vicar and his wife. Then there's Penny Callaghan—'

'She's that weirdy woman from the council,' Noakes interjected. 'Almighty pain in the arse. Never stops banging on about equal opportunities an' diversity.'

Burton looked as though she was about to say something then thought better of it.

'Correct, Sergeant. Though I think we'll stick to "Councillor Callaghan" as opposed to "pain in the arse", if you don't mind.'

'Sure, guv,' the other replied sheepishly.

'Jeff Coleman's a retired writer — Mills & Boon, apparently.'

'Hey, I recognize *that* name.' Noakes was quite excited. 'The missus is allus getting his books outa the library.'

Markham suppressed a grin. He suspected Muriel Noakes would prefer not to have it known that the writer of *The Panting Savage* and *Between the Covers* was her go-to author, as opposed to the Pulitzer Prize-winning variety.

'Is that so, Sergeant? I look forward to consulting with her in due course.'

'Coleman's in a wheelchair, ain't he, guv?'

'That's right, Noakes, though I don't have the full background on his medical condition.'

He returned to his notes.

'Simon Gailey's a retired solicitor. Doctor Lucy O'Connor works as a registrar at the Newman. Her partner Martin Henley is a staff nurse there. I believe he's also had some input into the delivery of mental health and wellbeing at Hope Academy.'

There was an audible groan from Noakes. *Not that bloody school again*!

'Then we've got Stacey Macmillan — middle-aged neighbour, divorced, used to work in the newsagent's round the corner. Kenneth Dowell, retired psychologist from The Anchorage.'

'Christ, this is like freaking déjà vu,' muttered Noakes balefully.

'Yep, I know, Noakesy.' His boss's tone was mild. 'Ghosts of cases past and all that.' The coincidences were starting to feel eerie, his team remembering only too well the role the private psychotherapy centre had played in an earlier investigation. 'You'll just have to approach this investigation with a clean slate,' he added bracingly.

The DS grunted and returned to slurping up the last of his hot chocolate. Burton's face wore a distinctly pained expression, but she had long learned to avert her eyes from Noakes's matutinal rituals. She supposed it could have been worse. Doyle could have brought burgers . . .

'Mary Atkins,' she ruminated, returning to the list. 'That name rings a bell . . . Doesn't she work at Hope?'

'Correct, Kate.' There was a mischievous glint in the DI's tired eyes as he added, 'Noakes and I had the pleasure of consulting with her during the community centre case.'

Noakes's thunderous expression at this piece of information would have done Captain Ahab proud.

'Oh, gimme a break!' he exploded. Seeing Doyle's interrogative glance, he explained, 'She's that assistant head from Hope — fat bird — ever so *caring*.' He made it sound like a communicable disease.

The DC smirked. 'Got off on the wrong foot with her did you, sarge?'

'She's one of them clipboard johnnies — dead smarmy, talks bullshit like you wouldn't believe . . .'

'Ms Atkins is typical of the new breed of school leader,' Markham said reasonably. Then, with a hint of steel, 'Not to everyone's taste, granted—' There was a muffled expletive from Noakes. 'But no doubt in a position to give us a good deal of useful information.'

'Yeah,' came the riposte, delivered with a sly grin. 'Got the feeling she wouldn't mind a one-on-one with *you*, guv.'

Burton didn't doubt this was true. Women tended to fall like ninepins before the handsome DI's lethal blend of old-world courtesy and reserved charm. But no one ever got past first base. Markham had an air of untouchability that enveloped him like an invisible forcefield. Only with Olivia Mullen did his guard come down.

Abruptly, Burton registered the gleam of lascivious speculation in Noakes's eye.

'What about the last name on the list, sir?' she enquired, keen to turn the discussion away from Markham's sexual magnetism. 'Julian Hoskinson?'

'I believe he runs a charity shop in the town centre . . . also a committed fundraiser for various community projects: environment, wildlife, LGBT and the like.'

Noakes looked as though his day couldn't get much worse, activists and tree huggers being guaranteed to bring him out in a rash.

'What's the plan then, guv?'

The DI consulted his papers.

'I want Kate and Doyle to set up an incident room in the management company's office — it's a little bungalow to the rear of the complex, next to the car park. You need to report to Gary Coslett from Laneside Properties. He'll get you sorted with keys and anything else you need. Requisition whatever technical support you need from CID. I'll clear everything with the DCI in due course.'

Burton felt a little wistful. That meant the DI would be doing an initial recce with Noakes. Then she gave herself a mental shake. Admin and practical stuff were her forte whereas spreadsheets and computers were anathema to her fellow DS. It was a miracle he ever squeaked through his annual appraisal given his dogged resistance to all forms of technical innovation. But that was likely down to some fancy footwork on Markham's part. His cast-iron loyalty to CID's resident pachyderm was unfathomable, but as yet no one had yet succeeded in shoehorning Noakes out of the department.

'Never fear, Kate. You'll get your chance at interviewing.' She blushed at the ease with which the DI had read her thoughts, self-consciously shuffling pocketbook and reading glasses back into the smart leather satchel to hide her confusion.

'You too, Doyle.' Markham's austere features held genuine affection. 'We need to throw everything we've got at this case.'

'What about the DCI, sir?'

'I believe he's in meetings for most of today,' came the bland reply. 'But of course I'll be briefing him as soon as the opportunity arises.' Mentally the DI resolved to square things with Sidney's long-suffering PA, Miss Peabody. For all her resemblance to a dormouse or some other diminutive creature, past favours meant she could be counted on to run interference and keep Sidney off his back. At least for the time being, while he got the lie of the land.

'What's New College Close like, sir?'

'Well, Kate, at the moment it looks pretty magical blanketed in snow. Picture-postcard in fact.' He produced some photographs from a folder. 'These are some estate agent's particulars, just to give you an idea.'

'Hmm . . . quite nice,' she said, contemplating yellow stucco walls and quirky porthole windows which gave the terraced cement properties a cosy feel. 'Looks like it's been done up recently,' she continued, taking in the trim window facings and concentric terracotta tiles radiating out from the portholes.

'Lemme see.' Noakes lurched to his feet and peered over her shoulder. 'Yeah, not bad . . . decent garden too. Mind,' he said beadily, 'the hallways in them flats are another story — right tatty, if you ask me.'

'True,' Markham agreed. 'Some of the communal areas *are* on the dingy side. The place is a mixture of rental and privately owned properties with some social housing, which may account for issues in terms of facilities management.' Crisply, he added, 'That's something I'd like you to go through with Mr Coslett, Kate. See what tensions may have arisen on the estate.'

'You don't think this is summat to do with a neighbour's vendetta do you, guv.'

Noakes plonked himself back down, rasping his bristly chin. 'Rolling pins at dawn . . .'

'Unlikely, Sergeant, but we need to explore all eventualities.'

'Coslett's a twat an' no mistake,' the DS observed.

'Would that be a term of art, Sergeant?'

The other grinned. 'C'mon, boss . . . reckon you didn't take to him neither.'

The DI recalled the facility manager's ferrety features and sharp-elbowed manner.

'Well, he was definitely spivvish, but in fairness to the man it was a godawful shock . . . two women found entombed like that.'

Burton shivered. 'Buried alive,' she mused. 'Everyone's worst nightmare.'

'Didn't the Victorians have safety coffins and things?'

Noakes stared at Doyle.

'*Safety coffins*?'

'Yeah, sarge.' The young DC was animated. 'Folk were so scared about being buried alive that they had strings attached to their bodies. The strings were connected to bells above ground. If the bells rang, it meant they were still alive.'

'Chuffing Nora.'

Doyle was pleased with the effect he had produced.

'Straight up, sarge. They used stuff like glass panels too . . . you know, to check if there was condensation from some-one's breath.'

'Freaking paranoid, if you ask me.'

'Well they weren't so advanced back then. Couldn't be sure the medicos would get it right.'

'Dawn MacAlinden tried to scratch her way out,' put in Burton, recalling them to the matter at hand.

They fell silent once again. The outer office was quiet now, sounds of revelry having subsided. Beyond the DI's window, with its unrivalled view of the station car park, large cottony snowflakes swirled and drifted against pewter skies.

'Feels all wrong, don't it?' Noakes said finally. 'Happiest time of the year — "Mistletoe and Wine" an' all that . . . Then two dead women turn up under a bed.' He scratched angrily at his head, causing frowsy tufts to spring upright like so many spines on a stickleback. 'I mean, what harm did they ever do to anyone? Jus' two harmless old biddies having a nice cup of tea an' a bit of a chat . . . an' next minute it's Hammer House of Horror.'

'The answer lies somewhere in their past, Sergeant,' Markham said decisively. 'Highly unlikely this a random attack.' His mouth twisted. No need to add, *whatever the DCI may think*.

'Are we gonna start the interviews today, guv?'

'I've arranged to call on Mr and Mrs Ledwidge first, Noakes.'

'The padre?'

'That's right.' Markham stifled a yawn. 'Apparently, Mrs Bussell was quite friendly with them. Brian Ledwidge has some pull with the current incumbent of St James's Church—'

'That sooty-looking building at the bottom of Chapel Street?'

'The very same, Sergeant. They've agreed we can use the church hall for interviews — hopefully sometime this afternoon. Anyone we don't manage to see today will be on the list for first thing tomorrow morning.'

'Any point checking in with Dawn MacAlinden's husband, sir?'

'You can try, Kate, but I doubt he's fit to be interviewed. See what the GP says.' He sighed at the recollection of the sandy-haired little man's devastation. 'I want you and Doyle to prepare preliminary profiles on the victims ready for tomorrow.'

'You don' think . . . well, they couldn't have been . . . I mean, it's not likely they were . . .' Noakes's face was brick red.

The DI gazed at him in mystification.

'Spit it out, Sergeant.'

'The killer wouldn't have been trying to say they were *involved* . . . in a relationship, like . . . what with them holding hands an' that . . . ?' Suddenly the cynosure of three pairs of eyes, he became even more tongue-tied. 'It's jus' that after the last investigation . . . there's nowt so queer as folk . . .' Realizing what he had said, the DS turned even redder.

Time to put him out of his misery.

'Ah, I see your point, Sergeant,' Markham said levelly. 'Quite right. We definitely need to be sensitive to the full sexual spectrum.'

Noakes's colour subsided, his complexion reverting from full-on coronary to its usual corned-beef hue.

Doyle was more nonchalant. 'It's not likely though, is it, sir? I mean, they'd have been well past that kind of thing, wouldn't they?'

Oh, the casual cruelty of youth.

'I don't think we can make any assumptions at this stage, Constable,' the DI said gently, to Noakes's evident gratification. 'Right, you and Kate can shoot off now. Any problems with Gary Coslett, just ring my mobile. Noakes and I will take the Ledwidges, then round up as many residents as possible for interviews. Get the incident room set up and join us at the church hall as soon as you can.'

Saluting smartly, the pair hastened to comply.

Left alone, Markham and Noakes contemplated each other across the DI's desk.

'This one's got you worried, guv.'

It was a statement.

'And then some, Noakes.' The DI crossed to the window and stared bleakly across the station car park. 'It was the sense back there in Marian Bussell's flat of someone deriving exquisite pleasure from that ghastly tableau, like some sort of wicked impresario. Revelling in the thought of them fermenting in the dark . . . toughened like cured meat . . . mummified for us to find.'

'Yeah.' The DS nodded his massive head. 'He musta known we'd find 'em . . . No amount of Febreze'd get rid of that pong.'

'They were like those bog bodies they dug out of the peat . . . but somehow fleshy,' Markham shuddered, 'with a half-digested look as if the maggots had got started on them.'

It occurred to Noakes that there was such a thing as having too much imagination. The half-formed request to swing by Greggs for a breakfast roll died on his lips.

The DI was still locked in his own morbid reflections. Unable to indulge his feelings in front of Burton and Doyle, he knew he could safely let down the portcullis with Noakes.

'I'll never forget those twisted faces, Noakes,' he muttered. 'God knows what agonies they must have endured at the end.'

'He wanted 'em to suffer alright . . . but,' the DS asked with honest perplexity, 'what could they have done that was so bad they had to die like that . . . ?'

*A secret in their past . . . a crime . . . an unavenged wrong . . .*

The DI shook his head as though to dispel the murk from his vision.

'Whatever it is,' he said determinedly, 'we're going to drag it into the light.'

He turned from the window. 'Come on,' he said. 'Let's be on our way.'

# 3. STIRRINGS

Even though it was mid-morning, the day was overcast, almost dark. But the snow was satisfyingly 'deep and crisp and even'. A small gaggle of students playing truant from one of the local schools were happily engaged in throwing snowballs at unsuspecting pedestrians and drivers but swiftly dispersed as the two detectives crunched across the car park. Normally Noakes would have read them the riot act, but the festive season had rendered him uncharacteristically benign and he merely grunted before unlocking his battered saloon with the usual muttering about missing ice scrapers and broken demisters.

Eventually they were underway, though at the pace of a funeral cortège given the state of the roads. The portable car heater belched out a steady stream of heat, creating a passable cosy fug.

'Won't you be wanting to speak to that lass who found the bodies, guv?'

'Good point, Noakes . . . Shona, wasn't it?'

He recalled the teenager's damp blotched face and desperate distress.

'Poor little bint,' the other said ruminatively. 'Kept banging on about seeing a robin or summat an' it being a sign of good luck . . . sounded a bit delirious.'

Markham remembered her poignant desperation.

'She'd spotted a robin redbreast in the garden,' he said sadly, remembering the sighting by St Chad's cemetery and his own very different interpretation. *Dies irae, dies illa.*

'Oh aye,' said his DS, unconscious of the other's dark reflections. 'Cute little fellas. Nothing beats one of 'em on a Christmas card. Mind, the missus says it's a scandal the way there aren't any proper religious ones in the shops . . . she wants a crib an' shepherds an' kings, the full monty . . . otherwise she says it's disrespectful . . .'

Thinking of the depressing procession of whey-faced Madonnas and clayey Infants he had received from Muriel Noakes in past years — 'Botticelli or bust', as Olivia put it irreverently — Markham couldn't help but feel there was something to be said for a nice, secular robin redbreast.

'Good kid that Shona,' Noakes continued. 'Sounded like she got on well with the old lady.' A frown darkened his features. 'My Nat said community service wasn't much cop an' she allus got the grumpy ones.'

Pneumatic, perma-tanned Natalie Noakes — a twenty-year-old beautician ('she felt university was overrated,' Muriel pronounced after less than stellar A level results) — was the apple of her doting father's eye. Doyenne of Bromgrove's less salubrious nightclubs, it was difficult to imagine her selflessly dispensing good cheer to the town's geriatric community. Her tastes ran in another direction entirely.

'Mind you, these days they prob'ly match 'em up better,' Noakes added. 'An' it's not compulsory like it used to be . . . so it's only the kids who really like that sort of thing end up doing it . . .'

'As you say, it sounded like she'd definitely formed a bond with Mrs Bussell . . . Enjoyed hearing her talk about what Hope was like "in olden times".'

'A sight better than what it is now,' the DS groused. 'I jus' can't be doing with all the PC bollocks an' management crip crap. I mean, listening to that Atkins woman, it's like she's speaking some foreign language. D'you remember what she was like in the community centre case, guv?' He broke into a shrill falsetto comically at odds with his normal guttural rumble. '"We have to give children ownership of their emotions and avoid binary thinking." What the bleeding hell does that mean? In my day, you jus' got on with it an' none of this namby-pamby stuff . . .' The DS didn't add, *It made me the man I am today*, but the words hung in the air.

Avoiding the well-worn theme of a terminal decline in educational standards, Markham observed, 'You'll just have to grin and bear it, Noakesy. What happened almost certainly has its roots in Mrs Bussell's past, including her teaching career. Ms Atkins could be a useful conduit for information, so we don't want to alienate her.'

'But where does MacAlinden fit in, then?' As the car skidded slightly, Noakes cursed the gritters in colourful language before returning to the fray. 'She was a student at Hope an' Mrs B used to teach her, right?'

'Correct.'

'So were the pair of 'em up to summat dodgy in them days or what . . . ? I mean, how did they manage to piss someone off so badly he decided to bury 'em alive?'

'Your guess is as good as mine, Sergeant.' Markham gazed at the blanketed landscape, once more feeling the ache to lie down in its chill, compacted ice. 'We don't know whether they were killed for something that happened at Hope or later after they had both left. It might have nothing to do with the school, but it's a coincidence that both women were there and I—'

'Don' like coincidences,' Noakes finished for him.

'Precisely.'

They were now approaching New College Close.

'If you head round the back, we should be able to park there,' Markham instructed. 'There's one of those unadopted lanes at the rear — Beech Drive, I think it is — and then you've got the playing fields behind.'

'It's a wonder the council hasn't snaffled 'em for development,' the DS said. 'Y'know . . . more flats or shops . . .'

'I believe there's an arrangement with various local schools for them to use those fields for sport and extra-curricular activities.'

'Smoking an' doing drugs more like,' Noakes muttered. His boss wisely chose not to hear.

* * *

The parking area was situated at the bottom of a fairly steep slope next to the undercroft ('For Residents Only').

As they pulled in, they were surprised to see a little knot of people, muffled up against the freezing temperatures, outside the modest bungalow to the right of the undercroft. Burton and Doyle were there too, along with a bored-looking Gary Coslett. There was some arm-waving and the sound of raised voices before an upright silver-haired figure shepherded the group away.

'What was all that about?' the DI enquired once they were back inside Laneside's HQ.

'Well they're angry, innit?' Coslett volunteered.

'Why might that be, sir?' Markham felt a strong antipathy towards the weaselly young man, whose close-set pebble-like eyes bore an expression of resentment and distrust.

'Feel the police aren't keeping them *informed* for one thing.'

'And for another?' growled Noakes.

'They want to know about extra security, police patrols,' the facilities manager replied, with a wary eye on the sergeant, who bore more than a passing resemblance to a distempered, dishevelled gorilla. 'With a murderer on the loose, it's about protection, right?'

'To deal with your first point, Mr Coslett, there will be a press conference shortly,' the DI replied stonily. Though God knew, residents were unlikely to find Sidney's preferred *modus operandi* — pinning it all on some crazed psychopath — particularly reassuring. 'We aren't currently in a position to say more than that two residents have been found dead underneath a bed in circumstances that we regard as suspicious. To speculate at this point would be irresponsible and might cause panic.'

'But look here, Inspector — we're talking serial killer, right?'

'I'll thank you not to bandy such terms about in my hearing, Mr Coslett.' Markham's voice was chillier than a Siberian wind. 'As things stand, we are dealing with *two* victims and awaiting the results of a post-mortem. This is not,' he added scathingly, '*The Amityville Horror*, and sensationalism can only cause distress to Dawn MacAlinden's widower.'

'Yeah, save it for the pub, mate.'

Noakes hoped Coslett would try and start something. Give him an excuse to deck the tosser.

But the DS was doomed to disappointment. The facilities manager merely muttered, 'What about extra security then?'

'There will be thrice-nightly patrols, Mr Coslett.' Sidney would go ape about the overtime, but there was no avoiding it. 'Added to which, I will be arranging a discreet uniformed presence in the close this week to ensure residents aren't pestered by journalists.'

'Or murdered in their beds more like.'

Markham ignored the sarcasm, deciding it was time to take the fight to the enemy. 'And what, pray, does Laneside propose to do for the residents' security and comfort?' The DI's tones were silky smooth but deadly. 'I understand there's been some . . . dissatisfaction over maintenance and repair.'

'The communal areas,' Burton put in helpfully.

'That's being attended to,' came the sulky response.

'You need new locks, buzzers — the whole caboodle, mate.' Noakes was starting to enjoy himself.

'Like I said, the company's on it.'

'Glad to hear it, Mr Coslett. You can rest assured I'll be taking a keen interest in progress.'

Markham allowed a moment for this to sink in, noting wryly that his interlocutor looked less than thrilled at the prospect.

'Right,' he said briskly. 'Have we got an incident room set up?'

'In the back, sir.' Burton pointed to a smaller annexe leading out of the room in which they were standing. Clearly the front room, wallpapered and carpeted in utilitarian grey rattan, was where Gary Coslett spent most of his time, with a ratty green sofa bed, television-cum-DVD atop a pine dresser, kettle and fridge comprising the essential creature comforts along with a large *Playboy* calendar at which Burton had already directed several disapproving glances. Box sets of various Scandinavian thrillers — *Wallander*, *The Bridge*, *The Missing* — littered a coffee table in front of the sofa.

'I like to keep the office stuff separate,' Coslett said defensively.

'Of course,' Markham said smoothly, accompanying his colleagues into the other room which had a desk, computer, phone line, heavily scarred oak table, gunmetal filing cabinet and four conference chairs that had seen better days. He was pleased to see Burton had already pinned up her trusty magic whiteboard and begun organizing files and paperwork into her customary neat piles. It was rather a cramped space — the gangling Doyle was already falling over his feet — and somewhat dispiriting with its blue flock wallpaper and cheap beige carpeting, but it would do. At least the radiators seemed to be working, so they wouldn't freeze.

'Have you got everything you need, Kate?' he said jovially, loud enough for their surly host, who was lurking in the other room, to hear. 'If not, I'm sure Mr Coslett will be able to help.'

She grinned. 'Mr Coslett's vacating the bungalow for the duration, sir — to give us a free run. He'll check in with us every day, though, to maintain continuity for the residents — a reassuring presence.'

Noakes rolled his eyes.

As there seemed nothing else to say, they re-joined Coslett.

'Where's the bog?' Noakes demanded. 'Or is it a Portaloo?'

'Round the side.' Coslett glowered at him. 'The lean-to.'

More mildewed cupboard than lean-to, Markham opined. He decided to dispense with a sanitary inspection.

'Do you have a visitors' log, Mr Coslett?' the DI asked.

'Not as such.'

'Why not?' Markham's glance was sharper than a skewer. 'I would have thought with security being somewhat . . . lax . . . and so many residents being senior citizens, you would want to keep a record — tradespeople, service engineers, deliveries and so forth.'

'Things kinda worked out without any need to sign people in and out. I'd get a call if there was a problem.'

'Only you didn't. Get a call.' His words came out flinty. 'Two women were murdered in Marian Bussell's flat and the alarm wasn't raised until days later.'

'Obviously our systems failed,' the other blustered.

'No, *you failed*, Mr Coslett.' The DI never raised his voice, but the air of menace was unmistakeable. 'Not your systems.' He almost hissed the words. '*You*.'

'Nothing's foolproof, Inspector.'

*Fool being the operative word*, thought Noakes.

Coslett took a step backwards. Markham stood very close to him. 'You will listen to me and you will listen well. I expect you to assist my officers in trying to establish who may have been on these premises last week. I also expect you to step up your security. As in *you personally*.'

Markham moved away leaving the manager visibly shaken.

Noakes winked at him. 'Less *Wallander* more caretaker, capeesh?' Okay, he'd been deprived of the chance for a spot of police brutality, but the guvnor had put the frighteners on that little shit good and proper. All in all, a job well done.

Back outside, they looked about them. Then Markham headed for the ginnel and cement steps which appeared to lead up from the car park to the front of the complex.

'Hey, boss,' Noakes was squinting behind him, uncertain.

'What is it, Sergeant?'

'I jus' thought I saw summat out there.'

'Where?'

'Far end of the playing fields . . . sort of blurry . . . like someone's out there . . .'

'Dog walker? Children? Snowman?'

'Nah . . . it's gone now . . . must've imagined it. Reckon I've got snow blindness or summat.'

Markham scanned the horizon. Nothing moved. All was filled up with snow. And yet, for an instant, he too had the curious sensation that they were in the crosshairs of a silent observer.

It occurred to him that the playing fields offered a panoramic view of New College Close. On a dark night, the estate would glow, drawing the eye like a stage set illumined for action.

'We'll check it out, Noakesy. But first I want to have a word with the Ledwidges.' He stamped his numb feet, watching his breath spiral upwards in a smoky cloud. 'No doubt there'll be a hot drink on offer,' he added artfully.

The DS didn't need telling twice.

* * *

The Reverend and Mrs Ledwidge lived at number sixteen in one of the close's terraced townhouses. Spread over three floors, it was clearly one of the close's more expensive properties. As in Marian Bussell's flat, the living room looked out over the car park towards the playing fields and the countryside beyond. With sanded oak floors, sleek minimalist fittings and high-end finish, the décor was somewhat at odds with the couple's old-fashioned appearance. 'Our daughter Catriona's an interior decorator,' Mrs Ledwidge explained when Markham politely complimented her on the property's delightful aspect. 'Gutted the house when we moved in and renovated it from top to bottom.'

*Prob'ly looking to cash in when Mum and Dad popped their clogs*, thought Noakes. Mind, she'd be waiting some time from the look of things. The couple were in their seventies or thereabouts, but spry and very much on the ball.

Brian Ledwidge was a soft-spoken man with a slight lisp. In appearance, he was not overly prepossessing, there being something lizard-like about the glaucous eyes behind thick bottle glasses and the way he punctuated his remarks with a croaky *heh-heh-heh*. His wife Eileen was a well-preserved bosomy woman with an ash-blonde beehive reminiscent of *Coronation Street*'s Bet Lynch. This must have been the attraction of opposites, thought Markham as she bustled off to make tea while her husband engaged in stilted conversation with the two detectives.

On her return — with a tray of coffee and Bourbon biscuits (which raised her several notches in Noakes's estimation) — the atmosphere lightened somewhat, though Markham noticed that Brian Ledwidge seemed ill at ease and jumpy. That was perhaps only to be expected given the nature of recent events on his doorstep.

Markham was grateful for the couple's self-imposed restraint and the way neither of them fished for details of the gruesome discovery at number seven. Of course, as a clerical couple, circumspection and discretion were doubtless second nature to them.

But it was time to cut to the chase.

'Can you think of anyone who might have borne a grudge towards either of these ladies?' he asked. 'Anyone they'd quarrelled with . . . a dispute?'

Eileen Ledwidge looked genuinely bewildered.

'They were both well liked, Inspector,' she said in her pleasant contralto. 'Obviously Marian wasn't so mobile any more, but Dawn dropped in on her regularly and people generally kept an eye out.' She bit her lip, suddenly looking upset. 'We should have done more . . . the thing is, we've both had bad colds and didn't want to risk infecting anyone else . . .'

Her husband's eyes were opaque behind the thick glasses. Markham found it disconcerting that they made it difficult to read his expression.

'Don't upset yourself, Eileen,' he said in a sibilant murmur. 'We weren't to know . . . and anyway, there was a volunteer from Hope Academy visiting every week . . . community outreach or something like that.' He looked enquiringly at Markham.

'Unfortunately, she had to miss a week . . . otherwise we'd know more about Mrs Bussell's state of mind in recent days.'

'The lass thought Mrs B seemed a bit jittery . . . nervous, like, the last time she saw her,' Noakes mumbled through a mouthful of biscuit.

The couple looked at each other. An invisible signal seemed to pass between them.

'I believe she'd been bothered by some hate mail a while back,' Eileen said tentatively.

'*Hate mail*?' Markham contemplated them thoughtfully. 'What sort of thing?'

'Oh, she just said it was poison-pen stuff . . .' The woman was vague. 'Didn't give any specifics. I think she just wanted to know if anyone else had been targeted, otherwise she wouldn't have mentioned it.'

'And *was* anyone else in the close targeted, Mrs Ledwidge?'

'Not to our knowledge, Inspector. I think it would have come up at the last residents' meeting if anyone had been bothered in that way.' She looked to her husband for confirmation.

'Oh yes,' he said. 'Mrs Bussell was unusually . . . well, reticent on personal matters . . . but I can't imagine others keeping it to themselves.'

'What about Ms MacAlinden?' asked Markham. 'Did she mention anything like that?'

'No, Inspector.' Brian Ledwidge's expression was inscrutable, but the DI noticed a muscle working in his jaw.

*Something* was bothering the Reverend Brian Ledwidge. But what?

He decided to change tack. Perhaps that would flush it out.

‘Have you noticed anyone hanging around the close lately, someone you haven’t seen before?’

‘No, nothing like that . . .’ But then Eileen Ledwidge seemed to recollect herself. ‘Hold on a minute,’ she said. ‘I *did* report a prowler to Mr Coslett . . .’

‘A prowler?’ Markham leaned forward. ‘Where was this?’

‘Well I couldn’t be completely sure. To be honest, I feel a bit foolish about it now.’

‘Don’t worry about that, Mrs Ledwidge.’ Markham’s voice was gentle and reassuring. ‘Any piece of information, no matter how slight, is valuable.’

‘Yeah, luv,’ Noakes’s guttural rumble echoed. ‘You’re our eyes an’ ears on this one.’

The woman looked pleased. ‘I’m the Neighbourhood Watch Coordinator for the estate,’ she said. ‘So I tend to notice anything unusual or out of place.’

The two detectives looked at her expectantly. Markham had the feeling that Eileen’s volubility was unwelcome to her husband, but for the life of him couldn’t imagine why.

‘It was down on the playing fields,’ she said at last. ‘When it was getting dark, I thought I saw someone standing there . . . very still, just staring up at our windows.’

‘Were you able to make out anything, Mrs Ledwidge? Anything about this person’s appearance?’

‘Not really,’ she said regretfully. ‘Though I think it *might* have been a woman. I could have sworn they were wearing a headscarf.’

*So likely not a Peeping Tom then*, thought Noakes.

‘An’ that was all they did, luv? Jus’ stood an’ stared?’ Noakes pressed her. ‘They didn’t have a dog with them, did they? Or any kids? Nothing like that?’

‘No, whoever it was . . . I never saw anyone else around.’

‘How many times did this happen, Mrs Ledwidge?’

‘Oh, it was only half a dozen evenings or so last month, Inspector. And to be honest, I could have been making a fuss about nothing.’ With some compunction she added, ‘When people are in trouble — going through bad times — well, they quite often like to go off by themselves for a walk, don't they? I suppose that's why Mr Coslett didn't think it was anything to worry about.'

*No, it's cos he's a work-shy git.* But Noakes held his peace.

'Mr Coslett didn't report it to the police, then?'

'Not as far as I know, Inspector. He told me it was probably like I said — a rambler, someone walking off stress — you know, Nature as healer.'

*Quite the philosopher, our Gazza*, thought Noakes sourly.

'But something about it made you uneasy, Mrs Ledwidge.' Markham regarded her steadily.

'Oh, it's probably to do with the time of year.' She laughed nervously. 'November being All Souls' month . . . ghosts and ghouls coming out to play . . .'

Sensing her discomfort, the DI decided to bring the conversation to a close.

'I believe you're the Chair of the Residents' Association, Mr Ledwidge,' he said. 'We're most grateful to you for arranging access to St James's for us.'

'Not at all, Inspector.' The other's relief at getting off the subject of prowlers was almost palpable. 'Most of us should be able to get down there later. Should we say from about one p.m.?'

'Excellent.'

'Was there some sort of argy-bargy with Gary Coslett before?'

*That's right, Noakesy, press the man's buttons, why don't you?*

The close-shaven sallow cheeks flushed.

'A simple misunderstanding.' His Adam's apple bobbed. 'There's been some concern about security on the estate. And with the . . . latest development—'

'Of course, Mr Ledwidge, of course.' Markham was emollient. 'The police will be liaising with Mr Coslett on this.'

Making sure the idle bugger finally pulls his finger out.

* * *

'What d'you reckon, guv?' Noakes asked once they were back outside. 'Think this prowler's our killer? Mebbe they're the poison pen too.'

'Certainly sounds suspicious, Sergeant.'

'The Rev was antsy.'

So the DS had noticed it too.

'Deffo summat he weren't telling us,' Noakes observed trenchantly.

Before Markham could answer, DC Doyle came panting up.

'How's it going, Constable?'

'The uniforms found something, sir,' the DC said without preamble.

The 'something' turned out to be a vintage lady's powder compact.

Exquisitely enamelled in silver and turquoise, it was of Art Deco design bearing the image of a 1920s hostess with shingled hair, dressed in a tuxedo and flourishing a cigarette holder.

'Where did they find it?'

'On the playing fields, sir. At the back towards the woods. The silver caught the light, otherwise they'd have missed it in the snow.'

Markham and Noakes looked at each other.

'Can you show us where?' the DI said.

And with that, the trio headed back towards the car park and the lonely fields beyond.

## 4. A SHOCK

'It's beautiful, Gil.' Olivia Mullen ran her fingers caressingly across the enamelled surface of the powder compact. Then suddenly she shivered convulsively.

'What is it?'

'Oh, I don't know.' She looked embarrassed. 'Just got goosebumps for some reason.' She dropped the compact on the table in front of her as though she had received an electric shock. 'A negative vibe,' she added weakly.

The DI was back with his lover in their apartment at The Sweepstakes, an upmarket complex off Bromgrove Avenue. They had just finished their supper — roast chicken with all the trimmings followed by apple crumble — and were onto coffee. Having avoided shop talk during the meal, Markham felt able to mull over the events of the day. The living room, with curtains snugly drawn against the freezing winter night, was cosy with a wood burner's aromatic scent and the desolate playing fields seemed a million miles away.

He adjourned to a comfortable armchair while Olivia curled up on a low stool with her back against his knees, long red hair cascading about her so that she looked more than ever like a faery princess of legend.

'By rights I shouldn't have brought it home,' he said, turning the pocket mirror round and round. 'Ought to have bagged and logged it.' He stroked the tumbling tresses. 'But I wanted you to see it,' he added tenderly.

'D'you think it's got something to do with the case, Gil?'

'Well, Eileen Ledwidge from number sixteen mentioned having seen a prowler hanging around the playing fields—'

'*A prowler*?'

'She struck me as a sensible woman — husband's the vicar at St James's.'

'So the killer could've been watching the close, spying on people and then dropped the mirror?' She paused. 'Or maybe the killer's girlfriend.'

'Anything's possible.'

'A woman . . .' Olivia regarded the trinket warily. 'High-maintenance at that. It's cloisonné, Gil . . . looks quite expensive from where I'm sitting.'

Markham contemplated the compact.

The workmanship was exquisite, and the face of the blonde flapper girl — assuming that's what she was — a marvel of androgynous airiness, as though illuminated by some divine aerosol.

'She's beautiful alright,' Olivia said reluctantly. 'Pure and mysterious . . . almost above sex somehow . . . Neither one thing nor the other.'

'Hmmm.' Markham revolved the compact once more. 'That pose with the cigarette holder's pretty suggestive.'

'Oh, I don't know, Gil. It's so stiff and unnatural . . . like Anubis or one of those deities you see on frescoes in the Egyptian pyramids.'

'Isn't Anubis the one with a human body and dog's head?'

'Yep — the God of death and mummification.'

Patron saint of embalmers. Horribly apt but somehow not exactly what Markham wanted to hear.

'Did anyone recognize it — any of the people who turned up to St James's?'

'Not a flicker,' he said glumly. 'No one has a clue where it came from.' He thought hard for a moment. 'Or else they made a damn good job of hiding the fact.'

Olivia picked up on his despondency.

'What were they like then?' she enquired cheerfully. 'The folk from the close?'

'That's just it, Liv. They were the epitome of suburban normality . . .'

Markham thought back to the afternoon in that chilly church hall warmed by convector heaters that had been supplied by the current incumbent.

The 'weirdy' Labour councillor Penny Callaghan hadn't joined them due to 'pressing business elsewhere'. (Spending taxpayers' money, according to Noakes.) Apparently, he would be meeting her the following morning with DCI Sidney when no doubt the focus would be firmly on civic damage limitation. He knew he could expect any suggestion that the double murder was connected with Hope Academy to be closed down in double quick time.

Of the others, no one had really stood out, though he'd quite warmed to the solicitor Simon Gailey and Kenneth Dowell from The Anchorage. Gailey was a slender, lean-featured man with the whippet good looks of a Battle of Britain squadron leader. Silver-haired and distinguished-looking, his natural air of command was allied to a self-deprecating charm which took some of the tension from the occasion. Dowell too was what he would call a 'player' — tall and rangy, though less conventionally good-looking than the solicitor on account of his beetling brows and beaky nose. 'Strange sorta trick cyclist,' Noakes muttered. 'The kind who'd say "pull yourself together" soon as look at you.' Not someone to mess with, though once or twice Markham caught the psychologist looking lost in thought, almost dazed, as though wrestling with some private conundrum.

Stacey Macmillan was a bubbly little woman with a peroxide perm and an expansive manner. 'Motormouth,' said Noakes *sotto voce*, but his expression was kindly.

Jeff Coleman, wheelchair-bound, was no one's idea of a romantic novelist. 'Fuck, it's Stephen Hawking,' DC Doyle observed when he set eyes on the hunched wizened figure. Burton's glare at this witticism was 'ball-shrivelling scary,' but Markham had to admit the description was apt. From snatches of overheard conversation, he gathered that Coleman, who looked to be in his seventies or thereabouts, had been a regular visitor to Marian Bussell. 'I think he might've been sweet on her,' confided Stacey, though Markham detected no marks of especial sorrow in the man. 'He said he was her — what d'you call it — mentor.'

'How'd you mean?'

'She wanted to try her hand at writing,' the other replied vaguely. 'Books about the past — right up her street seeing as she used to teach history.'

Coleman turned out to be suffering from motor neurone disease — Doyle threw Kate Burton a triumphant look on hearing this — 'but slow moving at the moment, Inspector,' the writer informed them, 'so I still have a reasonably decent quality of life.' The DI found his quiet stoicism and lack of pretension attractive. 'I was at the chalkface, too, in an earlier incarnation,' he said, 'but took early retirement.' His lopsided face, the once handsome features furrowed with pain, grimaced. 'Just as well all things considered. Teaching's hard enough for the able-bodied, let alone if you have a disability.' Clearly he had been fond of Marian Bussell, but Markham wasn't sure it went much further than that. 'She showed promise as a writer,' he told them with professional detachment. 'After I introduced her to my own editor at Harlequin, she emailed them some ideas . . . I believe they were very keen.' The DI made a mental note to check out the publisher in due course.

'My missus . . . she's a big fan of yours,' Noakes put in.

'What a delightful boost to my flagging ego,' the other replied with a disconcertingly impish grin. 'Clearly a lady of taste and discernment.' Noakes puffed out his chest as though to proclaim, *you hear that*! His satisfaction was mightily compounded when Coleman assured him, 'I'll be sure to get you a signed copy of my latest, Sergeant.' Cue much shuffling of feet.

'Could you put "For Muriel" in the cover?' the DS said, to his colleagues' ill-concealed amusement.

'It will be my pleasure,' came the gallant response, marred only by the wheezy cackle peculiar to sufferers of MND.

Doctor Lucy O'Connor was an attractive pony-tailed brunette who looked far too young to be a psychiatric registrar. However, her appearance belied the calm good sense that was no doubt an asset in her profession. She indulged in no gush or flowery platitudes about the dead women, contenting herself with a quiet but sincere expression of regret. 'I didn't know them very well,' she said, 'what with my hours being somewhat antisocial. But they always talked good sense at residents' meetings — forthright but kindly, if you know what I mean.' She flashed a smile. 'Not afraid of taking on Laneside and Gary Coslett either.' Markham made another mental note to get hold of the Residents' Association minutes from Brian Ledwidge — assuming, of course, that such records existed. Judging from what he'd seen of Ledwidge, the DI thought it more than likely they did.

Martin Henley, Doctor O'Connor's partner, was a good-looking young man who struck Markham as being well aware of the fact. Certainly, he seemed to enjoy the way Stacey Macmillan batted her eyelashes whenever he looked in her direction. The DI felt an immediate antipathy towards him but, aware that his dislike was instinctive and had no rational foundation, was careful to give no hint of his aversion.

Noakes, needless to say, felt under no such constraint. 'A male nurse, then?' he said in a disparaging tone which was only marginally on the right side of being offensive. 'Ain't that a bit *girly*? Not get the right grades to do medicine?'

An angry colour ran up under Henley's tan. '*Senior staff nurse*, actually,' he shot back and Markham heard a

Northern twang as the BBC accent momentarily slipped. Henley's sapphire blue eyes were chips of ice as he looked at the Neanderthal.

'You must forgive my sergeant,' the DI said pleasantly. 'The training on sexist stereotypes somehow went right over his head.' Noakes merely smirked. Henley was too cocky by half, but that flash of temper showed another side to him. From the uneasy way Lucy O'Connor monitored the exchange, it was clear she had to box clever round her man's ego.

Talking of ego . . . Mary Atkins, AHT from Hope Academy, was another one full of it. So woke and PC, she literally made Markham's teeth ache. But he tried to give her the benefit of the doubt, reminding himself that the ability to spout fluent gibberish was pretty much an article of faith for assistant headteachers these days.

And yet underneath all the twittering and come-hither coquettishness (for it was clear, as Doyle later told Noakes in the pub, that she thought the DI was hot stuff), Markham detected discomfort in her manner and in the nervous way her eyes darted round the room.

'Obviously Marian was at Hope well before my time, Inspector. Quite a character by all accounts . . . very feisty.'

*Feisty*. An interesting choice of word.

But before he could pin her down, she was off again.

'And so *sweet* that Dawn kept in touch with her old teacher — very *caring* of her.'

'Did you know Dawn well, Ms Atkins?' Burton interrupted the flow.

Markham sensed that, for some reason, this question was unwelcome, but the woman's professional patter was equal to it.

'Ships that passed in the night, unfortunately. Everyone's so *time-poor* these days, don't you find?'

Glutinously saccharine as ever, the DI learned nothing useful beyond the fact that Mary Atkins' admiration of him was apparently undimmed.

Olivia chortled appreciatively at his pen-pictures. Being a teacher at Hope, she particularly enjoyed hearing his impressions of the school's assistant head.

'Atkins *is* an awful woman, Gil, but pound to a penny if there's anything juicy in Marian Bussell's past — anything to do with Hope — she's bound to know about it. We call her the "keeper of secrets" cos she's got a mind like a freaking rolodex.'

Markham grinned.

'Well, whatever she knows, she wasn't giving me a sniff of it.' He kneaded his girlfriend's shoulders, a habit of his at such moments of introspection, as though it aided the deductive process. Olivia groaned pleasurably as the long sensitive fingers massaged away the strain of a day in the swamp of fear and loathing, as she was accustomed to thinking of Hope.

'I could have a word with Mat, if you like.'

Mat Sullivan was Hope's deputy head and a long-standing friend of both, in addition to being one of the few teachers not inimical to Noakes.

'That would be great, Liv.' Markham hesitated, only too aware how Sullivan had suffered after coming under suspicion in a previous investigation. 'But not if he feels it might compromise him.'

'Oh, he's good at managing Atkins.' Olivia chuckled. 'Him being gay's the icing on the cake . . . gives her a chance to flash those right-on credentials.'

'Well, if you're sure.'

'Leave it to me, Gil.'

By way of diversion, he told her about Noakes requesting Jeff Coleman's autograph.

'The others won't let George live *that* down in a hurry.' She chuckled before adding, 'Puts paid to Muriel pretending she reads nothing but Dostoevsky and Dickens.'

'It was quite touching the way Noakesy got it in. Though, as you say, I'm not sure "the missus" will thank him for it.'

The note of despondency was back.

'You sound bushed, dearest.'

'I'm no further forward really, Liv. They're the people who knew the victims best, but I just don't see any of them being killers. Though . . .' His hands tensed on her shoulders.

'What is it?'

'There was this moment when I had the strangest feeling of real *malevolence* in the room . . . a pulsing hatred . . . like some sort of forcefield.' He sighed heavily. 'And then it was gone.'

'And you didn't connect this . . . aura with anyone there?'

'No.' Another deep sigh. 'They all seemed perfectly decent and ordinary. Apprehensive and on edge, naturally, but no more than you'd expect.'

'What about alibis?'

'Well, we won't be doing formal interviews till tomorrow, but it looks like Mary Atkins, Kenneth Dowell, Doctor O'Connor and her partner, and Stacey Macmillan are strongest on that front since they were apparently all at work . . . assuming Dimples is correct on time of death.'

She looked up at him expectantly.

'Looks like it happened sometime late Thursday afternoon. Traces of Rohypnol in the vics' bloodstreams—'

'What?' Olivia was startled. 'The date rape drug?'

'A very effective muscle relaxant and hypnotic,' her boyfriend said grimly. 'Which explains how he was able to subdue them so easily. No signs of a struggle, so they were happy to let him into the flat.'

'Which means he must have been known to them.'

'Seems the most likely explanation.'

'God how *horrible*,' she said feelingly. 'And they were in that contraption for what . . . *four days*?'

'Mrs Bussell had a heart attack,' Markham said quietly. 'But in the case of the other lady . . . we're looking at suffocation.' He decided to spare Olivia the heartrending detail of those torn fingernails.

'*God*,' she breathed again, almost in invocation, then, 'What about the rest? Your other suspects?'

'I won't know about Councillor Callaghan till tomorrow. The retirees — that's the Ledwidges along with Messrs

Gailey and Coleman — seem to have been blamelessly occupied, though we'll need to drill down into the details. Oh, I almost forgot . . . some long-haired activist turned up just when everyone was packing up.'

'Activist?'

'Well that's what Noakes called him.'

'Ah,' this was said in a tone of deep comprehension. 'Nose-piercing and Save the Rainforest bangle, then?'

Markham laughed.

'Lip stud actually, but you're right about the bracelet — LGBT Pride, I believe.'

'*My*,' Olivia whistled. 'That'll have brought the old silverback out swinging.'

'Luckily Noakesy's mind was firmly on his chippy tea, so our friend got off lightly.'

'What kind of activist is he?'

'Name of Julian Hoskinson, runs that charity shop Lili's in town.'

'Oh, I know who you mean.' Olivia was animated now. 'Tall and thin, sallow-skinned with wide-spaced eyes . . . looks a bit like a heroin addict, but perfectly polite.'

'That's him.' Markham's voice was hopeful. 'D'you know the background?'

'He came to one of my evening classes at the university, but I never really got to know him. Quite shy and buttoned up for all the druggie look.' She thought for a moment. 'The shop's pretty nice actually, and he doesn't try to shove propaganda at you.'

'Why Lili's?'

'After Lili Elbe, you know, the Danish transgender woman.'

'Oh right,' he said uncertainly. 'Probably best if I get Kate Burton to recce this one.'

'Well, if George goes crashing in with his size twelves there'll be a mass exodus of customers followed by unwelcome publicity courtesy of the *Gazette*,' she agreed.

'Is it just Hoskinson runs the shop?'

'There's the odd student helper, but it's pretty much his own show. I think he gets a grant of some sort from the council.'

A conversational gambit for tomorrow's meeting with Penny Callaghan, then.

'Did you . . . did you tell the residents all the details, Gil?' She had shaken her abundant hair over her face so he couldn't see its expression. 'The Rohypnol . . . and how they died?'

'We kept it general . . . talked about them being trapped and how it appeared to be deliberate. Nothing about the school badge in Marian Bussell's hand.'

'I'd forgotten about that.' Now she pushed the masses of hair back, and he saw the apprehension in her eyes. 'There must be some link to Hope, Gil . . .'

'Not necessarily, love.' Markham knew his girlfriend was still traumatized by the earlier murder investigation at her school. 'We're dealing with a maniac here. Who can say what was going through his mind? We don't know if he brought the badge along on purpose. Or if it was already in the flat and he just snatched it up on an impulse — put it in Mrs Bussell's hand to throw us off the scent.'

'Or as some kind of sick joke.'

He yawned theatrically.

'Right, enough of the ghoulish speculation for one night. I vote we settle down to a boxset . . . something daft and mindless.'

'You're on.' Olivia's face brightened. 'I'll just clear away and then *Father Ted* it is.'

His laughter followed her into the kitchen.

* * *

The meeting next morning with DCI Sidney and Councillor Penny Callaghan was every bit as sticky as Markham had anticipated. Though there was some comfort to be taken in the fact that Noakes had jettisoned his fisherman's get-up and was wearing a more or less coordinated suit and jacket — at least, to the extent that they were both sludge-brown and did not provoke Sidney's long-lived wondering frown.

Ms Callaghan (definitely a *Miz*) was a thick-set woman with a badly dyed, pudding-bowl haircut and pendulous jowls. Sidney, needless to say, was deferential to the point of obsequiousness and only too eager to follow her lead in ruling out any possible link between the 'atrocity' in New College Close (she made it sound like the handiwork of some lone wolf Uber Bomber) and the local secondary school.

The DCI stroked his newly cultivated goatee — which hirsute accessory he no doubt fondly imagined counter-balanced his bald bonce yin/yang-style — and murmured agreement when she allowed him to get a word in edgeways. Markham noticed that Penny Callaghan featured prominently in several pictures on the photomontage in Sidney's office that CID wags had irreverently dubbed the 'Hall of Fame'. He also seemed to recall she was on the Police Liaison Committee, which was no doubt why Sidney was keen to keep her onside and do nothing to jeopardize the eventual award of his gong.

But Markham was damned if he was just going to roll over.

'Obviously at this stage we don't want to narrow our lines of enquiry, Ms Callaghan,' he said, ignoring Sidney's gimlet gaze. 'In the case of Mrs Bussell, social services were involved. There are also links between Hope Academy and both victims.' He beamed charmingly at his boss and Ms Pudding Bowl. 'Then there's the property management company Laneside, which maintains New College Close — on the council's list of approved contractors, I believe. There are connections to an outreach charity and local psychiatric facilities as well.' Pause for dramatic effect. 'Cases like this really go to the *heart* of the community.'

'I hardly think,' she began, but the DI cut her short.

'Of course, as you say,' though she hadn't, 'it's early days so we don't want to rule anything out.' A certain steeliness entered his voice. 'Least of all, lest this should give the *unfortunate* impression that the local authority sought to . . . *close down* legitimate avenues of enquiry.' He produced his most insincere smile and concluded with cheery insouciance, '"Without fear or favour", that's our watchword isn't it, sir?'

Sidney's expression turned thunderous and he looked as though he was about to let rip, when there came a soft tap at the door. Miss Peabody sidled into the room with her usual air of being attendant on a capricious and wildly unpredictable caliph.

'What is it, Miss Peabody? I told you *no interruptions*.'

She whispered in his ear and the two policemen saw him change colour.

'There's been a development, Markham,' he said finally in quite an altered tone of voice. He turned to Penny Callaghan. 'Councillor Callaghan, please accept my apologies but . . . investigative matters, you understand.'

Having bowed the stumpy, ill-favoured woman out of the office, the DCI turned to Markham and Noakes.

'A body's been found at the playing fields behind Beech Drive.'

'Who?'

'One Kenneth Dowell. I understand you met him yesterday.'

'*The psychologist*?' Noakes burst out. '*No way*!'

'Foul play, sir?'

'Your other DS,' Sidney glanced with distaste at Noakes, 'appears to think so.'

Markham realized it was as he had subconsciously feared all along.

That the murders of Marian Bussell and Dawn MacAlinden were just the start.

And a short time later, contemplating the corpse of Kenneth Dowell, strung out between the goalposts of the redundant football pitch with a gaping wound where his throat had been, he knew his fear to be well founded.

# 5. WHEELS WITHIN WHEELS

Afterwards, in the bungalow-cum-incident room, Kate Burton had been unable to stop shaking. The DI kept her busy organizing hot drinks and biscuits, and the bustle of sorting the refreshments seemed to do the trick. Gradually some colour returned to her cheeks.

'What took you out to the playing fields, Kate?' he asked once they were settled with mugs and chocolate digestives.

'I just thought I'd have a nosey round, see if anything else turned up — like that make-up mirror — in case someone was watching the close.'

Noakes and Doyle exchanged meaningful glances.

*Got a touch of the bleeding Miss Marple*, thought Noakes, but he refrained from comment.

'And then—' She came to an abrupt halt and took a gulp of well-sugared scalding hot tea. 'When I saw him, my first thought was some kids had been messing about, got a dummy from somewhere and put it in goal for a joke.' Another gulp of tea. 'Once I got closer, I realized it wasn't a dummy . . .' She trailed off.

'It's alright, Kate, take your time.'

The kindness in Markham's voice made her want to cry. Her eyes suspiciously bright, she continued, 'The head was hanging down, but there was something familiar about him. Then I clocked who he was — the psychologist. He was at that meeting in the church hall.'

'Big, scary-looking bloke,' Noakes said dunking his third digestive. 'Though he looked . . . I dunno . . . well, a bit *out of it* yesterday — like he'd seen a ghost or summat.'

It was a typically shrewd observation.

'Could just've been the shock of living next door to a double murder scene,' Doyle put in.

'Nah.' Noakes was decisive. 'It was more than that — like summat had dawned on him an' he couldn't take it in.'

'You mean, he suddenly twigged who the killer was?' the young DC pressed.

'Well he deffo looked gobsmacked . . . Couldn't get away fast enough at the end while the rest of 'em were up for a bit of a natter.'

'If he experienced some sort of revelation about the killer's identity, he could have wanted to be by himself,' Markham said thoughtfully, 'figure out what he was going to do.'

'Well the poor bastard obviously ruled out coming to the cop shop,' Noakes grunted.

'Blackmail?' This was Burton, clutching her mug for dear life. 'And the killer somehow lured him to a meeting on the playing fields?'

'Dowell looked like he could handle himself,' Doyle mused. 'I mean, six foot three or four. So the killer's gotta be strong.'

'Not necessarily, Constable.'

Doyle was all alert interest.

'If Mr Dowell was taken by surprise or somehow disabled, then it wouldn't have required vastly superior strength. Dimples said a woman could've done it given the right circumstances.'

'You're not saying a woman pegged him up, guv?' Noakes was incredulous. 'I mean, I could see it if it was just the throat slashing. But rigging him up like some creepy Jack Frost? That's gotta be a bloke.'

'Maybe the adrenaline made her super-strong or something,' Doyle suggested. 'You know, like those cases where folk lift cars off accident victims. I've read about it happening in America.'

'Huh, *America*,' Noakes snorted as though to say *I rest my case*.

'If it was a woman, she could have had an accomplice,' Burton offered. 'Or maybe someone else came by afterwards. Someone with a grudge who hated Dowell and,' she swallowed hard, 'did *that* to the body.'

'*Pur-lease*.' Noakes had heard enough. 'This ain't sodding *Jackanory*.' In his vehemence, he dropped half a biscuit into his tea. Burton fastidiously averted her eyes as he fished and slurped his way back to a state of equilibrium. 'It's gotta be a bloke.'

'We're not ruling anything out here, Sergeant,' the DI said in a tone of mild reproof. Uneasily, he added, 'Whoever our killer is, there's a morbid . . . *artistry* about the way they operate.'

The pathologist had agreed with him on that. 'Bit of a showman your boy,' he said contemplating the crystals which hung from the corpse in long spiky strands reminiscent of drizzle icing. 'I'd say he positively *enjoyed* this.' The body, head sagging forward, had been secured in its cruciform pose — like some horrible parody of Salvador Dalí's *Christ of Saint John of the Cross* — by a combination of guy ropes and crampons.

''S like summat out of an S & M movie,' was Noakes's more prosaic verdict. 'Santa's grotto with a twist.'

'More like *Satan's* grotto, you mean,' Doyle shuddered.

'Dimples believes Mr Dowell had ingested alcohol shortly before his death,' Markham told the team.

'What — you mean he had a drink with the killer?' Doyle boggled.

'Like the two of 'em were toasting each other out there in the snow . . . *Bring a bottle*!' Noakes chuckled grimly. 'Thought I'd heard it all, boss, but that beats everything!'

'No, hold on a minute.' Burton said with an intensity that made the others stare at her. 'Remember the Rohypnol they found in the women's bloodstream: a sedative to enforce compliance.'

'Yeah, but *c'mon*.' Noakes's scepticism was undiminished. 'It was easy-peasy with *them* — slipped into their cuppa . . . never saw it coming. But Dowell knew what was what—'

'He knew he was meeting a murderer,' Doyle agreed eagerly. 'Would have been cautious.'

'Fair enough,' Burton said. 'But if the killer's someone he knows — maybe even likes — he might have relaxed his guard. I mean,' she was warming to her hypothesis, 'a quick swig from a hip flask, accepting the offer of something to warm him up . . . Where's the harm in that when it's brass monkeys outside? And don't forget, we didn't tell anyone the women were drugged so Dowell won't have been thinking along those lines.'

'Even so.' But it was clear the DC was coming round.

'If Mr Dowell was distracted or disorientated, his usual warning instincts might not have kicked in,' Markham observed. 'As Noakes said, he looked "gobsmacked" at that meeting. Could have been so off-balance that self-preservation took a back seat.'

'What now, guv?'

'Well, Dimples is sorting the PM.'

He didn't want Kate Burton attending but, to his surprise, Doyle spoke up stoutly. 'I'll take that, sir. Good CPD,' he added as Noakes's shaggy eyebrows shot up.

'The killer chose the meeting place well.' Burton didn't want to show how relieved she was that her young colleague would be the one reporting to 'Stiff Central'.

'Yeah,' Noakes concurred. 'SOCOs'll get sweet FA what with all that snow.'

'I suppose we got nothing useful from the sweep of Mrs Bussell's flat, Kate?'

'No, sir,' came the gloomy response. 'Everything was wiped clean.' Her frown deepened. 'And in any case, half the close could've left trace evidence in there. Like Dimples always says, if it's a disorganized killer or a bloodbath then you'll get results with luminol or whatever else the techies have in their box of tricks. But otherwise . . .' She shrugged despondently.

'Proper little ray of sunshine, ain't he?' Noakes grouched.

'Just telling it as it is, sarge. Unless our man slips up or we get majorly lucky, forensics is a dead end.' She flushed. 'Sorry,' she mumbled, 'unfortunate choice of words.'

'What about next of kin?'

'Mr Dowell was single,' Markham said sombrely, 'parents deceased. There was a sister, but she's gone too. Breast cancer.'

'So he had no one, guv.' For all his external belligerence, there was a chord in Noakes that was easily touched.

'Well, I understand he was "wedded to his work".'

'Oh aye. Who came up with that?'

'I spoke to an administrator at The Anchorage. You and I are going to head round there, Noakes, and see if we can glean anything.'

'Like what?'

'His clinical interests, recent state of mind, any unusual calls or visitors . . . It may be that the killer's identity came to him like a bolt from the blue. But equally, there may be clues in his work profile.'

Noakes looked far from convinced.

'D'you remember what that lot at The Anchorage were like during the art gallery investigation, boss? They're so hung up on client confidentiality an' GDPR, it'll be a freaking miracle if we get anything out of them.'

'Nonetheless.' Noakes knew that tone of voice. It meant the guvnor was not for turning. 'We need a handle on Mr Dowell. If his routine altered in any way, or a colleague noticed something different about him, then I want to hear about it.'

'Mrs Bussell got some hate mail, didn't she?' Doyle piped up. 'Well maybe Dowell did too. Or he could've let something drop at work . . .' The DC faltered slightly under Noakes's mocking gaze which said *teacher's pet* louder than words. 'Something about the prowler . . . he might've seen them as well. Or maybe someone from the close visited him at the clinic.'

'Good thinking, Constable.' Doyle coloured with pleasure at the approval in Markham's voice. The DI's tone was notably drier as he added, 'Since we've got "sweet FA" from forensics, the best bet is to probe our victim's background.'

'Maybe we should be looking for a patient,' Burton said suddenly.

'Somehow I think it's more complicated than that, Kate.' Absent-mindedly, the DI crumbled the biscuit he had barely touched. 'Too risky for the killer given we could get a warrant for patient files. If Mr Dowell had anyone from the close on his books—'

'They'd be suspect *numero uno*,' Noakes concluded.

'Or at the very least we'd be taking a keen interest in them,' the DI agreed.

'Why the chuffing hell didn't Dowell come to us?' Noakes kicked the table leg angrily, almost oversetting their drinks. 'What made the daft git think he could sort it himself?'

'He was a psychologist, sarge,' Doyle countered. 'Prob'ly thought he had everything under control . . . Maybe it wasn't even blackmail and he thought he could make the killer turn himself in.'

It was an interesting perspective, thought Markham. Intellectual arrogance or hubris could work all kinds of mischief.

He noticed the wistful look on Kate Burton's face and recalled his resolution not to keep her at arm's length. Burton needed affirmation that she was as important to him as Noakes, even though his complicity with her fellow DS ran far deeper than he could put into words or even explain to himself.

'Kate, I want you and Doyle to go house-to-house here. Not so much to establish residents' movements — the killer'll have that off pat . . . More to suss out their reactions . . . You're our behavioural boffin, so check out the body language.' He paused before adding with grave deliberation, 'Whoever did this will have been on a huge high before crashing back down to earth. See if there's anyone who strikes you as being unusually worn-out or drained.'

'Right, boss.' She lit up at the prospect of some psychological profiling then hesitated. 'How much do we tell them about the way Mr Dowell died?'

'The bare minimum.' It was said with a grimace. 'Gavin Conors and the crew from the *Gazette* will come sniffing around, but get Gary Coslett to see them off. Put a couple of uniforms on it if necessary. As far as the residents are concerned, give it the usual — unexplained circumstances . . . don't have the full picture . . . unhelpful to speculate at this stage . . . press conference tomorrow, blah blah.' Channel your inner Sidney, in other words. 'Obviously it'll leak.' His mouth twisted. 'Too grotesque not to. But, in the meantime, be as vague as you like. Talk about exposure and hypothermia if you must. Let's keep them off-kilter, off-balance . . . and see what crawls out of the woodwork.'

The DI felt stiff and cold. Through the small window, which looked out across Beech Drive towards the playing fields, a leaden sky seemed to bear down oppressively upon the winter landscape. It was only early afternoon, yet the light was already starting to fail.

'Right, Noakes,' he said, 'Let's make tracks for The Anchorage. And after that we'll swing by Hope Academy.'

'Eh?' The DS was startled. 'What can *they* tell us about Dowell?' His face fell. 'Don't tell me *he* was a student there an' all. At this rate, we'll be looking for some psycho with history going back to the pigging playground.'

Markham gave a thin smile. 'Relax, Sergeant. I just want to have a word with Mat Sullivan. I understand he's somewhat in Mary Atkins' confidence, may be able to fill us in on Marian Bussell's career history.'

'Oh, I *geddit.*' The other sagged with relief. 'Jus' so long as we don' have to listen to Atkins spouting crap.' The tips of his ears turned pink. 'Any chance we'll see your Olivia around?'

'If we play our cards right, we should be able to talk her into having a quick cup of tea before she settles down to a mound of marking.' The DI smiled inwardly at his sergeant's susceptibility, which had to be the worst-kept secret in CID. The old mastodon was even brushing off his horrible tweed jacket and smoothing down his tufty hair as though to make himself presentable for Markham's girlfriend. 'First things first,' he said. 'We need to see what staff at The Anchorage can tell us.' With the lure of Olivia's company to come, Noakes submitted with better grace than might have been expected.

* * *

An hour and a half later found them with Mat Sullivan and Olivia in the latter's classroom on the third floor of the 'bunker'.

'Got a good view up here,' observed Noakes looking out towards Bromgrove South Municipal Cemetery. 'Lucky you an' the guvnor get off on graves an' things.'

It made them sound like a pair of necrophiles, thought Markham, watching with amusement as his colleague toured the classroom, stroking the spines of classics on the shelves of Olivia's little bookcase with shy curiosity. To Noakes it was as though the DI's girlfriend, with her slender delicacy and dreamy ethereality, was a priestess at the altar of Culture, a shrine whose mysteries simultaneously awed and repelled him.

'Here's your tea, George. Creosote, just as you like it. And yes, I've got Wagon Wheels — top drawer of the filing cabinet.'

'So,' she said as they drew chairs up to her desk. 'How goes it with the investigation?'

The two detectives exchanged glances.

'Oh no,' she breathed. 'There's been another one, hasn't there?'

Quietly and succinctly, Markham recounted the discovery of the morning. There was no softening the horror of it, his lover's lively imagination quick to supply all the fearful detail implicit in his sober account.

Mat Sullivan, the tall, lanky deputy head — a 'beanpole with specs' — looked equally appalled.

'My God, Gil. What's going on in that close . . . you got Hannibal Lecter running amok or what?'

'Oh, nothing as tasteful as fava beans and chianti,' Markham replied.

'Jus' burying alive an' throat slashing.'

'No leads on this latest victim, then?'

'None to speak of, Mat. He was a psychologist at The Anchorage. Married to the job by all accounts.'

'The admin woman passed us over to one of Dowell's colleagues. Awful woman.' Noakes rolled his eyes expressively. 'Doctor Skanky or summat.'

'Skelthorne,' Markham corrected him.

'Well, she was a right pain in the—' the DS looked at Olivia and blushed, 'proverbial. Same as last time.'

'Last time?'

'We had dealings with the lady during the art gallery investigation, Mat. Noakesy found that she didn't improve on acquaintance.'

'Too right. Talk about mealy-mouthed . . . It was all "confidentiality" an' "ethical concerns".'

Olivia laughed at the munchkin falsetto.

'You mean your well-oiled charm got you nowhere, George?'

'Well.' A sly glance at Markham. 'The boss sweet-talked her into telling us about Dowell's research stuff, which was better'n nothing.'

'Mr Dowell's main area of interest was body dysmorphic disorder or "BDD",' the DI elaborated.

‘Folk with hang ups about how they look.’

‘Something of a simplification, Noakes.’

‘Well yeah,’ the DS winked at the two teachers. ‘Miss Clever Clogs went all *University Challenge* on us.’ The falsetto again. ‘“Suicidal ideation” an’ “social interference”. But that’s what it boils down to. The missus says it’s the media’s fault . . . If it weren’t for . . . Instagram an’ all them daft sites, people wouldn’t get into such a state.’

As far as Noakes was concerned, The Oracle had spoken.

‘Muriel has a point about the role of the media,’ said Olivia tactfully. ‘It’s something Mat’s incorporating into our personal development curriculum . . . the extent to which social media makes kids unhappy with their bodies or pushes them into believing they’re in the wrong body. The unit on LGBT doesn’t just deal with sexual variation but looks at other stuff, so the kids understand it’s complex and there’s an overlap with BDD and conditions like autism.’

‘Yep,’ Sullivan confirmed before sighing, ‘but I have to tread carefully. Some parents kicked up a fuss last year over the LGBT scheme of work . . . decided it meant kids would be turning into drag queens or transgendering overnight.’

Noakes guffawed appreciatively.

‘In fact the whole point of it was to challenge online culture and promote honest dialogue—’

‘But the mums an’ dads jus’ thought you were pervs.’

Sullivan smiled weakly. ‘I’m beginning to feel it’s an occupational hazard.’

‘Too right,’ Olivia agreed fervently. ‘Here we are trying to combat all this “crowd madness” and warn against medicalizing kids because of fads . . . and then we get accused of promoting some creepy agenda.’

‘It was better in the old days,’ Noakes ruminated. ‘When kids learned what they needed to know behind the bike shed.’

Natalie Noakes certainly favoured the practical approach, thought Markham, doing his best not to meet Olivia’s eye.

‘It’s a hugely emotive field,’ Sullivan mused. ‘Folk mutilating themselves in search of some perceived ideal of beauty, gender dysphoria, trans activism . . . yes, really incendiary.' A thought struck him. 'Did your victim face any hostility from headbangers?'

Markham looked quizzical.

'Y'know, bible-basher types, people who think dysphoria's a delusion, anti-liberals, the ones who say it's all gone too far.'

'*Outraged of Bromgrove*,' Olivia laughed.

'It's interesting you should say that, Mat.' Markham stood up and walked across to the window with its view of the cemetery, a Jaffa-red winter sun sinking slowly down behind the crosses and monuments, gilding them with a lurid glow. For a brief moment, he contemplated the scene then turned back to his friends. 'Apparently, there *were* sporadic outbreaks of "unpleasantness" and the occasional "angry rant letter" but "nothing of any significance".'

'Didn't they keep the hate mail — in a 'nutters' file or something — just in case anything ever happened?'

'It would appear not, Mat.' Markham restlessly paced the room. 'It's not an NHS clinic. These private places are pretty much a law unto themselves. I think if there ever *was* anything threatening, it's been binned.'

'Or they're jus' not gonna talk about it,' Noakes added. 'Keep everything nice and shiny. According to them, it was all business as usual with Dowell. No unexpected visitors. No problems. No nothing.'

'*Don't frighten the horses*,' Olivia said wryly. She thought for a moment. 'Would the "unpleasantness" mean demos and placards, or criminal damage — that kind of thing?'

'I'll get Kate to check the station records,' Markham replied, 'but from the sound of things it was more a case of the local God Squad making their feelings known.' He paused next to a vibrant wall display entitled `Sex and Cross-Dressing in Shakespeare's *Twelfth Night*'. Weirdly apt in the circumstances. 'As Mat said, the whole LGBT arena can get pretty toxic. But I still think this case is about New College Close.'

'None of the residents happened to be on Dowell's books, I suppose.'

'Well, we eventually got sight of the appointments diary and drew a blank. Ran the list of residents' names past the administrator — ditto.'

'We c'n get a warrant for their records, guv.'

'True, Noakes, but I doubt it'll get us any further forward.' Markham re-joined them at Olivia's desk. 'This killer's three steps ahead of us, nothing to fear from a trawl.'

'Didn't you say Marian Bussell got some hate mail, Gil?' Observing the weary droop of her lover's broad shoulders beneath the immaculately cut pinstripe, Olivia saw her chance to give him a lift.

'*Hate mail?*' Sullivan sat up straighter. 'Now that *is* interesting . . .'

'How so, Mat?'

'We had a spate of that here a while back. Well, Mary Atkins did.'

Noakes twitched reflexively, eyes darting towards the door as if he expected his nemesis to materialize in a puff of smoke.

'Take it easy, George,' Olivia chuckled. 'She's off boring the governors right now.' Pushing the biscuits towards him, she added kindly, 'Have another of these . . . for the shock.'

'She opened up a bit when I got on to the subject of the murders,' Mat explained. 'Said some crackpot parent had been sending her nasty letters.'

'She definitely said it was a *parent*, Mat?'

'Not in so many words, Gil. But that's how I understood it. Apparently, they were the ranty type like poor Mr Dowell got. Y'know, accusing her of twisting kids' minds and encouraging sodomy.'

'I guess it's too much to hope that she kept them.'

'Sorry, mate. She told me she flushed them straight down the loo. The poor cow looked upset, so I didn't press it.'

'Why *her*, Mat?'

'Good question.'

'I c'n answer that.' It was Noakes.

'Be my guest, Sergeant.'

'It's cos she's a bleeding-heart pain in the you-know-what.' The DS warmed to his theme. 'No cause so nuts or new age she don' want a piece of the action. Allus getting herself plastered across the *Gazette* whenever they need a tree hugger to interview. Like being *wet* an' *woke*'s some kind of sodding religion. Didn't she do that wacko interview last year about us all needing to be more — what was it — oh, yeah, *child-centric* . . . an' stop judging kids who want to *self-identify* . . . The missus nearly choked on her cornflakes.'

Again, Markham carefully avoided meeting Olivia's eye.

'No argument there,' Sullivan conceded with a grin. 'But in fairness to her, *someone*'s got to trot out the progressive claptrap and at least she looks like she believes it.'

'Whereas you and I are just born-again fascists,' Olivia said deadpan.

'Something like that,' her friend agreed affably.

'Ms Atkins told me that Marian Bussell was "feisty",' Markham said suddenly. 'Any idea what she might have meant by that, Mat?'

'Not the foggiest . . . unless . . . hold on . . . I seem to remember someone saying she was the only one of the old guard who was remotely broad-minded.'

'Mad lefty, then?' prompted Noakes.

Sullivan smiled what Olivia liked to call his undertaker's smile. 'Not as such . . . But quite radical for the times . . . Keen on young people deciding their own destinies . . . Youth autonomy, that kind of thing.'

'Like I said. Mad lefty,' the DS grunted. 'An' we're not short of those . . . There's Penny Callaghan an' the charity shop fella Julian Hoskinson for starters. Mebbe this is all about some commie conspiracy.'

'Okay.' Markham threw up his hands in exasperation. 'So the killer's targeting anyone left of centre. In which case, where does Dawn MacAlinden fit in? Was that poor woman some kind of flag-bearer for individual rights?' He exhaled deeply. 'Or is this poison-pen stuff just a complete red herring and we're missing some other connection . . . something *crucial*.'

Mat Sullivan looked at his old friend in concern.

'Hey, Gil,' he admonished, 'don't beat yourself up. Or rather, why not take some time out and pound the flesh at Doggie's.'

'I second that,' Olivia echoed softly. 'You know you always feel better after a bout in the ring.'

'Never been able to persuade you to take it up, though, have I, Mat?' her boyfriend observed.

'Well, all that *Rocky* stuff's not really my scene.'

'Plus we need him for five-a-side,' sniffed Noakes.

'You can hold the fort for a while, can't you, George?'

As ever, the DS was putty in Olivia's hands.

'Course I can. I'll hook up with Burton an' Doyle, boss. See what they've got on the house-to-house . . . Let Miss here get on with the marking.' He cast a respectful look at the piles of exercise books, as though they were a portal to another world. *If only*, thought Olivia ruefully.

'Go on, guv,' Noakes urged. 'Burton c'n organize some photos of the residents and we'll get them across to The Anchorage — see if they recognize any of 'em. Then there's Dowell's finances . . . I'll get Doyle on that while I check out the climbing equipment the killer used.'

'You've succeeded in twisting my arm,' Markham smiled at his subordinate.

Sullivan got to his feet. 'I'll see you off the premises,' he said before adding mischievously, 'just to make sure you don't get abducted by any tree huggers in the guise of assistant heads.'

* * *

After they had gone, Olivia was too restless to start work. She made herself another drink and carried it over to the window. Night had fallen, but the snow still gleamed blue-black in the darkness. Somewhere out there lurked a killer, she thought. Someone with a shard of ice for a heart. With a little shudder, she turned back to her classroom and the light.

# 6. TIGHTROPE

Markham was well aware that his penchant for cathartic workouts at Doggie's — as Bromgrove Police Boxing Club was known — featured high on the list of his offences as reckoned up by DCI Sidney.

'Doggie' Dickerson was an army veteran whose antecedents no one cared to examine too closely (least of all the manner in which he had acquired his nickname). How he had become proprietor of the boxing club was wreathed in mystery, but his dingy premises in Marsh Lane were now as much of an institution as the police station itself.

Physically, Doggie was a cross between Fagin and some sort of military relict from the Napoleonic Wars, his accessories including a peculiar horsehair wig and an eyepatch, depending upon the effect he wanted to produce. With his wonky jaw, yellow tombstone teeth, twisted features ('nerve damage') and nicotine-stained fingers, he was no one's idea of a health guru. 'Looks like a pimp or a drug dealer,' Sidney spluttered. 'And as for the clientele — half the local villains go there.'

It was quite true that Doggie didn't exactly 'vet' his customers. But his formula — 'no names, no pack drill' — seemed to work, with youthful delinquents, ex-cons, a variety of malefactors and Bromgrove's finest all happily slugging it out side by side. Normally on opposing sides in the battle of life, they called a truce in the no man's land of the gym where only grit and physical courage counted. Markham found this bizarre freemasonry curiously soothing and never dreamed of abandoning it for more select purlieus such as The Sanctuary or Body Works.

Doggie had taken an instant shine to Markham, whom he was prone to call his 'fav'rite 'spector' (another black mark in Sidney's ledger). Over the years, they had become quite cosy, the old reprobate most recently sharing confidences of a romantic nature. Surprisingly, he was never short of girlfriends, the latest of whom — Marlene, bingo caller at The Pavilion with a décolletage that was one of the wonders of Bromgrove — had a keen interest in the supernatural, horoscopes and what Noakes derided as 'mystical hocus pocus'. In honour of which, Doggie had taken to wearing flowing kaftans reminiscent of an eastern Grand Vizier. Appropriate enough, given that the gym was pretty much his personal empire. A potent waft of Jack Daniel's told Markham that Marlene hadn't yet converted her seedy lothario to the joys of chai lattes and soya smoothies, which he found reassuring. An alcohol-free Doggie would be a step too far.

Now, after a therapeutic pummelling in the ring, Markham relaxed in what was euphemistically dubbed 'the sauna' — in reality, a manky locker room with a few shower stalls of dubious salubriousness and a grimy window that was invariably jammed shut. His opponent, DI Chris Carstairs from Vice, slumped down next to him breathing hard.

'By rights I should have had you back there, Gil.' Carstairs pinched his spare tyre ruefully.

'New squeeze bit of a domestic goddess is she, Chris?'

'Something like that,' the other grunted then waggled his eyebrows suggestively. 'Dynamite between the sheets, so I'll get another workout later on.'

'Too much information, mate.' But Markham's lean, angular face wore an expression of amused tolerance.

'Heard you've got your plate full with those New College Close murders.' Shop talk was generally verboten at Doggie's, but Carstairs was an old ally. 'I suppose Sidney's trotting out the usual playlist.'

'Pretty much.' Markham grimaced. 'You know how it is with him. Anything to avoid a scandal of the "pervs in high places" variety.'

Carstairs whistled. 'D'you think it'll come to that?'

'Well, we've got a smattering of local worthies in the mix, along with the local school and a psychotherapy clinic.'

'Ah. Tricky.'

'You can say that again.' Markham's muscles were aching, but it was a pleasurable tension. Unlike what awaited him back at the station. 'Then there's the LGBT angle . . .'

'LGBT . . . How come?'

'Well, I'm not clear how it fits together, but it looks like two of our vics may have got on the wrong side of the transgender debate.'

'*Uh-oh.*'

'Yep. And just for good measure we've got Councillor Callaghan, various church folk, a local activist and medics from the Newman all potentially in the frame. Plus subplots including poison-pen letters, prowlers and a dodgy caretaker.' Markham smiled wearily. 'You can imagine how much I'm looking forward to tomorrow morning's press conference.' As in not at all.

'Anything you need from me, Gil?' Carstairs was all sympathy.

'It's the usual story. I just need to blindside the press and Sidney really. Buy the team some time.'

'Wasn't there some kind of kinky element to these murders . . . ?' Carstairs paused delicately. 'Women in a box under the bed? That bloke strung up between goalposts . . . ?'

'Kinky's one word for it.'

'Well, I'll look out some of our unsolveds, rustle up a few stats from the S & M files. Might help to give it a sex maniac slant and direct attention away from folk in high places.'

'I don't want to start a panic, Chris. You can imagine the headlines: *Ted Bundy Comes to Bromgrove*.'

The other chuckled.

'Nothing like that, I promise.' He began to towel himself vigorously. 'Just enough to send them all haring off in the wrong direction. With any luck, you'll fan speculation it could be a case of sex games gone wrong.'

'What — two respectable women trapped like that and the local trick cyclist strung up with his throat cut?' Markham sounded sceptical.

'Give it a touch of sex, drugs, and rock 'n' roll,' his colleague urged.

Well, there *was* the Rohypnol . . .

'C'mon, Gil. Let your Uncle Chris help out.'

Markham laughed reluctantly.

'Seeing as I'm out of other ideas . . . I'll get Kate Burton over to you first thing tomorrow.'

Carstairs sighed theatrically. 'Not exactly Linda Lovelace, that one . . . more like a girl guide. But there's no denying she's thorough.'

'She's good at press conferences,' Markham agreed before adding heavily, 'knows how to handle the journos. Unlike Noakes.'

'Weren't there fisticuffs between him and Gavin Conors on that last case — the community centre one?'

'Pretty nearly.' Markham frowned, remembering. 'Sidney did his nut.'

'I'll bet.' Carstairs did a mean imitation of the DCI's honk, '"We're all on the same side in the fight against crime."'

'Noakesy'd rather be dead in a ditch than play nicely with anyone from the *Gazette*.'

'Well if you feed Conors and the rest of 'em a few choice titbits — strictly non-attributable — and chuck in a bit of Cracker-style analysis, it should get them off your back for a while and keep Sidney happy . . . Everyone's a winner.'

'Worth a try. Thanks, Chris.'

'My pleasure.' Then, with an air of exaggerated astonishment, 'Fuck me! It's the Marsh Lane Swami!'

Utterly unabashed, Doggie twirled his latest voluminous robe, embroidered with what looked like hieroglyphics, and beamed at the two detectives.

'Triffic, ain't it?' he said with his trademark snaggle-toothed grin.

'Where'd you get it, Dogs?'

'Marlene bought it from some shop in town. All new age an' Zen,' he said vaguely.

'Would that be Lili's by any chance?' Markham asked.

'Yeah, thass the one.' Doggie was clearly pleased its fame had gone before it.

'Kindred spirits, you two.' Carstairs waved cheerily and disappeared into a shower cubicle.

'D'you shop there as well then, Mr Markham?' There was a touching wistfulness about the enquiry.

'Not as such, Doggie.' Time to be diplomatic. 'But I understand it's very popular with the "in" crowd.'

The old villain nodded sagely. It was probably the first time anyone had ever intimated that he was on-trend.

''S a bit way out,' he volunteered shiftily, speaking out of the corner of his mouth. 'Y'know . . . *alternative*. I'm not into the makeovers an' dressing up. But Mar says it's got a bit of a vibe. Always smells nice, too, what with them joss stick thingies.'

Markham tapped the side of his nose.

'Never fear, Doggie, your secret's safe with me.'

To his relief, the other gave a nervous cackle — 'You will 'ave your little joke, Mr Markham' — and lurched off.

*Makeovers and dressing up*. For one awful minute there he'd been afraid Doggie was going to disclose he had a bit of a yen for drag.

It sounded as though Julian Hoskinson's emporium was edgier than he had been led to believe. Might be worth getting Doyle in there for a recce.

* * *

Twenty minutes later, showered and refreshed, he stood outside gulping down lungfuls of sharp, clean air. *Home*, he decided and then froze.

On his way into the gym, he had noticed a crudely fashioned, lopsided snowman on the pavement at the corner of Marsh Lane. Nothing unusual about that — it was the festive season after all. The local kids had used pebbles and bits of rock for its features, and a gaudy scarf was knotted about its neck.

But it wasn't these makeshift adornments that made him pause.

Something was there that hadn't been there before.

The snowman now sported a policeman's helmet. Tilted at a rakish angle, it seemed almost to be mocking Markham.

He looked up and down the street but it was deserted, all vanilla marzipan perfection with its carpeting of snow. Little flurries swirled about him as though trapping him in some toy Christmas globe. The effect was uncanny, making him feel momentarily as if Bromgrove were a phantasmagorical landscape.

Letting himself into his car, he sat lost in reflection for some time.

Snowmen, he recalled wryly, were one of George Noakes's pet hates. '*Sly*,' the DS was wont to declare emphatically. 'Like they're grinning about summat wicked.'

Oddly enough, Olivia shared this superstition. 'They give me the creeps, Gil. Half human, half demon . . . It's not so bad if they've got arms. But when they're just a *torso* plonked there staring at you. Like they're full of hate.' Markham had never really thought about it before, but now, under the influence of the time and place, he felt oddly unsettled. As though something malign was lurking just out of sight on the periphery of his world . . . watching and waiting.

The connection with Hope Academy — the 'ranty' hate mail sent to Mary Atkins — bothered him. There seemed to be a lot of bad feeling swirling around the school. But at least this time there was no danger of Olivia being caught up in the maelstrom, and he intended to keep it that way.

With one last keen glance along the snowy avenue, he started the engine.

* * *

In the event, the press conference on Wednesday, 11 December passed off better than Markham could have anticipated.

Chris Carstairs had been as good as his word, so it had proved relatively easy to lay a false trail for the little cluster of reporters who had braved the elements to attend.

Not that Gavin Conors hadn't tried it on, of course, circling the subject of Hope Academy with the relentless zeal of a truffle hog.

But Kate Burton had deftly sidestepped all the traps and stuck undeviatingly to her script. Without directly saying so, she suggested a scenario of randomized sex offences with possible links to other cases, throwing in a discussion of 'bottom-up geographical profiling' and 'locatedness'. Noakes might have called it 'moron-speak' but the press pack lapped it up, not least because of the flattering implication that these were exclusive insights unavailable to the common herd. 'You'll appreciate that at this stage we don't wish to jeopardize ongoing investigations,' Burton concluded smoothly after a mini disquisition on crime mapping, 'but the public can be assured we are pursuing a number of very promising leads.' Her tone conveyed the impression that further questioning would be in singular bad taste.

*Pursuing a number of very promising leads.*

She actually sounded as though she believed it, thought Markham lurking at the back of the room.

But the DCI was well pleased.

'Excellent, excellent, Sergeant,' he flashed his shark's smile at Burton who recoiled slightly. 'Crucial at this stage to keep an open mind and consider all possibilities.'

*Yeah right*, Markham couldn't help scoffing under his breath. If by considering all possibilities, you meant not incriminating anyone important.

Slimy Sid stroked the insignia on his upper sleeves. 'We bear a heavy responsibility,' he intoned, for all the world as if he was the CID equivalent of Atlas, thought Markham with bitter humour. Mercifully, after a few more platitudes and a beady-eyed glare at Noakes's disreputable-looking parka, he vanished into the upper regions.

'Thank Christ for that,' Noakes growled at Sidney's departing back. 'Did you see the way he kept admiring his reflection? An' flashing his gnashers at that bird from the *Courier* . . . prob'ly thinks the pips are a turn on.'

'Well done, Kate.' The DI ignored his subordinate's muttered imprecations. 'That bit about responsible journalism hit home, I think.'

'Yeah, well done,' Noakes echoed, giving credit where credit was due. 'Fannying about with all them statistics really threw them off the scent . . . An' you could tell they got off on all the psycho mumbo jumbo.'

There *had to* be a compliment in there somewhere, Burton thought desperately.

'Thanks, sarge,' she said weakly as Markham smothered a smile.

Doyle too was enthusiastic. 'Reckon they'll leave us alone after that.'

*Not for long*, thought Markham grimly.

'Right.' Noakes was rubbing his hands. 'After that, I reckon we deserve a bacon butty.' He looked at Burton who clearly wasn't up for a grease-fest. 'Or that granola stuff you like,' he added with the air of one making a vast concession.

'You've got *ten minutes* to grab something,' the DI said firmly. 'And then it's back to the close. I want an update on the residents' movements and then we can get some of them in.' He locked eyes with each of his team in turn. 'There's something uniquely horrible about the way our victims died. I'm worried about an escalation.'

Noakes stared at him.

'Like our killer's gonna go on the rampage, guv?'

'More like he'll eliminate anyone he perceives as a threat . . . and take a perverted pleasure in doing so.' Markham's voice compelled attention. 'This is an exceptionally dangerous individual whose camouflage has so far served him well. So we have to move *fast*, otherwise we're looking at more tragedies before Christmas.'

* * *

Their little incident room felt cold and bleak despite the radiators being on full blast. Burton had magicked up a fan heater from somewhere, which helped take the chill off the room. Gradually they began to thaw out.

'Have you got anything for us then, Sergeant?' Markham asked Noakes.

'No one at that poncey clinic recognized any of the residents,' came the reply.

'D'you want me to get a warrant for patient records, boss?'

'Might as well, Kate, but I doubt it'll yield anything. Whoever did this knows they've got nothing to fear from a paper trail.'

She scribbled industriously in her pocketbook.

'What about Mr Dowell's finances?'

'I'm seeing the manager of the Halifax later, guv, but sounds like he had no worries money-wise . . . His flat was mortgage free an' all.'

Still, thought Markham, it could have been a case of 'much wants more'.

'I want the flat searched with a toothcomb, Noakes.' Markham shifted impatiently in his uncomfortable chair. 'See if we can dig up anything useful in his papers . . . maybe something about that mysterious research of his.'

Observing Burton's expression of intense interest, the DI updated her on what they had learned from their visit to The Anchorage.

'BDD,' she said eagerly. 'I had to do a paper on that for my degree, sir. Well, it was about Pure O actually.'

Noakes and Doyle leaned in. Little Miss Holier-Than-Thou and the drugs scene!

'It's a type of obsessive-compulsive disorder that centres on intrusive thoughts . . . No obvious external signs like repetitive actions or hand washing.' She tried not to laugh at her colleagues' crestfallen expressions. Clearly they were hoping to learn she'd dabbled with hallucinogenics as opposed to the *Diagnostic and Statistical Manual of Mental Disorders.*

Markham's eyes met Burton's in a moment of amused complicity, and she felt herself turn red.

'If anything turns up in the house search, then you can check it out for us, Kate,' the DI said. 'It's a complex area,' he added before going on to relate what he and Noakes had learned at Hope.

'The transgender debate's gotten pretty vicious in recent years,' she mused. 'You get people on one side saying experts are making up the science — that the whole trans thing's a delusion and unnatural. And then on the other side it's like there's a tripwire, so anyone who says anything critical about the trans community is labelled transphobic and a bigot.'

Going by the expression on Noakes's face, Markham suspected his wingman would regard 'bigot' as the ultimate compliment. From the nervous looks Burton darted at her fellow sergeant, he could see she knew it too.

Oblivious to these undercurrents, Doyle chipped in. 'Yeah, you've even got students doing demos against lecturers who say you can't self-declare — y'know, decide you're a different sex.'

Markham didn't feel equal to exploring the brave new world of gender fluidity.

'The point is,' he interjected hastily, 'it's all very contentious . . . Passions running high on all sides.'

'So some religious fanatic — or someone with conservative views — may have been angry with Marian Bussell and Mary Atkins for being on the wrong side,' Burton said slowly. 'And with Dowell too.' She turned to Markham. 'But where does Dawn MacAlinden fit in, sir? Was she some kind of campaigner for trans rights? Or was she an accident — killed because she happened to be in Marian's flat and he couldn't let her get away?'

'That's exactly what I've been asking myself, Kate. How does Dawn fit in?' He raked a hand through his hair, achieving an effect of Byronic dishevelment as opposed to Noakes's startled porcupine look. 'You see, I don't believe she was just collateral damage . . . I think he wanted to kill her too. It was all part of the masterplan.'

'Maybe it's got nothing to do with all this transgender stuff and there's something else that links the vics.'

'You could well be right, Doyle. But at this stage it's a common factor. And the poison-pen element points to the killer being a committed hater.'

'What about them two from the Newman?' Noakes demanded. 'Doctor Wasserface an' the Boy Wonder.'

'Doctor O'Connor and her partner, Martin Henley,' Burton amended patiently.

'Yeah them.'

'Well, they're not specialists in gender reassignment or anything like that. Doctor O'Connor works in the field of oppositional defiant disorder while Mr Henley's field is autism and complex needs.'

'What's all *that* mean when it's at home?' Noakes asked rudely.

Before Burton could get started on the clinical details, Doyle said with a cheeky grin, 'Means they're not messing about with folks' bits, sarge.'

Noakes did one of his more theatrical eye-rolls.

'Which isn't to say they don't have experience of trans issues,' Markham pointed out. 'Or that their paths mightn't have crossed with practitioners in that field.' He turned to Burton. 'We need to check if Dowell was on their radar, or if he did any work at the Newman.'

Burton's shiny bob bent over the pocketbook again.

When she looked up from her notes, the DI asked, 'Any word from Dimples on time of death for Mr Dowell?'

'He reckons between ten and eleven on Monday night, sir.'

'Residents' whereabouts?'

'As you'd expect, sir. Safely tucked up in bed or watching the telly — except for Julian Hoskinson.'

'What was Mr Hoskinson up to?'

'Sampling the delights of Ducky.'

'Hmm . . . That's the new bar off Abercrombie Street, isn't it?'

'Yes that's it, sir.' A furtive look at Noakes. 'It's, er, pansexual.'

'She means anything bloody goes,' the other rumbled.

'Presumably we've got witnesses to corroborate.'

'Any number, sir.' She hesitated. 'Though I'm not sure how reliable.'

Noakes muttered something under his breath, eliciting a knowing smirk from Doyle.

'Anyone else out and about?'

A quick riffle through her notes.

'Oh, Doctor O'Connor was on call. And Mr Ledwidge was out at Bromgrove General — he's one of the chaplains there, apparently. sometimes gets asked to bring the sacrament, his wife said.'

'Anyone vouch for them?'

'Well, Doctor O'Connor drove home around ten thirty. Mr Ledwidge paid a visit to the hospital chapel and didn't get in till around midnight — said there wasn't anyone else in the chapel when he was there.'

'Any of 'em could've done for Dowell,' Noakes said grimly. 'Them alibis aren't worth diddly squat.'

The DI took a deep breath. Earlier feelings of wellbeing from his workout at Doggie's and the successful press conference were fast evaporating.

'What about the residents' whereabouts for last Thursday afternoon? Where are we up to with Mrs Bussell and Ms

MacAlinden?' Markham was punctilious about according victims due respect. Burton realized she had never heard him refer to the dead by just their surnames, though this was commonplace in CID.

'Dimples says the time frame's late afternoon to early evening. He can't be absolutely positive about when they were knocked out with the sedative, but their bodies went into the base of that bed around six or seven p.m.'

She began ticking off suspects on her fingers.

'Mary Atkins, Lucy O'Connor, Martin Henley and Stacey Macmillan were all at work in the afternoon.'

'Continuously? In sight of colleagues?'

'Looks like it, yes. Though O'Connor and Henley left around three because she wasn't feeling too well — coming down with something.'

'So they're each other's alibi then.'

'That's right, sir.'

His expression said it all. *Unsatisfactory*.

'Stacey was doing a few hours in the newsagents — McColl's — round the corner.'

'I thought she was retired.'

'She is. Just helps out now and again . . . Headed for home around 2 p.m.'

Again, she couldn't be ruled out.

'Mary Atkins had meetings after school. Didn't leave till gone eight.'

'How about the non-workers?'

'The Ledwidges were playing mah-jong with Jeff Coleman and Simon Gailey.'

Noakes snorted incredulously. ''S like one of them farces,' he said with heavy sarcasm. '*Anyone for tennis*?'

'Well Jeff Coleman isn't, sarge.' Doyle's eyes danced. 'In a wheelchair, remember?'

The DS ignored him. 'Very cosy,' he said sourly. 'What time did the party break up then?'

'They can't be sure about that, sarge, but Eileen Ledwidge thinks it was around three-ish. She went off to phone her daughter while the men stayed chatting for a bit.'

'What did they do after that?'

'Coleman went off to work on his latest book. Gailey wanted to watch *Judge Rinder* or *Judge Judy* . . . some legal programme.'

'What was Julian Hoskinson up to?'

'Minding the shop apparently. Says he closed early because it was quiet . . . about four thirty.'

'A perk of being your own boss, I suppose,' Markham sighed.

But singularly unhelpful in terms of establishing an alibi.

'Councillor Callaghan?'

'Closeted with the Works Committee down at the town hall . . . finished up two-ish.'

'*Jesus wept.*' Noakes could stand no more. 'They could *all* have done it.' He scowled at Burton. 'Can't Dimples narrow it down some more?'

'No can do, sarge.' She blew a stray lock of fringe out of her eyes. 'You know what he's like. Got quite narked when I tried to push it.'

'The bodies were semi-embalmed,' Markham pointed out.

Silence fell over them like a pall as their thoughts travelled back to those desiccated corpses.

'None of us were at the women's PM, right?' Noakes said finally. 'Happen Dimples is in a snit about it.'

'I doubt it,' Markham said drily. 'It's hardly a spectator sport, and you may recall we had our hands full at the time.' He turned to Doyle. 'I believe you attended Mr Dowell's, Constable.'

The young DC's wan expression suggested it was an experience with which he could well have dispensed, but he pulled on his game face. 'I've emailed you a summary, sir. There *were* traces of Rohypnol like DS Burton thought.'

'Thank you.'

'What now, guv?'

'Let's see who we can round up.' The DI's fingers drummed the table. 'Probe the cracks in their stories . . . Anyone strike you as looking unusually strained, Kate?'

'A couple of them, sir. But, to be honest, there's some sort of cold or flu bug doing the rounds that could account for it.'

'Hmm. Well let's press on anyway. We can start with Gary Coslett, find out exactly what he's been up to.'

*Good luck with that, guv.*

'Oh by the way, sir . . .'

'Yes, Doyle.'

'Sorry, I forgot to mention it before . . . There's a service for the victims later this afternoon — at St James's. Not a funeral, obviously — what with the bodies not being released yet — more like,' he looked around him as though for inspiration, 'a *memorial* service . . . for people to pay their respects, Mrs Ledwidge said.' He looked at his colleagues' glum faces. 'There'll be eats afterwards in the church.'

'Now you're talking my language, son.' Noakes turned hopefully towards Markham.

'Yes, we'll be there, Constable,' the DI said.

Outside, pewter skies held the threat of more snow.

Looking towards Beech Drive, Markham saw that the playing field goalposts had been taken down. As if the previous night's gruesome descent from the cross had never been.

# 7. IN THE BLINK OF AN EYE

The team decided to walk to St James's. Crunching along snowy Chapel Street, they felt secretly relieved to get away from New College Close, which had begun to feel increasingly oppressive. It was turning bitterly cold and a stiff breeze had whipped up, but the contrast with the stale fug of their incident room was invigorating.

'Do any of our suspects have criminal records?' the DI enquired as they tramped along.

'Gary Coslett got community service for assault,' Burton said. 'Spent conviction. Nothing since.'

'Figures,' grunted Noakes. ''S got "scrote" written all over him, that one.'

'So, our Mr Coslett has a bit of a temper. Hmm,' Markham reflected. 'Interesting . . . I need to see those Residents' Association minutes, find out if either Mrs Bussell or Ms MacAlinden had any run-ins with the management company.'

'I'll speak to Mr Ledwidge about it after the service.'

'Excellent, Kate. Anyone else known to us?'

'Julian Hoskinson, sir. Cautions for public order offences — went to a lot of demos, bit of an eco-warrior.'

'One of them nose-ringed crusties, you mean.' Noakes stomped along as though to trample the anathematized breed beneath his feet.

'What about the rest of the close — anyone else raise a red flag?'

'No one, boss,' Doyle chipped in. 'I've followed up on all the rest and run checks with the uni and social services . . . Clean as a whistle.'

'Call-outs to domestics, neighbours' bust-ups?'

'Someone rang in about a barney at the good doctor's.'

'Doctor O'Connor?' Markham was startled.

'Something and nothing, sir. From the sound of it, a nuisance caller, though they sent uniforms round to check.' Doyle had due reverence for the medical profession. 'Most likely an ex-patient making trouble.'

'Right.' Markham was thoughtful. 'Anything else?'

'Brian Ledwidge tends to get up people's noses from time to time,' Doyle said cheerfully. 'Y'know, all spit and polish, not letting standards slip . . .'

'Quite right too,' growled Noakes. 'Only way to make Coslett pull his finger out.'

'Oh, I don't think it worked, sarge. And him jackbooting around just pissed the rest of them off. He took a bit of flak for it. Marian Bussell nicknamed him "Mister Mind How You Go".'

And now she and her friend were dead.

'Some sort of feud was it?' asked Noakes.

'Nah.' Doyle was enjoying the conditions, kicking up drifts of snow like an overgrown schoolboy. 'Sounded like everyone just took the mick. The solicitor guy called him Captain Mainwaring.'

'Retired solicitor.' Burton was always punctilious about detail. 'Simon Gailey.'

'Yeah, that's the one. Him and Bussell were friends. The writer bloke went round there quite a lot too.'

'Jeff Coleman.'

*How does she do it?* Noakes asked himself. *Memorize all them names like some freaking index card.*

But, noticing how she nearly overbalanced into a deceptively deep rut that was concealed by the snow, he shot out a meaty ungloved paw and hauled her upright.

'Ta, sarge.' Huge myopic brown eyes blinked their gratitude and he found himself hoping to fuck they could keep her safe this time round. He still had nightmares over the team's investigation into murders of staff at the Newman psychiatric hospital when Burton decided to go it alone and nearly got herself killed.

Happily unaware of these dark thoughts, Burton went on, 'Jeff Coleman and Mrs Bussell had some sort of friendly rivalry going. It took him years to make it as a writer, but Harlequin — that's his publisher — were falling over themselves to sign her up. She liked to try ideas out on him and Gailey . . . *Ouf!*' She circumvented another treacherous dip. 'Dowell would call round now and again too.'

'Proper little writers' circle,' Noakes observed. 'An' now three of 'em have snuffed it.' He puffed and panted, squinting ahead with narrowed eyes like some overweight arctic explorer.

On that sobering note, he pushed open the frosted lychgate and led the little party up the path towards St James's Parish Church.

It was rather a beautiful building, Markham concluded, lagging behind the others who were in a hurry to get out of the cold. Two slender belfry towers, like minarets, jutted up from a triangular gable end. In the snow, the church's classical facade had the spun-sugar delicacy of a fairy tale castle. Around it on three sides, white-clad monuments and tombs formed a spectral honour guard.

Inside, he admired the vaulted ceiling with its aquatint coffering and the exquisite stained-glass east window behind the altar.

Noakes was less than impressed by what looked like a somewhat girlish King David in a flowery meadow playing his harp for an audience of pudgy cherubs.

'You don't know if he's Arthur or Martha in that get-up,' the DS grouched, contemplating the betunicked figure with pronounced distaste. 'At least if they've got beards, you c'n tell if it's prophets or whatnot.'

Markham steered his grumpy colleague round to another window on the far left-hand side of the church.

'There you go, Sergeant,' he said drily. 'Saint James. With beard.'

''S more like it,' the other replied. 'Looks a bit miserable, mind.'

'So would you if you were about to be beheaded.'

'Why's he holding that little plate with them prawn cracker thingies?'

'They're seashells. That's his symbol, Noakesy. He was a fisherman, remember?'

'Oh aye.' The DS revolved on his heels like a restless bullock. 'It's a bit fussy for C of E . . . all them blues an' pinks.'

By contrast, Markham found the décor unexpectedly charming, from the soft blush-pink of the three painted arches behind the main shrine and its adjoining bijou side-altars, to the blue-carpeted five-bay nave. Italianate-style statues of the saints with their respective symbols lined the ivory-hued walls at regular intervals. He spotted Saint Catherine with her wheel and Saint Cecilia bearing the palm of martyrdom. The embellishment and baroque attitudes chimed with his Catholic upbringing and made him feel oddly safe. He would have liked to wander the interior, taking it all in at his leisure, but became aware that Burton and Doyle were awaiting instructions, hovering warily in the porch as though they were in danger of 'catching' religion if they ventured too far into the interior. Suppressing a sigh, he made his way to the back of the church, trailed by Noakes muttering various uncomplimentary comments about 'weirdiness' under his breath.

'What time's kick-off?' the DS asked when they reached the others.

Burton glanced at her watch. 'They should be along in a few minutes, sarge.'

'Right,' Markham said. 'We'll make ourselves unobtrusive,' he glanced pointedly at Noakes who affected an air of sunny innocence, 'at the back.'

They shuffled awkwardly into a pew over to the left and waited.

It wasn't long before the residents of the close arrived in ones and twos.

As always, it seemed to Markham that individual identities were somehow subsumed — rubbed out — by the religious building. As though the church were simply swallowing them into its cavernous belly like Jonah disappearing into the whale.

Gradually, however, the small congregation became distinct to him, settling into their pews with the self-conscious awkwardness characteristic of attendees at such occasions. Brian Ledwidge appeared from a door at the back of the main altar wearing a dark purple stole and holding a prayer book.

Then the memorial service began.

It was a stilted affair, due in part to Ledwidge's stiff and mechanical delivery. Markham winced as the priest mangled a set of sonorously beautiful prayers for the dead before reminding himself, with a pang of compunction, that the man was labouring under a double burden of personal grief and pastoral responsibility. There were no eulogies, possibly because the mourners didn't trust themselves to speak. Formal tributes would doubtless wait until the funerals.

His eyes slid over the little group huddled at the front of the church.

Lucy O'Connor and Martin Henley had the lock-jawed look of a couple who have just concluded a quarrel. In light of what Doyle had told them earlier, the DI wondered if there might be trouble in paradise. Certainly, they seemed far from comfortable together, with the poker-backed posture of two people on the defensive.

Simon Gailey was dignified in a cashmere tailored coat. While Martin Henley was more obviously handsome, the older man's refined, ascetic features possessed a quiet distinction that made the other appear almost coarse. Catching sight of Gailey's profile, silver wings of hair brushed back from the temples, Markham was struck anew by his patrician good looks — the phwoar factor of a well-preserved Nigel Havers.

Stacey Macmillan would doubtless agree with this verdict judging from the surreptitious sidelong glances she was directing Gailey's way. It occurred to the DI that it might pay to cultivate Stacey, who struck him as an inveterate gossip.

No smiles were squandered by Stacey on Julian Hoskinson who sat on her right, though the charity worker's appearance was considerably less grungy than his signature style. He still had that famished, anorectic look, but there was no sign of any distracting lip stud or bracelet. His dark hair was neatly combed, and he wore a perfectly respectable charcoal herringbone suit topped with a chunky car coat. The entire ensemble actually looked quite expensive, causing the DI to ask himself whether Hoskinson might not be one of those trustafarian socialists.

Jeff Coleman had been wheeled into the church by Simon Gailey and sat in the right hand transept. The writer appeared startlingly worn and ravaged, his deep-set eyes like two burning coals against the pallor of his face. Markham wondered if there was any truth in Stacey's assertion that he'd cherished a secret tendresse for Marian Bussell. Or whether he resented her late-life flowering as a writer when, from the sound of it, his own path to success had been strewn with thorns and thistles. Either way, as Noakes put it not at all sotto voce, he looked like something out of a Transylvanian horror movie.

Eileen Ledwidge sat next to Dawn MacAlinden's widower who wore a glazed expression as though none of the proceedings made any sense. Markham knew from the family liaison officer that he was in a very bad way mentally, still clinging to his belief that Dawn's death was an accident despite all evidence to the contrary. Eileen's kindly face reflected her concern that the occasion might prove too much for him.

On the other side of the widower, with the air of a warder taking him into custody, was Councillor Penny Callaghan, her resemblance to Ann Widdecombe more pronounced than ever. Boot-faced, she bellowed out responses with her usual trademark bray.

Sitting in the row behind was Mary Atkins, enveloped in a monstrous black poncho. 'Bleeding hell, it's Zorro,' Doyle quipped as he craned to look before subsiding back into his seat at a glare from Kate Burton.

Poncho aside, Hope's assistant head looked distinctly subdued, even making allowances for the sombreness of the occasion. In fact, Markham thought she looked nervous. But then, it was hardly to be wondered at with a murderer on the loose.

And, with a cold sensation like icy water in the pit of his stomach, Markham felt a sudden, cast-iron certainty that the killer of Marian Bussell, Dawn MacAlinden and Kenneth Dowell was right there in church with them, joining in their prayers for the souls of the dead.

The little two-manual pipe organ wheezed into life and they made a stab at 'Abide with Me', the DI's melodious tenor doing its best to obliterate whatever noises Noakes might feel himself impelled to make.

At the end of the service, the team loitered once more at the back, making what passed for polite conversation with the mourners.

'Inspector.' It was Simon Gailey. 'This young lady would like a word.'

The DI recognized Shona Townley, looking waif-like in a blanket coat that was several sizes too big for her.

'Hello, Shona,' he said warmly. 'I didn't spot you before.'

'Me and a few teachers from Hope were in the side-chapel, Mr Markham,' she said shyly. 'We knew it was supposed to be for residents, but what with me . . .' she stuttered slightly, 'finding them . . .'

'Of course you wanted to be here,' Markham finished smoothly. 'And very fitting that staff from Hope came along too.'

She was clearly relieved but continued to linger, eyes riveted on him.

'Was there something else, Shona?'

Simon Gailey tactfully melted away.

'Do you want to talk to me on your own?'

At her nod, he steered the schoolgirl gently towards a recessed bay whose three lancet windows commemorated Bromgrove's fallen dead from the two world wars, with what looked like various archangels scooping up youthful heroes in a range of battle uniforms.

'What is it, Shona?'

She looked about her apprehensively, for all the world as though she didn't want even the inscrutable archangels to hear.

The DI checked behind him. Burton had clocked the situation and was ensuring no one approached.

'The coast's clear,' he encouraged her. 'Don't be frightened, no one's listening.'

'Did you find Mrs B's scrapbook, Mr Markham?'

His spine tingled.

'Nothing like that turned up, Shona,' he said with assumed casualness. 'Why — was it important?'

'Dunno,' she said uncertainly. 'But it might've been.' Her face fell. 'Jus' thought I should mention it . . . in case there might be a clue in there or somefink. She was going to show me it, y'see — her treasures an' all that. Pictures of school when she was there.'

Markham suddenly felt more convinced than ever that there was a connection between these murders and Hope Academy. But he allowed nothing of this to show on his face.

'Thanks for telling me, Shona,' he said. 'I'll look into it right away.' With a gentle pressure of his hand on her arm, he added, 'Of course, it might be that she was wandering a little in her mind. Maybe she wished she'd compiled a scrapbook without actually getting round to it.'

He wanted to draw the teenager away from the subject of the missing scrapbook. For her own safety. Equally, he didn't want to alarm her.

'Let's keep this to ourselves for the moment,' he continued easily. 'Sounds like the past was important to your friend.'

'Yeah, I reckon it was.' Her voice was sad. 'Now I'll never know if there was something special she wanted to show me, cos I missed a week an' didn't call round.'

'I'm sure your visits were a comfort to Mrs Bussell.' The DI's voice carried conviction. 'As well as being a link with the past.'

The wan features brightened a little.

'D'you really think so?'

'I'm sure of it.'

'I better go now. The rest'll be waiting for me.'

'When does school break up for the holidays, Shona?'

'Twenty-third of December, Mr Markham.'

'Goodness, that's late. They keep your nose to the grindstone all right.'

She smiled shyly.

'Oh, I don' mind . . . Want to go to uni, so I need to get the grades.'

'What're you hoping to study?'

'History.' Then, somewhat self-consciously, 'Mrs B got me interested. Told lots of good stories . . . about wars an' the princes in the tower.'

Markham's mouth twisted as he recalled how that particular episode of Plantagenet history had figured in a recent investigation.

'Well,' he said recollecting himself, 'history's about *all* our stories. I'm sure yours will turn out to be a good one.'

Another smile — more confident this time — and she was gone.

Noakes shambled over. 'Well, whatever you said seems to have cheered her up, guv. Don' look quite so peaky.'

Burton and Doyle joined them.

‘Shona mentioned Mrs Bussell having a scrapbook, some sort of album of mementoes from her teaching days.’

‘Nothing like that turned up when the crime scene was processed, sir.’ Burton was quick to see the significance. ‘You think the murderer took it because there was something incriminating in there?’

‘Possibly, Kate.’

‘Mebbe it was like a trophy or summat.’ Noakes had recently discovered the joys of Sky’s True Crime channel. ‘Like he wanted to keep it as a reminder of the kill.’

‘That’s another possibility, Sergeant.’

Doyle spoke up. ‘Or he could’ve been curious, taken a look and seen someone he recognized—’

‘You mean, from his schooldays?’ Noakes butted in. ‘Jesus, that’s all we need. Another nutcase from Hope . . . Traumatized from getting too many detentions from Bussell or summat barmy like that.’

‘Could be, sarge,’ the DC replied equably. ‘Or maybe there was just something in there that, well, struck a chord or something.’

‘Yeah, there’s no saying how a sicko’s mind works,’ his colleague agreed.

‘Whatever the motive, the scrapbook’s missing.’

‘Could it have been a figment of Mrs Bussell’s imagination, sir?’ Burton asked hesitantly. ‘Old people have fancies sometimes.’ She thought of her own aunt’s long decline as she said it.

‘From the way the residents spoke, it didn’t sound like she’d lost her marbles,’ Doyle put in.

‘Hmm.’ Markham looked back into the church, which had relapsed into silence and shadow. His eyes fell on a strange little icon of Christ with downturned mouth, sad hooded eyes and right hand raised in blessing . . . or was it warning?

‘Right,’ he said, ‘let’s be on our way.’

‘What about the eats? ’S only next door.’

Opportunities for refuelling invariably loomed high in Noakes’s order of priorities.

‘We’ll put in an appearance,’ the DI said heavily, ‘stay long enough to be polite — and for you to stock up on sausage rolls. But for God’s sake be discreet about it, Sergeant. It won’t exactly enhance our reputation if the locals see you hoovering up all the edibles in sight.’

Having obtained the green light from Markham, Noakes received this reproof with equanimity.

‘By the by, did anything useful turn up in Dowell’s flat?’

‘Looks like he lived for his work, guv. No social life to speak of an’ nowt juicy in the paperwork . . . Kept all his medical stuff at The Anchorage . . . ’cept for textbooks an’ stuff.’ The DS wrinkled his nose. ‘There were tons of those . . . Like some musty ole second-hand bookshop.’

‘Anything leap out at you?’

‘Nah . . . It was all tranny bollocks.’ As ever, the DS was setting out his stall with a vengeance, the DI reflected wryly.

Burton cleared her throat disapprovingly. ‘Largely material on gender variant young people and non-binary options, sir.’ A scorching look at her colleague. ‘Also, trans hostility and adolescent nonconformity.’

Noakes was having none of it. ‘Like I said. Bollocks.’

DC Doyle grinned as though to say, ‘you can lead a horse to water, but you can’t make it drink.’

The DI sighed. ‘Save it for the pub, Noakesy. In the meantime, let’s adjourn next door or there won’t be anything left . . .’

As it happened, Eileen Ledwidge had organized a generous spread: thick-cut sandwiches with a range of fillings, quiche, sausage rolls, canapés, scotch eggs, scones and two types of cake. Fresh percolated coffee, tea and soft drinks were also on offer. Parishioners from St James’s circulated with expressions of kindly hospitality, doing their best to infuse some warmth into the sad little gathering.

‘Full marks to the padre’s missus,’ Noakes said expansively. ‘There’s nothing stingy about this lot.’

And with that, he headed off to do the buffet justice, Burton and Doyle following the good ship Noakes like two tugboats in the wake of a steamer.

The DI didn't feel particularly hungry, but he enjoyed the coffee, which was excellent.

After a minute or two, Burton came over to him with a paper plate. 'Have a cheese and pickle sandwich, sir,' she said awkwardly. 'They're really good and,' with a faint blush, 'you need to keep your strength up.'

'That's very considerate, Kate.' He took one to oblige her. It was surprisingly tasty, and he felt revived.

'What next, sir?'

'Well, we didn't get very far with rounding up the residents earlier,' he said. 'At least, not those we needed to interview.'

'Sorry about that, boss.' She looked crestfallen. 'Everyone seemed to be lying low.'

That was one way of putting it.

'More like the bush telegraph alerted them to stay out of our way,' he said grimly.

'I've done you a briefing note on all the alibis, sir, but—'

'I know, they don't take us much further forward.' For a moment, his handsome face looked hollow with fatigue, high cheekbones seeming almost to pierce the skin.

'Gary Coslett did a good job of stonewalling us,' she said. 'It was obvious that he thought Mrs Bussell was an interfering old bat and there'd been a few run-ins, but he wouldn't be drawn on specifics.'

'Do you think he saw anything, suspects anyone . . . ?'

'Difficult to tell, what with "shifty" being his default expression.'

'You don't think he was planning to branch out — graduate from assault to burglary?'

'You think he could be our prowler, sir? What about the make-up mirror?'

'Maybe that find is unconnected, Kate.'

But even as he said the words, he recalled the cool, smooth sensation of the compact in his hand . . . his conviction that it had been dropped by the killer . . . that it was a talisman of some kind, just like the school badge clutched in Marian Bussell's dead hand.

'I'll check with Laneside, sir. Dig a little deeper — see if there have been any complaints about Coslett.'

Suddenly, Stacey Macmillan materialized at the DI's elbow. With a somewhat strained smile, Burton gestured vaguely in the direction of the buffet. 'Back in a minute, sir.'

Markham murmured the conventional pleasantries while observing the woman closely. There was something unusual about her, he thought. She seemed to be — *fizzing* — in a state of heightened emotional excitement.

Of course, he reflected, funerals and memorial services had that effect on some people, but this was something different. Almost an expression of one-upmanship. As though she was privy to some huge joke that tickled her fancy enormously.

Noakes ambled over. *Getting his second wind*, thought Markham affectionately.

The DS smiled affably at Stacey.

'Hit the spot that did,' he said. 'Reckon we needed it an' all . . . to gee everyone up, like.'

God, he made it sound as though next up was the hokey-cokey.

Mercifully, she didn't take offence. 'You're right,' she agreed, 'especially on a day like this.'

'You seem a very close-knit community, Ms Macmillan.'

'Stacey, *please*.' Noakes watched the interchange with an expression of lascivious benevolence, a reflection of his complete faith in Markham's pulling power.

The DI tried not to wince.

'Well, like any neighbours we had our ups and downs,' the woman continued. 'Always the way with strong personalities . . .'

'Who wanted to be top dog then, luv?'

Stacey blinked, clearly taken aback by Noakes's directness. Even so, she rallied smartly.

'Our two schoolmarms had words from time to time.'

'Oh yes?' Markham was all polite interest.

'Marian thought Mary Atkins was a bit . . . *showy*. Tended to put herself forward a bit too much, made the story all about *her* instead of turning the spotlight on the kids.' She screwed up her face as if trying to remember, though Markham suspected she recalled Mrs Bussell's words exactly.

'She "colonized campaigns" was how Marian put it.'

'Is that how *you* saw it, Stacey?'

She gave an affected titter that set his teeth on edge. 'Well, maybe Mary can be just the *teensiest* bit pushy, makes the odd *faux pas*.' She paused to let this sink in. 'Dawn said it was a case of reinventing the wheel. Mary had a habit of forgetting that *Marian* was the one who put sexual health on the agenda at Hope . . . and took a lot of flak for it too. Dawn said to hear Mary you'd think *she* discovered LGBT.' Stacey bit her lip as though worried that she had been indiscreet.

*Little drops of poison*, thought Markham. But did it amount to anything?

'Yes, Marian could be a bit . . . well, *sharp* sometimes. Didn't suffer fools, if you know what I mean. Ken was the same — never backed away from a good old ding-dong.'

'Really?'

'Oh yes. He lit into Julian a few times and had the odd spat with Martin, enjoyed setting people straight about medical matters. Got on well enough with Lucy and Jeff, though. And he respected Simon.'

So, there were occasional ructions between Kenneth Dowell and other residents — Julian Hoskinson and Martin Henley for starters.

'He was an atheist too, you know, so it was a bit sticky between him and the Ledwidges.'

'Indeed.'

'Which is why it's so *nice* of them to organize all this.' A careful pause. 'They never held it against him — or Marian.'

'Was she an atheist too?'

'Oh no, Marian was C of E. But she was like Ken in other ways . . . a freethinker, very independent. Whereas Eileen and Brian are *conservative*.' Another tinkle. 'Well, it goes with his job.'

Again, the DI detected a current of suppressed excitement bubbling beneath the surface of the woman's prattle.

There was something else, he thought. Something she didn't want to share with anyone just yet. But secrets could be dangerous. He knew that by now the manner of Kenneth Dowell's death was bound to have got out. The little butterball in front of him could be in no doubt that Dowell had died because he knew too much.

Noakes too had picked up something in her manner.

''S important you don' hold out on us, luv,' he said. 'If there's owt you need to tell us, now's the time.'

For one second, she seemed to waver, her eyes flickering round the room. But then she laughed confidently. 'You can count on me for that, Sergeant. *Ooh*,' she squealed, '*coffee cake*. Must just get myself a slice.' And she sashayed away.

They looked after her retreating figure.

'Reckon that one's got a hot date,' Noakes said.

'You don't think she's sitting on something to do with the investigation?'

'Well, she was more'n keen to spew venom about Atkins an' the rest of 'em . . . like a right little puff adder. If she knew summat, I don' see her keeping it to herself.' He scratched his chin thoughtfully. ''Sides, she wouldn't have been all Happy Larry if she knew who the murderer was . . . not after what happened to Dowell.'

It was true, and yet . . .

The DI was lost in thought, but that made no odds. Noakes was used to it and waited in companionable silence till the guvnor was 'back on terra cotta'.

'I need you and Doyle to keep her in sight, Noakes.' Markham came to with a start and glanced about him.

He realized that the room had emptied during his reverie. 'They're clearing up.'

'I'll jus' . . .' The funeral baked meats had not yet disappeared.

Markham eyed his subordinate resignedly.

'Alright, alright. Stuff your pockets . . . get Mrs Ledwidge to do you a doggy bag. But I want you—'

He broke off in consternation.

'What is it, guv?'

'*Hold on a minute* . . . I can't see her, Noakes.' He muttered to himself. 'Surely she can't have finished her cake that quickly . . .'

From the other side of the room, Burton registered the body language and was at the DI's side.

'Sir?'

'Kate, I want you to check the cloakrooms. See if you can locate Stacey Macmillan for me — quick as you like.' Burton promptly headed for the exit.

He turned to his other DS. 'Noakes, get hold of Doyle and check where everyone went.'

'He said he was gonna help with the wheelchair. Coleman came with the Ledwidges . . . Think the padre asked for a hand.'

It felt as though a shard of ice was lodged beneath Markham's breastbone.

'He's got her,' the DI said.

## 8. HIDDEN WATCHER

'What? You mean the *murderer's* snatched her?' Noakes was startled. ''S not possible, guv.' The grizzled head swivelled from side to side. 'She was here a minute ago . . . stuffing her face . . .'

But his expression was uneasy. Unbidden, a segment from Sky's True Crime channel rose to the surface of his mind. A documentary on Ted Bundy, the serial killer who slipped through university campuses, sports resorts and schoolyards, preying on his victims in plain sight. He remembered one case in particular: a young woman, two days into a week-and-a-half ski trip, who got into a hotel lift and was last seen walking along the corridor to her second-floor room in search of a magazine while her fiancé waited downstairs in the lounge. Caryn Campbell, that was her name. They interviewed scores of folk, searched lift shafts and crawl spaces, kitchens and utility rooms, but never found hide nor hair . . . until her frozen corpse eventually turned up in a snowbank four miles away.

Bundy's nickname was the 'Phantom Prince' . . . was that what they had on their hands here? A killer who'd slipped like a ghost in and out of a church hall and spirited Stacey Macmillan away?

'I tell you he's got her,' the DI repeated hoarsely. 'Right under our noses.' Markham's long, lean body was taut as a bow spring. '*Think*, Noakes,' he said urgently. 'You said Stacey looked like she had a hot date . . . Well, she *did* — with her murderer.'

'You mean cos she had summat on him?'

'That's right . . .' Markham looked tormented. 'Only I don't think she realized the significance of what she knew.'

'She looked excited about summat for sure . . . kind of keyed-up an' pleased with herself. But she wouldn't have been all smug an' cheerful like that if she thought this bloke had killed them women an' Dowell . . . I mean, *no way* . . .'

It was true. Stacey Macmillan struck Markham as possessing a healthy sense of self-preservation. But this time it had let her down.

'She didn't realize the danger in time,' Markham said again. He whirled round on his subordinate so fast, the latter jumped. 'Get out there with Doyle . . . I need the premises sealed off.'

But he feared it was already too late.

As Noakes headed for the exit, Burton reappeared.

'No sign of her in the cloakrooms, sir.'

'Did anyone clap eyes on her?'

'One of the parishioners said she thought she'd seen her by the Ladies'.'

'*Thought* she'd seen her?'

Burton grimaced. 'Sorry, boss. To be honest, I'm not sure it's a reliable sighting . . . more like the old dear was trying to be helpful.'

'And that's it . . . no one else noticed her?'

'Most people have made tracks — worried about the weather and wanting to get back indoors. There's a couple of helpers stayed behind to clear up but otherwise . . .' She gestured helplessly.

Noakes was back.

'Doyle had loaded up Coleman an' the Ledwidges before I got there,' he muttered. 'Proper little boy scout.'

'So they've left,' the DI said flatly.

'Yeah, guv.' Noakes looked sheepish. 'The rest of 'em set off walking round the same time . . . prob'ly halfway down Chapel Street by now.'

'*All* of them?'

'Far as I can tell, yeah. Looks like it . . . Leastways, I checked with one of the Mrs Mops an' she was positive they'd done a bunk.' The DS shrugged. 'Can't blame them what with it being brass monkeys.'

'Shona and the teachers from Hope as well?' It was a forlorn hope.

'The whole caboodle, guv . . . Filled their boots an' then scarpered.'

'So no witnesses.' The DI's heart sank.

Doyle came panting in, glowing from his exertions.

'No joy, sir?' And on Markham signalling a negative, 'I clocked the others leaving together — in a little gang.' The young DC bit his lip. 'But Stacey wasn't with them . . . I figured she was helping to clear up.'

'She was talking to me and Noakes. Then she mentioned getting herself some cake.'

'Coffee cake,' the DS put in with a reminiscent smile. 'Home-made an' all.'

Somehow Burton fought down an acid rejoinder.

'Did she say anything interesting?'

'She was batting her eyelashes at the boss . . . all come-hither, like.' Noakes burlesqued a Lothario leer.

'Anything apart from that?'

'Bitching about the neighbours really.'

'Oh?' Burton's antennae were on high alert.

'Yeah, had a bit of a rant about Mrs B an' Mary Atkins squabbling over who did the most for them LGBT weirdoes.' His colleague frowned. 'Y'know, like, who did the most campaigning,' he hastily amended. 'Sounded like Dawn MacAlinden put her oar in too . . . saying Atkins was a loudmouth, allus wanting to be queen bee an' needed to put a sock in it.' He rolled his eyes. 'I kinda got where she was coming from.'

'Anything else?'

'Jus' that Mrs B was a clever clogs . . . an' Dowell too.' Noakes scratched himself vigorously under his off-colour cable-knit sweater like a restless yeti. 'Plus she said it was a bit sticky with the Ledwidges on account of them being God Squad.'

'How d'you mean?'

'Dowell was an atheist an' Mrs B . . . well, no disrespect,' he said quickly, 'but she was a bit of a lefty.'

Markham was growing impatient.

'Nothing stood out, Kate,' he said heavily. 'Mildly malicious titbits by way of spicing up the conversation.'

Once she saw a snogeroo with the handsome inspector wasn't on the cards any time soon, Noakes privately concluded.

'Maybe we're barking up the wrong tree, boss,' Doyle said frankly. 'I mean, an abduction . . .' He gestured round at the virtually empty space where two middle-aged women were busy at the far end of the room wrapping leftovers in clingfilm, casting the odd furtive glance at the detectives. 'How could he have grabbed her without anyone noticing?'

'There's a little pantry affair back there,' Burton said unexpectedly. 'With a fridge and microwave. Round the back of the loos.' She wrinkled her nose. 'Bit unhygienic if you ask me . . . it's only a cubbyhole really.'

'Show me.' The DI's face was dark and urgent.

The church hall's reception room was on one side of a narrow hallway with cloakrooms on the other. Burton led them past the loos and opened the door to a pokey utility room. There was barely room for the four of them to squeeze inside.

'I see what you mean,' Noakes grunted. His Muriel's lot organized things much better down at the Women's Guild, he reflected complacently, what with them being allowed to use St Mary's Cathedral. Lots of space in that nice bright kitchen behind the crypt. Not slumming it like in here with the smell of overcooked cabbage and Dettol. *Rank.*

At least they had a stacked washer-dryer. Fairly new by the look of it. Happen it came in handy with the down and outs. Noakes had only the vaguest idea about parochial outreach — and what it comprised — but he knew from the missus that smelly laundry played its part . . . and one time there'd been that cat got stuck in the dryer. Smudge, that was its name, daft little beggar . . . he remembered Muriel saying it gave her quite a turn.

Afterwards, he hardly knew what made him shuffle sideways past Markham and the others for a closer look at the appliances. Like a magpie, he was always drawn to shiny things and the unit sported a gleaming chrome surround that looked strangely out of place in the malodorous little storeroom.

Or maybe it was thinking about the cat spinning round and round . . .

At any rate, he bent down to give it the once-over.

Then '*Over here, guv.*' All signs of lethargy gone.

'Oh fuck.' Doyle swayed in shock, clutching Burton so tightly his fingerprints were still visible hours later.

A face was pressed up against the window of the bottom unit, its features squashed and distorted as though reflected in some diabolical hall of mirrors. More gargoyle than human being.

They had found the missing woman.

* * *

Markham had initially feared Stacey Macmillan's remains would have to be scooped out of the washer like some sort of human soup.

But the machine had not been switched on and the pathologist recovered her intact.

'Strangulation and then shoved inside,' Dimples Davidson put an end to their fevered imaginings. 'A small woman, so it wasn't difficult.' Tight-lipped, he added, 'Dislocation of various joints, but she was beyond pain by then.'

Doyle's complexion was greenish-white.

'Her face behind that window . . . all swollen and bulging,' he stuttered, 'like a helium balloon. It looked like she was *gurning* at us.'

'Not going to throw up on me are you, lad?' Dimples eyed him beadily, fearful for his well-polished brogues.

'He'll be fine, doc.' Noakes put a steadying hand on his colleague's arm. 'Once he's got a few pints down him.' The DS's invariable anaesthetic of choice.

Watching as the body was stretchered away, Burton found herself thanking God it wasn't a case of disarticulated remains. Ever since her very first murder case — the sex killing of a teenage girl whose skeleton eventually turned up in the woods on Bromgrove Rise — she'd been haunted by the cries of a desperate parent: 'How will we put her together again!'

Once the sombre little procession was out of sight, Davidson bringing up the rear, Markham turned back to his team.

'How did he manage it, sir?' Burton measured the distance from the loos to the little utility room. 'It's only yards, but even so . . .'

'Must be one strong son of a bitch,' Doyle burst out with unusual vehemence.

'Not necessarily.'

They all looked at Noakes.

'It's the element of surprise, see . . .' The DS was clearly gratified by their attentiveness.

'No need for muscle if they don' see it coming.' He cleared his throat portentously. 'Like with that Ted Bundy bloke . . . He got 'em in car parks an' corridors, even nabbed one university student as she walked down a path with her boyfriend watching from a window. In the end, they only got him cos he slipped up using some stolen car plates.'

'That's right,' Burton's interest was piqued. 'He was a clean-cut law student, wasn't he?'

'Yeah . . . volunteered at a crisis centre an' all. Sort of American version of the Samaritans an' no one suspected a thing . . . Some woman who worked there with him wrote a book about it.'

'How'd he pull it off then?' Doyle was momentarily distracted from thoughts of tumble dryers.

'Smooth-talking psycho,' Noakes replied sagely. 'Plus he used different disguises to make folk trust him — arm in a sling, crutches, that kind of thing. My missus read about it.'

For all the horror of the scene, Markham felt a twinge of amusement watching this outbreak of amity. Next thing, they'd be setting up a CID book club.

But Burton was never one to stray too far from the job in hand.

'Stacey was streetwise,' she said thoughtfully. 'But she never saw it coming.'

'Must've trusted the killer,' Doyle ran with it. 'He lulled her into thinking she was safe . . . she had nothing to worry about . . .'

'Took a hell of a risk, though.' Noakes ran a hand distractedly through his frowsy thatch, looking more than ever like a demented middle-aged rapper rather than a lean, mean, crime-fighting machine. 'I mean, lifting her in broad daylight.'

'On the other hand,' the DI said, 'he gauged it well. The party breaking up . . . people anxious to get home . . . everyone a bit distracted . . . disorientated after the service.'

That's how it was with the predatory animal, calculating the moment of peak vulnerability before cutting the weakest from the pack.

'It would have been the work of seconds,' Markham continued, 'provided he held his nerve.'

'A cool bastard alright,' Noakes concluded with reluctant admiration. 'But if Stacey didn't realize he was the killer, why'd she have to die?' Another scratch of the head. 'She was a chatterbox . . . chuntered on a bit, but no real harm in her.'

'She *knew* something, Noakesy,' the DI said quietly. 'Hadn't joined up the dots, though . . . Didn't make a connection with the murders—'

'But he couldn't risk her blurting it out,' Burton concluded eagerly.

'That's right, Kate.'

'So whatever she found out was crucial, then?' Doyle re-joined the fray. 'A clue?'

'Correct.'

Markham thought back to the gossipy little woman making doe eyes at him over the buffet.

'Whatever she knew,' he said, 'it *titillated* and intrigued her.'

'Something scandalous?'

'Hmm . . . I think that's quite probable, Kate. She was a *News of the Screws* type . . . the sort to pore over sensational stories in the tabloids . . .'

'Shame Gavin Conors wasn't onto her then,' Noakes groused. 'Sounds like she could've given him summat well juicy for *Conors Confidential*.'

It was gallows humour. Noakes was as shocked as the rest of them and no fan of the *Gazette*'s sleazeball gossip columnist.

'Maybe she just enjoyed holding something over one of the other residents,' Burton speculated. 'Something embarrassing . . . something that put them in her power . . .'

'You mean blackmail?' Doyle asked.

'Not exactly . . . or more like emotional blackmail rather than the financial kind. Something that gave her the upper hand.'

'Yeah okay,' Noakes said, won over by this reasoning. 'She was divorced, bored . . . on the pull . . .'

'Are we looking for a bloke then? I mean, if she was trying to use this . . . *secret* or whatever it was to hook a guy . . .'

'I think we have to be wary of making any assumptions.' In the dim light of the corridor, the DI's face was all planes and angles. Could do with getting some cake down him, Burton thought idly, then cringed at her own triviality. Luckily the gloom hid her tell-tale blush.

'Yeah.' Noakes was warming to his role as CID's true crime pundit. 'Could be some lesbo set-up . . . Like with that Rose West.'

Burton was sufficiently distracted by this reference to the Cromwell Street serial killer as to overlook the distinctly un-PC designation. For his part, Doyle simply boggled. 'You think Stacey wanted a wingding with one of the residents, sarge?' he said faintly.

'Mebbe,' his colleague replied complacently. 'She could've been desperate enough.'

There were so many things wrong with this assertion that Burton literally didn't know where to start. Before she could read Noakes the riot act, Markham cut in.

'We're not ruling anything out,' he said firmly. 'And there was apparently some tension between Stacey and Mary Atkins.'

'Not the sexual sort surely, boss,' Burton qualified with a shudder.

'No, more *ideological* you might say.' Seeing the mystified look on her face, the DI hastened to explain. 'She didn't like Ms Atkins claiming all the credit for promoting LGBT rights down at Hope.'

'Said Atkins was hogging the limelight,' Noakes added bluntly. 'An' Mrs B didn't like it.'

'Ms MacAlinden wasn't enamoured either,' the DI continued. 'There was that remark about "reinventing the wheel".'

'I can see Stacey being happy to get one over on another woman . . .' Burton reasoned it out with herself. 'But,' she shook her head, 'I don't see Atkins for the murders.'

'P'raps that were Stacey's mistake,' Noakes countered lugubriously. 'Jus' couldn't get her head round the idea of it being a teacher an' then . . .' He mimed strangling someone.

'But where does Dowell fit in?' Doyle was bewildered. 'Nobody's said anything about bad blood between him and Atkins.'

'True, Constable.' Markham sounded weary. 'Stacey said there were a few spats between Mr Dowell and various residents . . . He was a man of strong opinions from the sound of it.' His heavy sigh seemed to whistle eerily in the deserted building. 'But nothing about that points to Mary Atkins.'

Silence fell over the little group. By common accord, they returned to the main reception room where two scared helpers watched round-eyed as paper-suited investigators bent to their work. To Burton's overwrought senses, the SOCOs looked like extra-terrestrials from another planet.

'Get rid of the women and anyone else still hanging around please, Doyle,' Markham said. 'Take contact details and the rest of it, but after that they're free to go.'

Looking through the bay window that fronted Taggart Terrace at right angles to Chapel Street, Markham saw that it was already growing dark outside, the orange street-lamps' neon phosphorescence lighting the winter landscape so that it seemed to pulse with an unearthly radiance.

He wondered if that snowman on the corner of Marsh Lane was still standing. The one with the policeman's helmet. Irrationally, he found himself hoping it had melted or someone had knocked it down. The thought of it squatting there like a malevolent troglodyte made him shiver.

Noakes was stamping his feet impatiently. The ugly wall-clock said 5:30.

Markham took the hint.

'Right,' he said. 'Briefing at six sharp tomorrow morning before I update the DCI.' He turned to Burton. 'I want a media blackout, Kate, so square it with Barry Lynch, will you?'

Noakes grimaced. Old Octopus-Mitts would be only too eager to corner Kate Burton in the press office.

She kept her expression studiously neutral. 'Better take Doyle along for protection,' the DI added, eliciting a reluctant grin.

'On it, boss.'

'What a chuffing mess, guv,' Noakes said once the other two had left. Then, 'What're we gonna tell Sidney?'

'Well, even with Chris Carstairs' help, we can't blind him with criminal profiling mumbo jumbo forever.'

'Him and that Callaghan bint don' want shit on their doorstep.'

It was an accurate if crude summing up of the situation.

'Tough.' It was the nearest Markham got to a snarl. 'Let's head back to the close, Noakesy. We can track down Gary Coslett while the SOCOs do their stuff.'

'Thinks he's Jason Statham or summat, the cocky little git,' his DS muttered. 'Swaggering about down there doing sod all. *Hey*,' a thought struck him, 'd'you think Stacey gave him the glad eye?'

'As you said, she was bored and lonely.' There was compassion in Markham's voice. 'It wouldn't surprise me if she engaged in some banter . . . Bit of a long shot, but it's possible she might have let something slip.' Impatiently, he brushed a dark lock of hair out of his eyes. 'Then there's Dawn MacAlinden.'

'What about her, guv?'

'Well, she's faded into the background somewhat. But I don't think her murder was accidental.'

'Not "collateral damage".' Noakes brought it out with a flourish.

'Precisely.' Markham paused. 'She was a nurse at the Newman . . . I'd like to know more about her work. If it was psychotherapy, then she may have crossed paths with Kenneth Dowell.'

'Plus she'd have known Doctor Lucy an' the Boy Wonder.' The DS snorted. 'Them two didn't look quite so loved-up today . . . I'd put money on them having had a barney right before they came out. He said summat when they were by the buffet an' she looked daggers at him.'

'Interesting.' Markham rubbed his tired eyes. 'We'll get Coslett to round up the residents for tomorrow afternoon.' His expression was bleak. 'Not much likelihood of cracking anyone's alibi for Stacey, but at least we can rattle a few cages.'

And hope that eventually someone makes a mistake.

As the two men trudged back the way they had come, Noakes said, 'Funny ain't it, guv . . . how we call her "Stacey" not "Mrs Macmillan". Not all correct like with the others . . . y'know, Mister an' Missus . . .'

'True.' Markham glanced at his subordinate, whose corned-beef complexion had acquired a purplish tinge, especially round the nose.

'Mebbe it's cos they were poshos but she was more, well, down to earth.'

'And also because we spent time with her, Noakesy. Whereas the other murder victims are an unknown quantity.'

'Yeah.' The DS huffed and puffed to keep up with Markham's long strides. Considerately, the DI slowed his pace to match the older man's. 'You're right, guv. Makes a difference when you've talked to 'em . . . seen 'em close up.'

Noakes relapsed into silence. But Markham knew that Stacey Macmillan's voice would join the invisible victims' chorus that formed the soundtrack to their professional lives . . . Like a sonar device whose frequency was inaudible to their fellow men.

* * *

Later that evening, Markham updated Olivia on the events of the day, grateful for the wood burner melting the icy chill that had somehow seeped into his very bones.

He hadn't realized how hungry he was until his girlfriend dished up a steaming beef casserole followed by bread-and-butter pudding and a deliciously runny brie with his favourite *Châteauneuf du Pape*. By mutual consent they stayed off the subject of murder until it was time for coffee, at which point Markham adjourned to his favourite wing-back armchair while Olivia curled up at his feet, stretching luxuriously with the sinuous grace that characterized all her movements.

'Be sure to bring George back for a meal some time, Gil,' she said. 'You can lure him with the promise of jam roly-poly or one of those nursery puds he likes.'

'He's meant to be on the straight and narrow after that health scare, but you should have seen him at the memorial do — tucking into the buffet good-o.'

Olivia chuckled. 'Well, he was off the leash, wasn't he? Right now, Muriel's probably dishing up chickpea cobbler with broccoli on the side.'

'Talking of Muriel, we should really have them *both* round.'

His lover looked resigned to her fate. 'Fair enough, but she'll only flirt with you all evening in that awful arch way she has while implying that I snared you by unspeakable sexual chicanery.'

Markham laughed. 'Think of it as team bonding . . . And anyway, we owe it to Noakes.' A mischievous grin. 'He's desperate for the two women in his life to get on.'

'When hell freezes over,' Olivia replied philosophically but her eyes were twinkling. 'Our Muriel believes I'm a brassy piece . . . "on the make". She's just waiting for you to come to your senses.'

'Then she'll wait a long time.' Markham's eyes were tender.

'Was it very bad today, Gil?' Her voice was soft with concern.

'There's been another one, Liv.'

He recounted the day's events and the discovery of Stacey Macmillan's body, but he kept to himself the image of those bloated features stamped with the imprint of the woman's final agony.

'She won't have suffered, Liv. Choked from behind according to Dimples. No defence wounds. It would have been over very quickly . . . before she even knew it was happening.'

Pray God that it was so.

'But *how*, Gil?' An echo of DC Doyle's bewilderment. 'Grabbing her in a corridor . . .'

'I think Stacey's card was marked,' Markham said slowly. 'She was a blabbermouth and she'd come across something important . . . something the killer couldn't risk getting out. So she had to die.' He took a long draught of his coffee before continuing. 'And then suddenly, he saw his chance.'

'You think he hadn't planned to kill her there, then?'

'Who knows what he had in store for her.' Markham repressed a shudder. 'But that moment in the church hall was too good an opportunity to pass up.'

'But what if he'd been interrupted? Caught with his hands on her? It was taking such a risk . . .'

'My bet is he'd have carried it off. Said she was sick and he was helping her . . . something like that. With the memorial service, people would have assumed she was overcome with emotion.' His gaze was brooding, reminiscent. 'Thinking back, she was hyper . . . almost giddy. I got the feeling she might have had a drink or taken something before the service.'

Olivia nodded slowly. 'Dutch courage, Gil? Something to pep her up . . . for a romantic encounter?'

'Yes,' he agreed. 'Could well have been.'

And then those gloved hands lifting her off her feet, fastening like talons round her throat, snapping the hyoid bone . . .

'Poor woman,' she said. 'Poor, poor woman.'

'They're processing the scene, but we won't get anything,' he said leadenly. 'This one's forensically aware. Plus the world and his mother have tramped through that building.'

'Tomorrow's another day,' she said gently.

'Groundhog Day more like, given that I've got Sidney first thing.'

'Can't you throw him a bone, Gil?' Olivia had no great opinion of the DCI's intelligence. 'Something to get him off your back . . .'

'I suppose I can play up the prowler angle.'

*'Prowler?'* She caught herself. 'Oh right, now I remember. You mean the Peeping Tom or whoever dropped that compact mirror in the playing fields.'

'That's the one.' He hesitated as though wondering how much to tell her.

'Go on, Gil. I can tell there's something else.'

'Well, Gary Coslett told us an odd little story before we called it a night.'

'Coslett . . . the creepy caretaker, right?'

'And all-round sexist pig.' Markham's brows contracted as he recalled Coslett's indignant rejection of any understanding between himself and Stacey Macmillan. *You're joking, aincha . . . She's ancient! I'm not that hard up!*

'What did Coslett have to say?' Olivia interrupted his brown study.

'That Dawn MacAlinden and Mary Atkins both reported seeing a pair of gloved hands coming through the top of the curtains when they were in their living rooms on their own late at night.'

She stared at him. '*Hands*? As in, an intruder . . . burglary?'

'That's the odd part.' His face was troubled. 'They just reported seeing these hands and nothing else.'

'So what happened?'

'Well, apparently they screamed and then the hands disappeared.' He grimaced. 'It was obvious Coslett thought they'd been at the gin . . . Made them feel daft, so they didn't go to the police.'

'Were there any signs of a break-in?'

'That's just it. Both flats have French doors. They weren't sure they'd locked them properly, dah-di-dah . . .' He sighed heavily. 'In the circumstances, it was easy for Coslett to brush them off.'

'What do *you* think, Gil?'

'Possible attempted burglary . . . or some local sicko trying to spook them.' Even as he said this, he knew he didn't believe it.

Olivia did not press him, though the image of those snaking hands disturbed her.

'There you go,' she said lightly, 'the bushy-haired stranger. Sidney's villain of choice.'

Markham sent her a look that was full of gratitude.

'By the by, Gil,' she continued, 'it's the carol concert at school tomorrow evening.' She flashed him a winning smile. 'Our esteemed assistant head has corralled half of Bromgrove into attending . . . What you might call a three-line whip. There'll be mince pies and mulled wine, so no doubt tongues will be loosened.'

Noakes's belt would certainly be loosened once he heard about the mince pies, Markham reflected wryly.

'Might be a chance to catch Mary Atkins and the rest of them unawares,' she said persuasively. 'Plus you might pick up some titbits about Marian Bussell.'

'You had me at the mince pies,' he grinned.

She gave him a mock slap.

'Marvellous. Having you and George there will make it more bearable.'

And with that their talk turned to other things.

# 9. A LIT FUSE

Thursday morning dawned cold and crisp with a hard frost.

There was no sign of a thaw as yet, Markham noted with a sense of relief as he drank piping hot black coffee. He hated it when the snow turned to black sludge.

Idly, he wondered if they would have a white Christmas, as opposed to a rain-puddled washout, and smiled to himself as he thought of Olivia's child-like eagerness on that score. The snow's crystalline delicacy entranced her, so for his lover's sake he hoped the town might wear its mantle a while longer.

His smile faded as he looked out of his study window at the blanketed cemetery and recalled that there would be no more Christmases for four souls in Bromgrove.

He had passed an uneasy night in which an old childhood nightmare resurrected itself.

*Hands coming out of darkness towards him.*

*Hands invading, burrowing . . . molesting . . .*

Last year's investigation in Bromgrove's art gallery had featured hands too. Pale hands gleaming in the darkness . . . Reaching out to snatch a little boy . . .

And now he was on the track of another faceless wraith. He needed just one magic irrefutable connection to this phantom killer. And still it eluded him.

*Come on, Markham, snap out of it,* he told himself. With Sidney to face, this was no time to get fanciful.

But the interview with Gary Coslett the previous evening had unsettled him.

Noakes, predictably, had been sceptical. 'Grade A creep, guv,' he'd growled. 'Prob'ly into a bit of prowling hisself . . . perk of the job. Looks the type to get off on women's knicker drawers.'

But no sweat beaded on Coslett's forehead and the man's body language betrayed little tension. His close-set eyes, beneath the heavy hooding of their upper eyelids, watched the two detectives with blank passivity. He might as well have been made of clay or plastic for all the animation he displayed.

And Markham remembered what Dimples Davidson had said about the *artistry* of these murders — the sense of there being some malign choreography in play, a puppeteer enjoying his string-pulling.

What if those hands snaking through the living-room curtains represented the eruption of an urge that could no longer be repressed? An urge that was subsequently channelled into the staged murders of Marian Bussell, Dawn MacAlinden and Kenneth Dowell?

Stacey Macmillan's murder felt different from the others. Impulsive. Hurried. No time to savour, to *enjoy* his handiwork — his *revenge*. Just that moment when he yanked her from her life into oblivion. Trapped like a rabbit in a snare.

If the killer was decompensating, unravelling, then they were up shit creek without a paddle. No knowing where he might strike next.

Was there any chance of them making an arrest by Christmas? Or would the killer be sitting down to a turkey dinner and opening presents with a clear-eyed smile, hiding what lay beneath his mask?

What were they up against here? Some brilliant maniac who could take on experienced detectives and thumb his nose at them? A sociopath destined to slip through the cracks?

He thought of Dawn MacAlinden's widower, struggling to hold his world together even as it shattered into shards, and the blind unfairness of it all. It was down to him and the team to give the victims a voice.

But Markham hadn't the faintest clue how he was going to stave off Sidney. Olivia's bushy-haired stranger theory was all well and good, but when Chris Carstairs' pool of potential candidates ran dry, it'd be back to square one. And their superior would only dig his heels in at any suggestion of a link with the local community. As far as Slimy Sid was concerned, anything was better than that — even if it came down to a Ted Bundy wannabe. Though somehow Markham couldn't see the DCI settling down to a nice cosy chat with Noakes about their top ten serial killers!

They'd have to resort to the usual palaver — run a dummy investigation alongside the real one. Funnel the kooks and whack jobs Sidney's way while digging deeper into New College Close and the residents' backgrounds.

He'd arranged with Coslett to conduct further interviews this afternoon when hopefully some of those alibis could be tested. Impossible that somebody somewhere hadn't picked up on any unusual behaviour or something that seemed out of place.

Markham frowned as he recalled Coslett's surly intractability. Having finally got hold of the Residents' Association minutes, it was clear he'd gotten into any number of ill-tempered altercations with virtually all the inhabitants of the close, but nothing stood out as supplying a motive for murder. It seemed site security was a perennial grumble among the residents, but again this was more of a running sore than all-out war.

The only remotely useful piece of information was Coslett's reference to reports of an unidentified woman having been seen on the premises 'behaving suspiciously'.

'Chuffing red herring,' had been Noakes's verdict. 'Jus' wants to get the fuzz off his back . . . Any strange woman's most likely some slapper he's bonking.'

And it was true that Coslett had been notably short on detail. 'Some bird in a headscarf . . . looked posh,' was all he volunteered.

'Did you see the lady yourself, sir?' Markham persisted, resisting a wild impulse to slam the man up against a wall and beat the information out of him.

'Nah, but the sky pilot at number sixteen was positive they'd seen her.'

'I take it you mean Mr Ledwidge?'

A dangerous look in Markham's eye convinced the other that discretion was the better part of valour.

'Yeah . . . him and his missus do the Neighbourhood Watch stuff.'

Afterwards, when the DI had sent Coslett about his duties, Noakes exploded. 'Just as well the Ledwidges kept an eye out,' he fumed. 'What with that one holed up watching porn back at base.'

'Scandi noir as I recall, Sergeant.'

'*And the rest!*'

Noakes was still mulling the latest nugget. 'You don' think it's got owt to do with the murders do you, guv? Sapphire an' Steel at number sixteen could've imagined they saw summat . . . y'know, got carried away playing bobbies.'

'Hmm. Fuss-pots they might be, but the Ledwidges strike me as being on the ball.'

'Mebbe it's one of them gyppos — er, travellers, boss . . . The council's trying to shift 'em from Hollingrove Park . . . Happen one of 'em came this way on a thieving spree.'

'But whoever it was "looked posh", Noakes. Doesn't sound like your average petty criminal.'

'Won't be anyone Coslett's banging neither . . . that'd be some bimbo with one of them Oompa Loompa fake tans.' Ironically, this description was a perfect match for the charming Natalie Noakes, apple of her father's eye.

'Well, whoever this mystery lady is, we need to rule her out.'

In the meantime, perhaps this would suffice as a bone for Sidney to chew on . . .

Downing the dregs of his coffee, Markham roused himself from his thoughts and let himself quietly out of the apartment, making his way round to the garages at the back of The Sweepstakes. The raw air scoured his lungs and made him catch his breath, but he was grateful for the bracing shock. It would keep him in the zone — where he needed to be.

For a moment in the carpark he started at the sight of an unfinished snowman.

'Just kids,' he muttered to himself, 'just kids.'

But as he headed towards the station, he remembered once again the effigy on Marsh Lane with the policeman's helmet set atop its lumpy head like a challenge.

*I'm watching you. I'm watching.*

* * *

At the station, he found Noakes nose-deep in a tin of Quality Streets.

'Sheryl from typing,' he said in answer to the DI's enquiring look. 'Early Crimbo prezzie.'

'Well, go easy on the toffee fingers, Sergeant. There's the little matter of your sugar intake, remember.'

'The missus is on it,' the other said glumly. 'Pigging green veg every meal an' *fruit salad* for afters . . . I mean, I ask you!' The new regime clearly constituted a cruel and unusual punishment.

'Cheer up . . . Olivia wants you and Muriel to come round for supper. She'll do all your forbidden treats — no sprouts or spinach, I promise!'

'Champion.' His DS beamed at the implied compliment to his wife. Markham had never been able to fathom the bond between easy-going George Noakes and his overbearing, snobbish spouse, but there was no doubting his devotion. Markham suspected the woman's brittle affectations concealed a vulnerable core. But, in the meantime, her shrill

'*Gilbert*' affected him like the scraping of fingernails down a blackboard. Still, it was a small price to pay to see his wingman happy.

'Right,' he said. 'Down to business. We've got an appointment with the DCI in half an hour.'

The two men walked into Markham's office where Kate Burton was waiting for them, perched on one of the chairs in front of his desk — her bum half on, half off, as Noakes put it to himself, *like there was summat in the police training standards against taking a load off.*

The DI made an approving inventory of Burton's wardrobe: wine-coloured trouser suit with softly flared cuffs and a mandarin collar; crisp fitted T shirt; black ankle boots. Nothing to raise anyone's hackles. While Noakes on the other hand . . . well, the best that could be said for his crumpled off-white chinos and fawn sweater was that they didn't sport the wearer's usual breakfast detritus all the down the front. And the appalling bobble hat appeared to have been ditched. His ensemble should just about pass muster with Sidney, though the mere sight of Markham's number two generally elicited a dyspeptic reaction from the DCI.

Suppressing a sigh, the DI settled himself behind the desk while Noakes lurched over to the window. He turned his face away, staring moodily out at the station car park.

'Morning, Kate. What've we got? Anything for the DCI?' *As in, smokescreen*, he wanted to add.

'I did some digging on Gary Coslett, sir.' Faintly pink-cheeked despite the chill of the office, she riffled through her notes.

'Oh yeah?' Noakes was all interest now. Kicking the refractory radiator as though he wished it was the caretaker, he ambled over and took the other chair. 'What's he been up to then?'

'Nothing criminal as such,' his colleague replied carefully. 'But there has been the odd issue with student volunteers . . .'

'Like Shona, you mean?' Noakes's face darkened. 'The lass who visited Mrs B . . . community service, right?'

'Well, it wasn't Shona who reported Coslett, but there were a couple of other sixth formers who complained he was always hanging round . . . stood too close to them, invaded their personal space, that kind of thing. And one girl said he liked to sneak up on her and scare her.'

'Scare her how?' Markham's voice was sharp.

''S not clear, sir. She got cold feet and backed off . . . said it was all a misunderstanding. Apparently, a couple of times he appeared round the side of the building and said, "Boo!" Or came up behind people without warning.' Burton cleared her throat. 'To be honest, I'm not sure there was all that much to go on . . . Another kid said Martin Henley tried to chat her up.'

'He'd be the type to fancy his chances.'

'It didn't come to anything, sarge . . . and you know how silly girls can be at that age. I've put Doyle on it, though, just in case. But anyway, Mary Atkins arranged it so they visited in twos. For some reason Shona wasn't paired up with anyone for her visits to Mrs Bussell.'

'Anything else, Kate?'

'Apparently, Brian Ledwidge "had a word" with Coslett and Henley . . . nothing heavy, just the usual about being extra careful around any teenage visitors.'

'How about the other residents?'

'No problems with Julian Hoskinson. Apparently he was "cool".'

'*Getting down wiv da kidz*,' Noakes sneered, but Burton affected not to hear.

'There was a girl who said Jeff Coleman "freaked her out".' More air quotes.

'Bleeding snowflakes.' Again, Burton ignored CID's very own Greek chorus.

'Any specifics?'

'Unfortunately not, sir. The feedback was all part of something called *Student Voice*.'

'Kids having a whinge.'

This time, Burton grasped the nettle.

'It's how they do things down at Hope, sarge . . . letting pupils have their say.'

Noakes's scowl made it abundantly clear what he thought of such democratic sentiments.

'Letting 'em make mischief, more like. I mean, take that poor fucker in the wheelchair . . . What did they reckon poor ole Stephen Hawking was gonna do to them!'

Burton's lips were tightly compressed, but she didn't rise to the bait.

'It's all about safeguarding these days,' she said patiently.

'Guilty till proven innocent, that's what it is.'

'So you're saying you'd give Gary Coslett the benefit of the doubt then, sarge? Seeing as kids are malicious and make stuff up.'

*Touché.* Markham's lips twitched at the mutinous expression on Noakes's face.

'Enough,' he said. Then, 'Well done, Kate. It's enough to make Coslett a — what do they call it on those cop shows? — *person of interest.*'

Of interest to Sidney at any rate.

'Well, he raises a few red flags, sir.'

Burton had a keen interest in clinical models of deviant behaviour, with a habit — deeply irritating to Doyle and Noakes — of drawing on the American Psychiatric Association's *Diagnostic and Statistical Manual of Mental Disorders.* The DI was willing to bet she'd be brushing up on 'sociopathic signifiers' — window peeping, cruelty to animals, fire setting, bed wetting — the minute he and Noakes left the office. He wasn't sure she'd get anywhere with Coslett in terms of useful backstory, but the truth was they didn't have any other promising suspects.

Kate Burton sensed Markham's despondency, acutely conscious that he didn't have a trace of ego and cared only for those whose lives had been devastated by murder. She knew all too well how any perceived failure to save victims ate away at him. They were forever imprinted on his memory as real human beings, not just numbers or notches on a scorecard.

'There's a few strange characters in that close,' she went on. 'Real eccentrics.'

Markham was diverted. 'Who might those be, Kate?'

'According to the Ledwidges, there was some incident at that charity shop in town . . .'

'Lili's?'

'That's right, sir. Julian Hoskinson had a meltdown . . . cut some dummies into pieces . . .'

'*What*?' Noakes leaned forward, piggy eyes alight with interest. 'How come?'

'No one knows what upset him . . . But a friend of Mrs Ledwidge was in there — said he started slashing mannequins in the window display or something.'

'*Slashing*.' Her fellow DS had all the eagerness of a mastiff on the scent. 'Scratch the surface with them brotherhood-of-man types an' there's allus summat right nasty underneath.'

Having long since come to terms with Noakes's world view, she observed mildly, 'I'm not sure we can read all that much into it, sarge . . . But it's strange alright.'

Her face was thoughtful.

'What is it, Kate?'

'Brian Ledwidge, when he was talking about the murders . . . He kept repeating that God had his purpose and it wasn't for them to second-guess what happened.'

'Well he's a padre, ain't he? It's the sort of stuff they spout . . . in the job description, innit?'

She looked doubtful. 'It wasn't so much what he said but the way he said it . . . sort of cold and mechanical . . .'

'Shock affects people in different ways, Kate. And remember, these aren't people in the prime of life.' The DI smiled at her. 'But this is all very interesting. Sounds like you've been busy.'

She blushed with pleasure at his warmth while Noakes watched with a jaundiced eye. How the guvnor didn't notice she had a thumping great crush was beyond him, but that poor sap of a fiancé was bound to figure it out eventually.

'Well, I just dropped in on a few of them, boss . . . said I wanted to check they were okay after the memorial service.'

'Good thinking.'

'How were the medicos?'

'Well, Doctor O'Connor had gone back to the Newman but the boyfriend was in.' She made a moue of distaste. 'Smarmy character but seemed pretty relaxed. Said there's a lot of sick people out there.'

'He's pinched Sidney's line,' growled Noakes.

'Indeed,' the DI said with a thin smile.

'So we're gonna play along with this psycho-on-the-loose bollocks are we, guv?'

'That's not quite how I would have put it, Noakes, but essentially yes.' He contemplated his two sergeants intently. 'Of course, it's true that our killer *is* sick. I'd say violent images and fantasies have been part of his thought processes for a long time.'

'Maybe he's slipped under the radar and committed other crimes, sir.'

'That's one possibility, Kate. So we need to check all unsolved and cold cases.'

'On it, boss.'

She would be. Mentally, Noakes made a variety of faces.

'Was Martin Henley able to give you anything about Dawn MacAlinden's job at the Newman?'

'Just that she was a nurse with the adolescent mental health team.'

'Gender identity?'

'No, boss.' A quick flick through her notes. 'Eating disorders and developmental delay.'

'So, it's unlikely she crossed paths professionally with Kenneth Dowell.' The DI's frustration was clear.

'Looks that way . . . Mr Henley said they really only knew Dawn and Kenneth Dowell as neighbours.' She shrugged. 'Seemed like he was being straight up about it.'

'What about Henley and his missus?' Noakes asked, recalling the couple's demeanour at the memorial service. 'Pick up any signs of trouble?'

'Not really, sarge. I mean, they're both in stressful jobs and all relationships have their ups and downs. He's a bit in love with himself, but didn't seem uncomfortable or antsy . . . laughed it off when I brought up the student who complained . . . Totally laid-back . . . Though, hold on a minute—' More thumbing through her notes. 'He *did* say something about some nuisance calls.'

'Nuisance calls?'

'Don't know how relevant it is, sir. He just said they'd had a couple of calls a few months back where someone rang up . . . The caller didn't say anything. It was just a weird high-pitched shriek or maybe hysterical laughter . . .'

She looked helplessly at the dark, intent figure of her boss whose six-foot-two frame fairly vibrated with the desire to find something that would turn out to be physical evidence they could link to the killer they were hunting.

'Henley didn't seem to attach any great significance to it . . . said they had the odd crackpot ring them, but they took it in their stride. This one stood out — maybe cos of how they cackled down the phone.'

*I wonder*, Markham thought, *I wonder* . . .

'Did Mr Henley have anything to say about the other residents?'

'Not really. Mind you . . .' A thought occurred to her. 'He said something about Jeff Coleman being an old fraud.'

'How so?'

'Stacey Macmillan told him Mr Coleman's capable of walking unaided. He's got motor neurone disease but it's not end-stage yet, so he can manage a few steps. Apparently he "likes to have everyone dancing attendance".'

'God, that's poisonous,' whistled Noakes. 'Any idea if it's true?'

'I'll follow it up, but I don't see Coleman having the strength for these murders. And anyway, he was out in the car park with the Ledwidges and Doyle when Stacey was strangled . . .' She consulted her notes again. 'Simon Gailey's friends with Coleman. I'll try sounding him out.'

'Gailey? Oh yeah, the solicitor bloke.' Noakes dug some dirt from under his fingernails, a process which the DI devoutly hoped would not be repeated in front of the DCI. 'Bit of a silver fox that one. From the way she was eying him up, I reckon our Stace fancied her chances.'

Burton said carefully, 'She'd be barking up the wrong tree, then. He's a confirmed bachelor, apparently.'

'What, you're saying he's a *poof*?'

Burton's self-control these days was ironclad — at any rate, proof against George Noakes. 'From something Martin Henley said,' she continued, 'he's not a ladies' man.'

'Bleeding waste with them looks.' Noakes could hardly be described as a connoisseur of male beauty, but Simon Gailey had clearly made an impression.

'Anything on Gailey, Kate?'

'Nada, boss. I got the impression he doesn't miss much but is too discreet to spill any beans. Penny Callaghan rates him.'

Noakes blew a raspberry, signalling this was hardly a recommendation in his book.

Markham rose and walked to the window, his back to the other two. In the carpark below, two PCs were chucking snowballs at each other before suddenly becoming aware of the figure watching from CID. Self-consciously, they headed for their squad car.

In truth, the DI barely registered their presence. He was thinking of birdlike Stacey Macmillan choking in her death throes — eyes and lungs on fire before the blood vessels burst and flooded into the brain and there were no more words . . .

He turned to his colleagues. 'Where are we with the media, Kate?'

'Blackout since yesterday, sir, but Barry Lynch says that *Crime File* reporter from the *Courier*'s got wind . . . tip off from someone at St James's.'

'Okay, tell him to release it . . . but *low-key*, with the minimum of detail — "A woman was found dead yesterday", that kind of thing. No further information till next of kin informed, et cetera.' He regarded her levelly. 'The ex-husband's in Australia along with a sister. No other relatives.' He gave a mirthless smile. 'But the journos don't need to know that.'

'Dimples is doing the PM this afternoon, sir. I've said I'll attend . . . It's alright, boss, honestly,' she said before he could raise any objection. 'I *want* to do it.'

*Thank Christ for that,* Noakes thought. Watching the pathologist Stryker-ing away to Classic FM always gave him the creeps.

'Right then.' Markham looked at his watch with a sinking feeling. 'Time for our appointment with the DCI, Noakes.'

The other grunted.

'Hook up with Doyle, Kate, and see what's out there in terms of cases in the same ballpark as ours.' Deadpan, he added, 'So we can give the DCI A, B and C categories in due course.'

And with that, the meeting broke up.

As her distinguished-looking boss crossed the outer office area trailed by Noakes, Burton reflected with amusement that they resembled some kind of variety act.

It didn't augur well.

* * *

Forty minutes later, the two men contemplated each other glumly across Markham's desk.

'This case is starting to feel like a chuffing powder keg, guv.'

Noakes had never said a truer word.

The DI's ears still rang with Sidney's hectoring tones.

'*You* do *realize, Inspector, that any time a murder is still unsolved within forty-eight hours of its discovery, the chances of its being solved diminish in direct proportion to the time that passes.*'

No shit, Sherlock.

'*If you're in over your head, Markham, then you should say so . . . No detective should become overly possessive of his case to the detriment of the real goal.*'

No wonder Olivia had nicknamed the DCI first cousin to Judas Iscariot, so transparent was his jealousy of CID's rising star.

*'We have to stop this bandwagon rolling, Markham.'*

*Bandwagon, bandwagon!*

It had been vintage Sidney and a toss-up as to which of his two subordinates most wanted to beat him to a pulp. In the event, despite both men slowly tautening with anarchic fury, neither had cracked.

'D'you think he's really going to sic Mystic Meg on us, guv?'

This referred to Sidney's latest suggestion that they should be open to all offers of help including, apparently, the services of an importunate psychic who insisted she 'saw things' and felt a connection with the victims.

Unusually, considering the nutty Norahs that CID investigations attracted as a rule, this one came with impressive credentials, being the well-to-do widow of an ex-councillor who also happened to play bridge with the DCI's wife.

'So far as one can tell, all she's come up with to date is some dotty vision of a heart dripping with blood,' the DI said heavily.

'Mebbe we c'n give her that make-up thingy we found on the playing fields,' Noakes sniggered. 'See if she gets any vibes off it.'

'Or why not go the whole hog and have a séance?' Markham said acidly. 'Ask her to make contact with the Other Side and see if the victims can point us in the right direction . . . tap once for "yes" and twice for "no".' He brought his hand down on the table with a thump. 'What a sodding *mess*.'

It was rare for the guvnor to swear and there was a discernible *thrum* beneath his regular voice, but Sidney had been more aggravating than usual. Worse even than his Gypsy Rose wheeze was the reference to a criminal profiler who came 'highly recommended'.

'Let's get out of here, Noakesy,' the DI burst out, 'before Sidney's psychic and this boffin from the university descend on us.'

Nothing loath, the other replied simply, 'Where to, guv?'

'New College Close. I want to check in with Mr MacAlinden and see where we're up to with the witness statements. Then this evening we've got a carol concert at Hope.'

'Very nice,' his DS replied without notable enthusiasm.

'There'll be mince pies.'

'Once in Royal David's City' and 'Hark! The Herald Angels Sing' suddenly acquired new lustre.

'Reckon we could do with summat Christmassy.'

The DI turned away to hide a smile.

'Come on,' he said. 'Our suspects await.'

# 10. STASIS

The MacAlindens occupied a ground-floor flat whose living room looked out on the communal garden.

As the two detectives made their way up the path, Markham was struck by the gloom of the day. There was precious little light and it would be dark before 4 p.m. Somehow, it matched his mood. He didn't share Olivia's enthusiasm for Narnia-like snowfields. The peaty embers of autumn were far more to his taste, and he invariably felt a pang when they were succeeded by monochrome winter tints. Perhaps he had seasonal affective disorder, winter depression or whatever they called it these days, but more likely it was just a reaction to the way this time of year made everything seem shrunken, hard and dry . . . like the corpses of the dead stiffening in Bromgrove General's morgue.

That interview with the DCI had been more dispiriting than usual. To have his efforts disparaged was a bitter pill, though on Sidney's watch he had grown used to being undermined. And now he'd have to fend off paraprofessionals like this criminal profiler, though he could probably get Kate Burton to deal with that . . .

He checked himself guiltily. Kate needed more experience in the field as opposed to being used to deflect Sidney.

But there was no denying she was good at it. The DCI had gone a bundle on that stuff about potential questioning techniques for their suspect — the only problem being that they didn't as yet have anyone who fitted the bill.

Ahead of him, Noakes was stamping his feet impatiently at the MacAlindens' front door.

Jolted out of his reverie, the DI moved to catch up.

* * *

It was a stuffy, overheated flat. Fussy and cluttered, the interior festooned with crocheted doilies and Franklin Mint china. Dawn's widower seemed even more desiccated and diminished than the last time they had seen him, while a monstrous yucca plant thrived in the corner of the front room as though sucking up all the oxygen.

At least the family liaison team seemed to have brought him round to some sort of acceptance of what had happened to his wife.

'I know she was murdered, Mr Markham,' he said with a trembling of the lip. 'And most likely the same person did for Marian and Ken.' He made no reference to Stacey Macmillan, and the DI felt profoundly thankful the grapevine hadn't yet brought him the news of her death. As soon as they were finished here, he'd alert the lead victim support officer so she could break it to him gently.

'I saw her in a dream the other night, you know . . . my Dawn.'

'Happen the missus jus' wanted to check in with you . . . see you're alright,' Noakes said comfortingly. For someone who affected to have no truck with Mystic Meggery, the DS was adjusting rapidly.

It was the right thing to say. The widower brightened. 'We were walking down Beech Drive together. I could hear her talking, though I couldn't see her mouth move. She kept smiling at me and I heard her say over and over, "I'm okay, I'm okay now, Dan. Don't worry about me, everything's okay."'

Noakes was touched. 'Sounds like she really wanted to give you a lift, mate,' he said gruffly.

'She kept pointing to her heart too. Like she was saying, "I love you".'

Suddenly, Markham remembered the psychic's vision of a heart dripping with blood. *No more than a coincidence*, he told himself, but he could see Noakes, too, was struck by it.

'Your Dawn was the caring sort,' the DS said with unwonted softness.

'Well, she wasn't a pushover . . . called a spade a spade, if you know what I mean. But yes, she was one of life's givers. That's why she found it hard to cut off at the end of the day . . . tended to bring the job home with her, so we got into the habit of going for a walk down the lane at the back last thing before turning in. She said being outside with nature helped remind her what was important . . . get things in perspective.'

To Markham's ears, it sounded like a good prescription. But it hadn't helped Dawn MacAlinden to lead a long and happy life. Listening to the bereft widower, Markham felt an uprush of anger at the killer so strong it almost made him choke. But he fought it down. The last thing the man needed was to see the lead detective in his wife's case succumb to undisciplined emotion.

Noakes gestured to a photograph album open on the coffee table in front of Dan MacAlinden's armchair. 'Nice to see 'em in a proper book,' he said approvingly. 'Can't be doing with all that digital messing about.'

'That's exactly what Dawn used to say. She had no time for folk showing pictures on their smartphones or whatever they're called.'

Confidingly, the man handed the burgundy leather volume over to Noakes. 'I was looking at pictures from when Dawn was a student at Hope,' he said. 'That's her with the long, dark hair . . . the one with plaits . . .'

The two detectives leaned in curiously.

'She was a bonny lass,' the DS observed. Then, 'That's her best friend?' he asked, pudgy finger pointing to a slim, fragile-looking girl with delicate features and ash-blonde hair. He turned over the pages. 'Seem to be quite a few of 'em together.'

'Yes, that's right. Joined at the hip in those days apparently . . . Can't remember the name . . . Sian . . . Silvia . . . something like that.'

'My Nat was like that when she was at Hope,' the DS said complacently. 'It was Tracey this an' Tracey that.' A slight frown. 'They drifted apart when her mate went to uni.' There was something in his manner that suggested the wrong girl got the breaks.

'Dawn kept up her connections with school.' Dan MacAlinden handled the album almost reverentially before replacing it on the coffee table and suddenly Markham recalled the scrapbook that had vanished from number seven. 'Marian Bussell was one of her old teachers . . . They were pretty thick together.'

'That's a tribute to them both,' smiled Markham. 'I'm not sure *my* teachers would be quite so thrilled if *I* came calling!'

'Marian was feisty, Mr Markham.' It was the same adjective Mary Atkins had used to describe the murdered woman. 'Very progressive in her attitudes . . . quite a social conscience. Dawn always liked that about her.'

'Did they . . . er, campaign together then?' Noakes phrased his question with unusual circumspection. 'Go on demos . . . that kind of thing?' The DI suppressed a smile. Clearly his subordinate was entertaining visions of a monstrous regiment of hairy-legged dungaree-wearing women descending on Bromgrove's civic institutions.

'Not really.' The other smiled affectionately. 'I used to call them the "armchair rebels" cos they were so civilized about it.'

Noakes waited expectantly.

'It was more about writing letters to local papers and pestering the council than anything else. Marian was quite vocal about minority rights . . . made a fuss about getting Section 28 repealed, that sort of thing.'

'The legislation that banned local authorities from promoting homosexuality in schools,' Markham explained. Then, before Noakes could ask what was wrong with that, he went on, 'I understand Mrs Bussell was at the forefront of broadening the school's pastoral curriculum.'

'Yes, that's right. She was into LGBT rights and all that, long before the local authority ever made a thing of it. There was a cousin of Marian's who committed suicide at boarding school . . . Don't know if it was on account of him being gay or transgender or what, but it kind of fired Marian up.'

So, a personal tragedy was the key to Marian Bussell's zealotry.

'An' your Dawn was into the LGBT stuff, right?' It was obvious Noakes struggled to understand the appeal of this particular crusade, but his tone was respectful. 'Was it summat to do with her job . . . helping kids . . . ?'

'It wasn't her specialism strictly speaking, but she saw quite a few children who were being treated for gender problems.' He paused. 'I think she worried some of them might've been rushed into taking pills . . . puberty blockers and other stuff . . . without them having a proper chance to see if it was what they really wanted . . .'

'Did she raise her concerns with the hospital authorities?'

'Oh, it didn't get that far, Mr Markham, though I remember the subject coming up at one of our residents' socials.' He grimaced at the memory. 'Dawn got slapped down by Doctor O'Connor and Ken Dowell. After that, she decided to leave it to the big boys. "Not really my bag is it, Dan?" she said. "Better not make waves."'

'But Mrs Bussell didn't mind making waves?'

Dan MacAlinden gave a weak laugh. 'Oh no, she was up for anything. Never say die!' Suddenly, his face crumpled as he realized what he had said.

Noakes's voice was kinder than Markham had ever heard it.

''S good your Dawn an' Mrs B had each other at the end . . . for comfort, like.'

The widower looked at Markham's big awkward sergeant and blinked. 'Yes,' he said, 'it helps to remember that.'

* * *

Markham decided the man had had enough for one day.

'We'll be on our way, Mr MacAlinden. Don't want to wear you out.'

'I haven't offered you any tea, Mr Markham.' It was poignant to see how he suddenly woke to the obligations of hospitality.

Never in the history of their long association had the DI known his subordinate to willingly pass up the chance of sustenance, but on this occasion he was firm. 'Don' you be worrying about that.' Noakes patted MacAlinden's arm reassuringly. 'We'll be drowning in it by the end of the day.'

As they passed into the hall, Markham asked casually, 'By the way, sir . . . Nothing to get alarmed about, but have you ever happened to see an unfamiliar lady in a headscarf about the place? It's just that we're just trying to trace any unidentified visitors and other residents have mentioned her.'

Keen eyes watched Dan MacAlinden steadily.

'Now you mention it, there *was* someone,' he answered vaguely. 'It was a while back . . . Dawn said she only saw the woman from behind, but she was sure she knew her from somewhere . . . something about the way she moved . . .'

'Jus' the once was this?' Noakes too was very casual.

'I'm not sure . . . might have been a couple of times. Dawn didn't think anything of it. I remember her laughing and saying Gary Coslett must have gone upmarket — dating Sloaney types — because she'd seen this elegant piece who walked like a dancer.' He screwed up his features, remembering. 'We figured maybe she was married and that's why she was sneaking in and out.'

'Ah, the eternal triangle!' Markham chuckled.

He had a gut feeling the mysterious headscarfed female — who matched the description of the prowler given by

Eileen Ledwidge — was somehow central to their investigation. But he could not as yet see how.

In the vestibule, on a ledge by the door was a glass case with what looked like skeletonized vertebrae.

'Fossils,' Dan MacAlinden said following the DI's gaze. 'Dawn was into beachcombing. A regular Mary Anning . . . never found a T-Rex, though.'

Markham found that the sight of the tiny bones affected him disagreeably, reviving memories of jumbled human remains retrieved from sludge. The little hallway suddenly felt unbearably hot. But he forced himself to linger, to make inconsequential chit-chat with the bereaved man for whom he sensed visitors would now increasingly be a rarity. His Dawn had been the umbilical cord that connected him to the bustling outside world, and now that cord had snapped.

'How've your employers been?' Noakes asked fiercely, as though fully prepared to take up the cudgels against any uncompassionate jobsworths down at Bestway Cash and Carry. 'They've been great.' But MacAlinden's voice was hollow. 'Told me to take as long as I need.'

'See you do, mate,' the DS urged him.

They were just at the threshold when the man clutched at Markham's sleeve.

'You'll get him won't you, Mr Markham, the one who did this to Dawn and the others?'

Markham wondered how much he knew about Kenneth Dowell's equally ghastly end and could only hope the family liaison team had sugar-coated it as much as possible.

Gaze and tone steady, he replied, 'I promise you, Mr MacAlinden, we'll get him.'

* * *

The rest of the day flew by in a kind of dream.

Before they knew it, the team was taking stock in what Doyle called the 'hut', which felt colder than ever despite Kate Burton's convector heater sputtering away in the corner.

Outside it was now completely dark and deserted, though throughout the afternoon there had been a steady stream of residents passing through the incident room.

Doctor O'Connor and Martin Henley had arrived together.

Lucy had been cool and collected.

Markham's hopes that she might yield insights about Dawn MacAlinden and the LGBT debate were dashed, as it seemed barely to have registered on her radar. 'The subject might've come up in passing,' she said, 'but I honestly don't recall . . . Dawn and I moved in different circles.' Professionally and socially was the implication.

It was pretty much the same with her partner. Mention of Dawn MacAlinden elicited no more than blank indifference. But there was a flare at the back of Henley's cold blue eyes when it came to Marian Bussell. 'Bit of a busy-body,' he said tightly. 'Too much time on her hands.' When pressed, he backtracked. 'Oh, I suppose there was no great harm in her. She was just one of those women who never got used to retirement . . . too interested in other people's business.'

'I wonder what "business" he meant?' Burton wondered after they had left.

'Mebbe Mrs B fancied herself a marriage guidance counsellor . . . them two deffo don' look like they're getting along.' Noakes chuckled. 'P'raps that bird in the headscarf was having a fling with Henley . . . He's the sort to play away.'

'Neither of them reacted when we brought up the subject of the mystery woman, Sergeant. They genuinely didn't seem to know anything about that.'

'Henley looked shifty when you mentioned Stacey though, guv.'

Aware that the latest murder would shortly be hitting the headlines, Markham had chosen to inform residents of Stacey Macmillan's death as succinctly as possible: Stacey's body was found in St James's parish hall and police were treating the circumstances as suspicious.

'It's possible Mr Henley and Stacey enjoyed a flirtation.'

'Not likely he killed her though, boss. Not with the missus sticking to him like superglue.'

Jeff Coleman seemed even less promising as a suspect for Stacey Macmillan's murder.

'Not unless he suddenly moved like the clappers . . . I mean, throttling Stacey an' then back into the wheelchair cool as you like . . .' Noakes was sceptical.

The DI looked interrogatively at Doyle who frowned with concentration.

'Brian Ledwidge said Coleman had gone to use the disabled loo, sir. We met up outside and got him into the car. I guess it's *possible* . . . people were dashing around and Eileen Ledwidge was flapping about getting off before it got dark, so everyone was a bit distracted.' He whistled. 'But even so . . . It's quite a stretch given Coleman's condition.'

'Don't forget what Stacey said to Martin Henley . . . according to her, he has some mobility,' Burton reminded them.

Coleman himself had been entirely unfazed when this was put to him. 'I can manage a few steps on occasion,' he agreed. 'And I use crutches too. But mostly it's the wheelchair.'

'I checked with the orthopods at Bromgrove General where he goes for physio, boss.' Burton again. 'There are periods of remission when he's able to walk, but it's irregular.'

The writer's upper body was strong and muscular. Could he somehow have dragged Stacey Macmillan off her feet and into a chokehold? His alibis for the two other women and Kenneth Dowell weren't watertight, so could this be their man?

Coleman claimed to have been friendly with Marian Bussell and Kenneth Dowell, but Markham sensed a certain waspishness beneath that urbanity of his. Had he been jealous of Marian Bussell for overtaking him as a writer? Of Dowell for those bona fide academic credentials which trumped his own achievements as a lowly teacher? Had jealousy curdled into something murderous, lit by some as yet unidentified touchpaper? Or had there been some personal dynamic at work between them, and if so where did Dawn MacAlinden fit in?

There was no mistaking Brian Ledwidge's prickly resentment of Mrs Bussell and Kenneth Dowell, though it wasn't until he was called away to an ailing parishioner at St James's that his wife became confidential. 'My husband's a good man,' she said defensively. 'Marian and Ken had a habit of cutting him down to size . . . taking cheap, intellectual pot shots.' Markham gained the impression they had looked down on her as well for being a housewife and wondered how much she had really liked these people with whom she lived cheek by jowl.

'Must get tiresome allus having to do the Mrs Vicar bit,' Noakes observed shrewdly after they had left. 'Turning the other cheek an' all that.' But the couple's horror at the news of Stacey Macmillan's death appeared unfeigned. It was impossible to glean their genuine opinion of the woman, though a certain tightening of Eileen Ledwidge's lips at the mention of her name suggested she wasn't a fan.

Julian Hoskinson had displayed a surprising degree of emotion when speaking of Stacey. 'She could be catty,' was his verdict, 'but she was a lot of fun too and very kind . . . no side to her.' It was an interesting remark. 'It wasn't easy for me to fit into the close,' he continued. 'But Stacey took me just as I was.'

'And other people didn't?' Markham prompted.

'Well, Marian kind of wanted to turn me into a *cause*, Inspector.' The charity worker sighed. 'I was quite closeted when I moved in and she tried to . . . well, *co-opt* me . . . get me to come out, on the basis that I owed it to myself to be truthful. Always quoting Ian McKellen or some other luvvie activist at me — all that born-again gay bollocks. I just couldn't be doing with it. Stonewall, Peter Tatchell, LGBT, all the "change from within" speechifying . . . it's just not me.' Noakes was surprised to find himself rather warming to Hoskinson by this point.

'Stacey accepted me for what I was,' the young man repeated. 'She and Simon were good listeners when my love life went off the rails.' Ah, thought Markham, the slashed mannequins.

'They didn't judge, whereas Brian and Eileen . . . well, you'll know what they're like by now . . . good people but deep down not keen on queers.'

'What about Mr Dowell?'

'Oh, he was very much in Marian's camp . . . used to lecture me about how the country would be healthier if people who were LGBT let society know about it and lived without disguise. God,' a spurt of bitterness, 'as if it's not hard enough being gay without folk making a *religion* of it . . . like we all have to become bleeding leaders of men or something.'

'Must've been rough, mate.' Noakes surprised everyone, not least himself, by this muttered admission.

'Ken was so intense . . . made me wonder what skeletons were lurking in *his* cupboard.' Suddenly, he flushed. 'Sorry, poor taste,' he mumbled.

'That's a bloke with a lot of baggage,' Noakes mused after he left.

'No alibi worth mentioning, what with him being his own boss,' Burton added.

'Located anyone able to vouch for him yet, Kate?' The DI found himself hoping they could rule Hoskinson out.

'Sorry, sir.' A wry smile. 'They all know him down at that nightclub place — Ducky or whatever it's called — but I can't pin anyone down to specifics.'

'All off their faces.' But Noakes was less vociferous than might have been expected.

Simon Gailey confirmed Hoskinson's occasional boyfriend trouble. He looked troubled when Markham raised Eileen Ledwidge's story about the slashed mannequins. 'I don't know anything about that,' he said slowly. 'Julian took some homophobic flak when he opened Lili's. There was trolling too . . . internet abuse,' he explained, 'so maybe it had something to do with that.'

'Bit of an, er, emotional fella.' Noakes felt the ground cautiously.

'True. But he's had a tough upbringing. Got a lot of guts.' Gailey, with lawyerly discretion, did not expand on this, but Markham saw the sympathy in his eyes.

'I take it he didn't want to be a poster boy for LGBT.'

The other grinned, eyes crinkling with amusement. 'God no, Inspector. Jules is too much his own man for that.'

*Jules*. Noakes was sniffing the wind. 'Are you and he close then, sir?'

'Not in the biblical sense, Sergeant,' came the riposte. Noakes was visibly unprepared for such frankness. 'We bonded over mutual interests . . . cinema, theatre, the arts generally.' Another grin. 'Plus he was able to vent to me when Marian and the others got too much. Hearts in the right place, but they could be a bit . . . relentless. Jules is a very private person — quite secretive until he trusts you. Once you've prised him open it's different.'

'Think Gailey's a wooftah as well, guv?' Noakes got down to brass tacks though the solicitor was barely out the door.

'If he is, he's not telling.' The DI certainly didn't see the sophisticated retiree as a habitué of Ducky. 'Sounds like he was a peacemaker — good at smoothing down ruffled feathers.'

'*Jesus*,' Noakes paced the pokey room morosely. 'None of 'em seems to be a fit . . . even though most of their alibis are *shite*.' He was like a caged animal at the circus, thought Burton idly.

'I'll brew up,' Doyle said to no one in particular, padding out to the bungalow's front room in search of Coslett's kettle before heading to the manky lean-to for some water.

Markham had never thought he would experience actual nostalgia for the creature comforts of Bromgrove CID, but at that moment he felt positively homesick for his sliver of an office with its unrivalled view of the station car park. At least there was always the chance of scrounging a half decent coffee from somewhere, whereas *chez* Coslett it was like bivouacking at Dunkin' Donuts.

And indeed, right on cue, the DC returned with three mugs of builder's and a paper bag of cinnamon buns.

'Good thinking,' Noakes said approvingly while Burton declined with a slight shudder.

'Sorry, sarge.' The young detective turned to her apologetically. 'They didn't have any samosas.'

Just as well. The mere thought of it made Markham feel quite nauseous.

'Anything in the unsolved files to help us, Kate?' he enquired.

She shook her head dispiritedly. 'Nothing so far, boss.' Her shoulders sagged. 'But no doubt the DCI's profiler will say our killer's in there somewhere.'

'Bleeding Cracker types,' Noakes growled through a mouthful of bun. 'They don't allus get it right, y'know. There was the Jigsaw Man—'

'The *what*?' To Doyle, it sounded like a serial killer's moniker.

'Smartarse psychologist who screwed up after that poor lass was murdered on Wimbledon Common.'

'Oh yes,' Burton perked up. 'I remember that. The Rachel Nickell case. We did a module on it at uni . . . The profiler helped the police set up a honeytrap operation, but the judge said it was illegal and there was a big hoo-hah about it . . . and anyway, they got the wrong man because the real killer was in Broadmoor all along.'

'Thass right.' Noakes winked at her as if as to say, *We students of the human mind.*

The DI's lips quirked.

'Well, we'll have to pay due deference. But in the meantime—'

'We've got sod all.'

'Quite, Noakes.'

'Jus' saying, guv.'

A thought occurred to Markham. 'That album or scrapbook Shona mentioned — the one with mementoes of Mrs Bussell's career — did it ever turn up?'

'No sign of it, sir.' Burton hesitated. 'Maybe it never existed in the first place.'

'Oh, I think it did, Kate.' And he recounted the visit to Dawn MacAlinden's widower.

'Dawn kept lots of photographs from her childhood and schooldays,' he concluded. 'I'm willing to bet Marian Bussell was the same . . . It was a shared pleasure for them, reminiscing about the past.'

'Remember the Ashley Dean case,' Doyle said unexpectedly. 'In the end, it all came down to a photo, didn't it?'

It was true. An earlier investigation at Hope Academy was blown wide open after Burton and Noakes came across an old school picture on the microfilm reader in Bromgrove Central Library. Markham had never forgotten that electric moment when the killer's face swam into focus from the grainy newsprint.

Was history repeating itself? Did Marian Bussell's missing album hold the crucial clue that would see all the pieces slip into place? Or had the killer simply seized it on a whim . . . ?

'None of our suspects seem to be showing any outward signs of tension,' he said at last. 'Or at least, no more than you'd expect from people caught up in a murder investigation.' Then, he tried another tack. 'Have we gleaned any more about the woman in the headscarf?'

'No, sir.' Burton narrowed her eyes thoughtfully. 'Maybe Coslett's trying to send us in the wrong direction.'

'But Eileen Ledwidge mentioned her too, didn't she?' Doyle pointed out. 'When she was talking about a prowler.'

'And Mr MacAlinden said Dawn caught a glimpse of her,' Markham added.

Noakes guffawed. 'Thought she might be some posh totty of Coslett's, sneaking in and out the back way . . . *as if*!'

'You know what they say about some women liking rough trade, sarge.'

'Get out of it! She'd have to have been desperate . . . I mean,' the DS gestured at the bungalow in disbelief, 'does this look like a love shack?'

From the look on Burton's face, she certainly considered the location to be less than aphrodisiacal.

'An accomplice?' she said desperately. 'In it with Coslett?'

'But where's the motive, Kate?' Markham leaned back in his rickety chair, trying to ease his aching back muscles. 'Coslett's a singularly unattractive character who's fallen out with most of the residents at some time or other . . . But a *killer* . . . I just don't see him for it. There was a finesse about those first murders . . .'

Even as he said this, the DI heard Sidney's dulcet tones in his ear.

'That "copper's hunch", Markham . . . Don't let it lead you by the nose . . . Good solid legwork's the thing . . . None of your famous *flair*!'

'Maybe this woman's the killer.' Doyle looked uncertainly round at his colleagues. 'An outsider with a grudge . . . and then Stacey caught on to her.'

'We're going round the pigging mulberry bush here,' Noakes scowled. The sugar rush was making him irritable. 'Next thing we'll be pinning it on Princess Di back from the dead or summat.'

'You're right, Noakesy. Better stick with what we've got.'

Which was a big fat zero.

'Let's divvy up the witness statements,' Markham said finally, 'and see if anything jumps out.'

'I've got background on the other residents here too, sir. Tracked most of them down via the uni and social services. All accounted for . . . alibis seem to be in order.'

'Not like this chuffing lot.' Noakes cast a baleful look at the sheaf of papers on the table in front of them.

Conscientiously, they applied themselves to silent scrutiny and for the next hour there was peace, interrupted only by the odd postprandial belch from Noakes or the assiduous swish of Kate Burton's highlighter pen.

Suddenly, the DI's mobile pinged. He glanced at the incoming text.

'Olivia,' he said simply, with the transfigured expression that always caused Kate Burton a wistful pang. 'Reminding me of our hot date with the carol singers at Hope.'

'I've got the PM on Stacey,' she said, glad of an excuse to avoid seeing the two of them together.

'Are you sure, Kate?' The DI's expression was solicitous. 'It's been a hard day and you look done in.'

His kindness made her want to cry, but she answered woodenly enough, 'It's good experience, sir.'

There was no arguing with that.

And no question of her fellow DS attempting to dissuade her.

*More mince pies for the rest of us*, his face seemed to say.

At the sight of her pinched pallor, some latent chivalry stirred in Doyle.

'I'll come with you, sarge,' he offered.

He was amply rewarded for this good-natured impulse by Markham's warm smile of approval. 'Excellent. Always go for safety in numbers when dealing with Dimples.'

* * *

Out at his car, Markham tossed the keys to Noakes.

'You drive, Noakesy. I've got spots in front of my eyes from all that paperwork.'

Nothing loath, the other settled himself at the wheel of the BMW with the air of a man who knew how to appreciate a top-of-the-range automobile.

'D'you reckon we'll get the chance to have a word with the gruesome twosome . . . Mary Atkins an' Councillor Callaghan, guv?' He ran his hands almost caressingly over the steering wheel. 'We didn't manage a go at them this afternoon.'

'Oh, I should think so.' Though the mere thought of it set a pulse beating at his temples. It promised to be a long evening . . .

'*What the fuck!*'

Noakes braked so suddenly that Markham's head bounced off the headrest.

A woman was rapping frantically at the rear window.

The DS was out of the vehicle in an instant. Wrapping his arms around the distraught figure, clad only in a flimsy housecoat and slippers, he bundled her into the back of the car.

'Mrs Ledwidge!'

The woman was wild-eyed, almost unkempt, the normally immaculate beehive straggling about her face in untidy strands.

'What is it?'

'Brian,' she stuttered through lips that were blue with cold. 'He's gone missing.'

# 11. CLOSE TO HOME

Markham swiftly shrugged off his cashmere overcoat even as Noakes was tugging at his disreputable parka.

'You're alright, Noakesy. Put mine round Mrs Ledwidge.'

Watching in his rear-view mirror, he waited while the DS shuffled Eileen Ledwidge into his guvnor's coat with little pats and clumsy words of reassurance.

The woman looked less pinched and wretched now, though her teeth continued to chatter, from a combination of shock and the cold.

'In a moment, we're going to get you back inside, Mrs Ledwidge,' the DI said easily. 'Don't want you catching pneumonia.'

Noakes was now chafing her livid hands between his big paws.

'Your Bri would never forgive us,' he said.

'There's a carol concert at the school.' The words came out thickly. 'We're supposed to be going.'

'There's plenty of time.' Again, the easy, relaxed tone belied the tension Markham was feeling. 'We were heading that way ourselves for a look round, but the concert doesn't start till half eight and it's not six o'clock yet.'

'Loadsa time, luv.' But Noakes's eyes met Markham's in the mirror and telegraphed, *this ain't looking good.*

'We'll come back with you to number sixteen, Mrs Ledwidge. I reckon you could do with a hot drink, and then you can talk us through your husband's movements. In the meantime, I'll put out an alert.'

Her hands clutched convulsively at Noakes.

'It's jus' routine, luv.' The DS was as soothing as possible. 'Don' fret yourself.'

'Do you feel able to stand, Mrs Ledwidge?' Markham asked gently.

A dumb nod.

'Right. I'll come round to your door, then the sergeant and I will get you indoors. It's just a few hundred yards.' He smiled at her. 'I can carry you if necessary.'

'Yeah, the guvnor's a dab hand at the fireman's lift.'

Most women would have killed to be in Eileen Ledwidge's shoes and enjoy a 'me Tarzan, you Jane' moment with the dishy DI. There wasn't likely to be much of that going on with the Rev.

Where the chuff *was* Brian Ledwidge? He was the type you could set your watch by . . . Noakes was starting to get a very bad feeling about it all . . .

* * *

Once inside the Ledwidges' tastefully appointed townhouse, Markham set Noakes to sorting well-sugared tea and biscuits. 'Reckon she could do with summat a bit stronger,' Noakes observed. 'There's whisky on that drinks trolley in the dining room.'

'Alright, you can put a shot in her tea but don't go overboard, Sergeant. I need her coherent.'

'Got you. Don' worry, guv. She won't be sparko.'

Thankfully the Ledwidges' living room was toasty warm. Markham noticed there were cups and saucers yet to be cleared away.

‘I had some of the neighbours round earlier,’ Eileen Ledwidge said awkwardly, like a hostess who had slipped up. ‘It’s a bit messy.’

‘Mrs Ledwidge, if that’s your idea of mess, then there’s no hope for the rest of us!’ Again, he kept it light and charming. ‘No, don’t get up,’ as she made to rise from the black leather sofa. ‘I’ve taken the liberty of pointing my sergeant in the direction of your kitchen. It’s all equal opps in CID these days, so it’s turn and turn about when it comes to making the tea. He does quite a decent brew.’ A wry grin. ‘He’ll be rooting through your biscuit tin as well.’

Some colour returned to her face.

‘You’re welcome, Inspector.’ This appeal to her nurturing instincts was well judged. ‘I expect you’re having to eat on the hoof at the moment.’

‘Well, Noakes’s requisitioning skills are second to none, so we do pretty well. Ah, talk of the devil . . .’

The DS lumbered in carrying a tray laden with mugs of tea and a plate of custard creams. As he handed Eileen Ledwidge her mug (mercifully, he hadn’t used her best bone china), the DS gave his boss a surreptitious wink, from which Markham deduced that the necessary medicinal ingredient had been added.

Number sixteen’s curtains weren’t drawn and in the distance the snowy playing fields gleamed an eerie ivory. Markham wondered whether Brian Ledwidge, like Kenneth Dowell, had somehow blundered out there into a deadly ambush.

He gave Noakes an imperceptible nod. Following the DI’s gaze, the other went to draw the heavy maroon drapes. ‘Don’ want any draughts getting on you, luv,’ he muttered, though the triple glazing made this unlikely.

For a few minutes, they sipped (or slurped) their tea.

Markham willed himself to be patient as the minutes ticked by.

‘I feel a bit idiotic,’ Eileen Ledwidge said finally. ‘Making a fuss when it’s most likely nothing.’ The familiar surroundings had recalled the woman to herself, but she still had a wild-eyed look and her voice pleaded for reassurance. 'It's just so unlike him. He went out . . . but he said he'd be back by quarter to six . . . and when he says he'll be back by a particular time you can always count on it . . .' A shaky hiccough. 'He always says, "Punctuality is the politeness of kings."'

'An excellent precept, Mrs Ledwidge.' The DI held her eyes. 'When did you last see Mr Ledwidge?'

'He went over to see Dan MacAlinden around four . . . sort of a pastoral call.'

Poor old MacAlinden. Noakes did his inward eye-roll. Probably the last thing the man needed was the likes of the Rev praying over him. All psalms and preaching.

'Brian really missed that side of his ministry after retiring,' she continued, making Noakes flush guiltily, as though she had caught him out. 'Being alongside people in their hour of need . . . That's why he enjoyed the hospital chaplaincy work . . . there was time to make a connection.'

'And after he'd been to see Mr MacAlinden?' Markham prompted.

'He arrived back around four. Most of the residents were going to the concert, what with Mary making such a thing about it . . . there's to be some kind of tribute for Marian and Dawn, and Brian was going to help with the prayers.'

Her hands had started to shake. Gently, Markham relieved her of her mug and set it down on the tray.

'To be honest, no one felt much like a carol concert,' she said tremulously. 'All pretty shell-shocked about Stacey, you see . . . and then the police interviews . . . and everything.'

'That's totally natural, Mrs Ledwidge. You'd been through the wringer.'

'Simon rounded up the neighbours for me. I think they were glad to have something to fill up the time before going out. Nothing fancy,' she added timidly, as though worried it might be considered tasteless to throw a party after four people had died. 'Just coffee and cake . . . more for comfort than anything else.'

Noakes needed no convincing that cake was the perfect antidote to misery. Scouting round the kitchen, he'd seen the remains of a coffee and walnut confection but had heroically restricted himself to the custard creams. 'Good on you, luv,' he said kindly through a mouthful of biscuit. 'Thass what I call looking out for folk.' Markham was amused to notice the DS punctiliously sweeping the crumbs from his trousers onto a plate, as though to convince Eileen Ledwidge he was a fit person to be entertained in her elegant drawing room.

'So they were all here, were they?' Mentally, Markham positioned the protagonists.

'Yes, that's right . . . even Lucy managed to get time off work . . .' she faltered slightly, 'in the circumstances.'

Yeah, it's not every day four of the neighbours snuff it.

But Noakes's voice was soft and encouraging as he took over the questioning. 'So, were folk still noshing — er, having refreshments when Brian came back?'

'Well, someone said they should be making a move and see you at Hope, that kind of thing.'

'Okay, so the party was breaking up,' the DS pressed her. 'Did you notice anything unusual . . . anything about your fella or one of the others?'

She put a hand to her straggly hair, ineffectually attempting to tuck it back into a semblance of neatness.

'Well, Brian looked a bit dazed.'

'*Dazed*. How come?'

'He came in and looked round at everyone . . . then he went quite pale and sort of stiffened. Like he'd seen a ghost or been shot in the back or something.'

'You're sure about that, Mrs Ledwidge?' Markham interposed.

'He definitely wasn't himself. I thought it must have been too much for him going round to see Dan MacAlinden . . . too emotional. Or maybe it was what happened to Stacey . . . delayed shock or something.'

Noakes took up the reins again. 'What happened next?'

'Oh, nothing really. Brian just said a quick hello to everyone and went upstairs to . . . well, freshen up, I suppose . . .'

*Freshen up*? Why did posh folk always have to talk like that when they meant using the bog? The DS shook his head at this eccentricity before zeroing in on the tableau Eileen Ledwidge had described.

'He didn't talk to anybody in particular?'

'No . . . they were leaving and anyone could see he was wiped out.'

'When he did this shot-in-the-back thing, did you notice if he was looking at any of 'em?'

'Not really, Sergeant.' She twisted her wedding ring round and round. 'The light caught his glasses so I couldn't tell.'

Markham remembered the thick specs and Ledwidge's exophthalmic stare.

'So, Mr Ledwidge was upstairs . . . getting washed and changed?'

Trust the guvnor to buy into all that middle-class crip crap.

'That's right, Inspector.' She hesitated, the wedding ring rotating ever faster till it looked as though she must be about to wrench her finger off. 'I didn't want to crowd him. I decided to have another coffee before tidying up.'

'Go on, Mrs Ledwidge, you're doing well.'

'Well, Brian came downstairs about ten minutes later—'

'What time was this?'

'About quarter past four. His colour still wasn't good. I told him we could pass on the concert . . . said I'd ring Mary. But he said it was nothing, just heartburn, and he'd be fine but there was something he had to do first.'

'You're sure those were his exact words, Mrs Ledwidge?'

'Something he had to do or someone he had to talk to.' She looked anguished. 'I wasn't really paying attention . . . I suppose deep down I was relieved I didn't have to ring Mary to cancel. She wouldn't have been best pleased.'

From what Markham knew of Mary Atkins, he reckoned it was an accurate prognosis.

'Did your husband say anything else?'

'He was holding his mobile and it pinged, so I knew he'd got a text.'

'What did he do?'

'He read it and put the phone in his jacket pocket. Then he told me he had to go out for a bit but he'd be back in time for the concert.'

'He didn't say where?'

'I didn't like to ask. He looked so strange . . . almost as though he'd had an out-of-body experience . . . or something surreal had happened.' The words tumbled out with startling vehemence, 'You must think me a strange sort of wife, but that's how it is being married to a clergyman. You learn not to pry . . .'

'Nowt weird about that.' Noakes was matter-of-fact. 'It's in the job description for a vicar's missus.'

Eileen Ledwidge visibly relaxed. 'Pretty much,' she said. 'Though it took some getting used to.'

*Well done, Noakesy*. The DS had his own inimitable brand of TLC to which everyone, be they juvenile recidivist or elderly curmudgeon, invariably responded.

'Did he take the car, luv?'

'Yes, he did. I thought there must be some crisis at the hospital and they needed a chaplain . . . for anointing the sick.'

Personally, Noakes couldn't think of anything he'd like less than Brian Ledwidge popping up at his sickbed, Bible at the ready, but he preserved a sympathetic expression.

'Your husband didn't actually *say* he was going to the hospital, Mrs Ledwidge?'

'No, Inspector . . . I just assumed. He often gets called out like that at short notice.'

'Did you see him leave, Mrs Ledwidge?'

'Yes, I waved to him in the car park, but he didn't see me . . . probably concentrating on his driving with the weather being so bad.'

'You didn't notice anyone with him? Didn't see him stop to speak to anyone?'

'No, he just drove away . . . I tried his mobile later on, but he must have switched it off.'

Markham nodded reassuringly, as if perfectly satisfied, though a gnawing sense of fear was tightening its grip on him.

'I'm going to get someone over here to stay with you, Mrs Ledwidge.'

Instant alarm in her eyes.

'Something's happened, hasn't it? Something bad.' She looked from one to the other. 'You think *he's* got my Brian?' She was half out of her seat.

'Easy, luv.' Noakes laid a restraining hand on her arm and, with gentle force, pressed her back down. 'We need you here, back at base . . . in case your fella phones the main line or comes home while we're out doing the rounds.' Sincere compassion softened the hangdog features, making them almost handsome. 'You're far better here, luv, believe me.' He didn't want her accompanying them to a grave site . . . or worse. 'We're gonna do everything we can.' As solicitous as any nurse, he whisked a chenille throw off the sofa arm and tucked it round her. 'Me and the guvnor are going next door in the kitchen.' He extended a stubby thumb and little finger. 'Gotta few phone calls to make an' then we'll be right back. You try an' have a bit of shut-eye in the meantime.'

* * *

Ten minutes later the two men eyed each other across Eileen Ledwidge's high-spec granite worktops.

'So, no sign of him at the hospital . . . No medical emergency or call-out.'

The DI looked at his watch. 'Nearly twenty past seven, which means the residents will most likely have headed out to Hope.'

'Yeah, so they c'n chow down on them mince pies before all the caterwauling an' speechifying.'

The doorbell rang. Trust the Ledwidges to have 'Edelweiss'.

A sturdy young uniform announced herself as PC Lynda Hart and was duly installed in the living room to keep Eileen Ledwidge company.

'Distract her . . . put the telly on, fetch a snack . . . whatever it takes,' Noakes hissed. 'We'll give you the nod once we're off.'

Then it was back to the kitchen.

'No point sealing the close, guv?'

'Our man's long gone, Noakes. That text to Mr Ledwidge's mobile was to set up a meeting . . .'

'Cos he realized Ledwidge *knew*.'

'Yes, I think as he walked in on his wife's guests and saw one of them, something clicked in his mind . . . The pieces fell into place and he suddenly guessed the killer's identity.'

'Got such a shock, he couldn't hide it.'

'That's right.' Markham swivelled a breakfast bar stool with a force that betrayed his frustration. 'A eureka moment . . . but we don't know what triggered it.'

'An' the doofus thought he could handle it hisself. *Shoot me now*!' Noakes groaned.

'Doubtless he took a *pastoral* view.' The DI's sigh was almost as despairing. 'Or maybe he hoped he was mistaken . . . wanted an explanation.'

'Wanted to — what did his missus say back there? — make a *connection*. Well, he's likely managed that alright . . . connected hisself to summat sharp an' pointy, I shouldn't wonder.'

Now Noakes too was spinning the bar stools like a manic juggler spinning plates.

'What next, boss? We ain't got the first idea where he was meeting Ledwidge?'

'I think it might be Hope.'

'Why the school?'

'Because that's where all the residents are headed this evening. Everyone's expected at the concert — three-line whip, courtesy of Mary Atkins — no excuses. *Think about it*.'

The handsome face was suddenly flushed with animation. 'Perfect cover.'

'An' we know he c'n move quickly . . . jus' has to slip away for a mo . . . an' hey presto, it's problem sorted. *Fuck*,' the DS burst out, 'so you're saying we're too late, guv, is that it?'

Markham's flush receded, leaving him ashy pale. 'Would to God I'm proved wrong, Noakes, but it would make sense for the killer to corner Ledwidge at Hope. No need to worry about an alibi since that's precisely where he's supposed to be.'

'Hey up though, boss. Schools are big on security these days. Folk have to be swiped in or wear a lanyard, an' all that jazz. Tougher than frigging Alcatraz . . . So anyone turning up early to have a mooch around the place would stick out like a sore thumb.'

Distractedly, Noakes rumpled his hair into myriad porcupine quills. Not a good look.

'The concert's not due to start till half eight with eats first . . . an' Ledwidge told his missus he'd be back here at quarter to six to get ready. It's only about ten minutes by car from the close to Hope, so that gave him more than an hour for a meeting before he had to get gussied up.' The DS rasped his stubbly chin. 'But someone's bound to have asked what they were doing there, guv. They couldn't have snuck in without being noticed . . . There'd be a teacher or receptionist or the caretaker . . . or *someone* . . . I mean, it's wall to wall nosey parkers in all them places cos they're obsessed with paedos an' pervs . . . *Nah*,' he sounded decisive now, 'couldn't be done.'

'I think it *could*, Noakes.'

The DS waited. That intense light was back in his boss's eyes.

'Mr Ledwidge would have had no trouble getting in . . . retired clergyman from St James's . . . special assemblies, bit of kudos for management. He'd be given the run of the place, no questions asked . . . Ms Atkins would have seen to that.'

Now Markham was running his hands through his hair, though the effect in his case was distinctly more Byronic.

Noakes couldn't but be infected by his superior's conviction.

'Well, I s'pose he *was* doing the prayers an' that tribute malarkey . . .'

'Exactly. What could be more natural than him being around to supervise things . . . kids gone home for the day . . . staff sloping off early. Nobody would have batted an eyelid. All totally respectable and above board.'

'Okay, that's Ledwidge sorted . . . but how'd the killer sneak in?'

'Remember the Ashley Dean investigation, Noakes? That place is a warren, full of nooks and crannies . . . lots of back doors and stairwells. I reckon if someone managed to get their hands on a set of keys, they could be in there in a trice. Or with everything going on this evening, it'd be a cinch to blag their way past the front desk . . . especially if they were a familiar figure—'

'Cos Atkins bullied 'em into helping out with stuff in the school.' The DS contorted his pudgy features into a pious simper. '"*Let's do it for the kids.*" God, they've probably *all* had their arms twisted.'

'Precisely, Noakes.' Markham's face darkened. The thought of that figure on the playing fields behind the close, watching the residents unseen, had never gone away. 'Whoever it is, nothing was going to deter him. And the timing was good . . . almost the holidays . . . everyone demob-happy . . . normal vigilance relaxed. Hell, there might not even have been anyone on the front desk. When we called on Mat and Olivia, we just strolled in with another teacher.'

'Thass right . . . they swiped us in cos that airhead receptionist was gassing to one of the kids . . .'

The DS looked at Markham with blank-eyed horror.

'Christ, boss, we can't jus' close the place down. I mean, we ain't got anything to say Ledwidge is in there . . . somewhere . . .' He swallowed hard. 'Sidney'll have you doing

Traffic for the rest of your natural if you kibosh that concert an' then we got nowt to show for it.'

It was typical of Noakes's Sancho Panza-like devotion to the DI that *Markham's* career prospects were his predominant concern. As Olivia put it, beneath that rough-hewn exterior was a diamond.

'We'll go to the concert, Noakes.'

The DS knew that look of old. It meant wild horses would not deflect the DI from his chosen course.

'There's an alert out for Brian Ledwidge. I want you to get on to Burton and Doyle and have them meet us at the school . . . no fuss, no blue lights, no sirens.' He drew a deep breath. 'Once the tra-la-la-ing's started, we can search the building.'

'How do we square it with Atkins?'

'We don't . . . I'll have a quiet word with Mat Sullivan and get the caretaker on side.'

'Thank fuck it ain't Jim Snell.'

For a moment, Markham fell silent, oppressed by unwelcome thoughts of that other hideous investigation at Hope. Then, the light of battle in his eyes, he said, 'Are you up for it, Noakesy?'

'Behind you all the way, boss.'

'Right, let's make our farewells to Mrs Ledwidge and get out of here.'

'We're looking for her Brian's body, ain't we, guv?' Noakes's fists were clenched. 'The poor sod was a goner as soon as that bastard saw that look on his face.'

'Yes, I think Ledwidge was dead not long afterwards . . . maybe even before his poor wife told us he was missing. But,' the concentrated pain in the DI's face was palpable, 'I want Eileen to get him back intact.'

Not mutilated or desecrated or chucked away like so much rubbish.

'D'you remember the first time we met the Rev, he was twitchy . . . nervous about summat, guv?'

'Yes, that's true. Something was definitely bothering him.'

'Mebbe he was already feeling antsy about one of the neighbours . . . had his suspicions about one of 'em. Mebbe he knew summat weren't right . . .'

'That's a definite possibility, Noakes. I think it's very likely something had been tugging at his subconscious and then it crystallized when he saw the residents all together in his front room.'

'Why didn't the daft beggar *tell* us? Talk about playing God . . .'

'Come on, Sergeant. We need to be on our way.'

Markham looked as though he had the weight of the world on his shoulders but, standing outside Eileen Ledwidge's living room, he straightened up and composed his features. His wingman watched in admiration as the guvnor dealt with Brian Ledwidge's desperate wife and telegraphed the state of play to PC Hart.

In less than five minutes, they were back in the car heading to Hope Academy.

The DI had always felt there was something magical about twinkling baubles and Christmas trees in the darkness, even if his number two grumbled that decorations seemed to go up earlier with each passing year. But now, with a terrible sadness weighing on his heart, he knew these festive fripperies were lighting the way to the Reverend Brian Ledwidge's final bourn . . .

* * *

The feeling of unreality persisted once they arrived at the school.

Normally the place struck him as a cross between a giant fish tank and a women's prison. However, the bunker-like building, with its awful sixties' architecture, had received some sort of overhaul, boasting an enormous real fir in the main foyer and a nativity scene next to it.

'Nice to see they remember whose chuffing birthday it's meant to be,' the DS muttered. 'Makes a change from all them "winter festivals" with pixies an' elves . . . I reckon half the kids round here think it's summat to do with the Goblin King.'

Predictably, Noakes's anti-Christmas syndrome had kicked in. It was always the same. He would loudly protest his intention to 'boycott the whole sodding circus' before eventually succumbing as wholeheartedly as any child.

There seemed to be nobody about.

'You were right about the reception desk, guv.' Noakes glowered at the vacant-looking blonde sporting a pair of red novelty antlers. 'Didn't even check our credentials . . . prob'ly been getting stuck into the Prosecco all afternoon.'

The DI suspected this was not far from the truth.

'Let's check out the LRC,' he said. 'That's usually where they lay out the food.'

But there was no one in the learning resource centre apart from a disconsolate teenager, also wearing reindeer headgear. Sitting at the librarian's desk, she appeared clamped to her iPod. Tinsel and crêpe-paper streamers festooned every spare corner, as though management was determined to squeeze every last drop of faux jollity out of the occasion.

'They're in the gym,' she said listlessly to Markham, unclamping herself from Beyoncé. 'But there's plenty of mince pies left . . . an' some chocolate log . . .'

The prospect of free provender had quite lost its allure for Noakes, given the nature of their mission.

'You're alright, luv,' he said kindly. 'Has it started yet . . . er, the singing an' what have you?'

'Yeah, I think so . . . there were a few last-minute problems had to be sorted.'

Like no one to lead the prayers.

It was beginning to dawn on the lethargic teenager that they weren't the usual run of visitors and definitely not parents.

'Is everything okay?' she asked nervously.

'Tell you what, luv . . . We're after Mr Sullivan. Any chance you could nip over there an' tell him Mr Markham needs a word?'

With a doubtful glance at the thick-set man who nonetheless had a fatherly air about him, she headed for the corridor.

'This lot need to buck up their ideas,' the DS growled on her departure. 'The lass didn't even ask to see our ID. We could've been *anyone* . . . I mean, what happened to stranger danger an' all that?'

There was something soulless and creepy about a school out of normal hours. Like a stage set deserted by the actors.

They didn't have to wait long.

'Gil!' Mat Sullivan had arrived, looking unusually smart in his academic gown. 'I know, I know,' he said forestalling Noakes's raillery. 'Mary insisted, so ours not to reason why.'

'Is the head around tonight, Mat?'

'Don't you mean the *executive* head?' Sullivan grimaced. 'He's down at Medway High.'

'Ah yes, your partner school . . . Don't tell me, they've got something on as well.'

'Yep . . . impeccable diary planning as always . . . but at least it means he's out of our hair for tonight. God knows, Mary's hard going but this time of year he's like the Duracell Bunny on speed.' Sullivan registered something about their demeanour. 'What's up, Gil? Has there been a break in the case?' Then looking at them more closely, 'Oh no . . . *not another one*.'

'Brian Ledwidge is missing.'

'*Ledwidge*? Oh right, I'm with you . . . He was meant to be doing the Advent Prayers but no-show . . . Mary had another tame clergyman in reserve, luckily. We just assumed Ledwidge had been called out to the hospital.'

'He had a call-out, but it wasn't Bromgrove General. Let's just say we're concerned for his safety . . . think he may have been lured over here.'

'What can I do?'

That was the great thing about Mat Sullivan. For all his languid appearance, he was cool and incisive in a crisis. No explanations necessary.

'Can you get hold of the caretaker for us, Mat . . . casually, without raising a hue and cry. We need to do a search.'

'No problem. You've got at least another fifty minutes before they wind up in there. Mary's in full gush mode . . . all that smarming to the governors and Councillor Callaghan should help spin things out.'

'Good man. And Mat,' Markham's face was anxious, 'no need to alert Liv. After last time, I figure she doesn't need to be in on this.'

'Don't worry. She's busy prompting her hopeless Year 9s — *Journey of the Magi* like you've never heard it before!' He placed a hand on Markham's arm. 'Seriously, it's okay. She was disappointed you didn't make it to the drinks, but it's been manic trying to deal with all those teenage divas!'

'Kate Burton and DC Doyle should be along shortly, but they know to play it low-key.'

'Right you are.'

'Ledwidge could be *anywhere*, guv!' Noakes exclaimed as Sullivan hurried off. Then he noticed the DI's unusually absorbed expression. 'What is it?'

'Remember what Dimples said about the killer . . . that he was "a bit of a showman" . . . someone who enjoyed posing his victims.'

'Arty-farty type.'

'Yes, Noakes. *Artistic* . . . I think I know where he told Ledwidge to meet him.'

The caretaker came bustling in. As unlike his predecessor as possible, he was young, personable and crisply efficient. And blessedly incurious.

'Where do you need to look, Inspector?'

'Can you show us to art and design?'

'No problem. It's in the new building.'

Hope's art and design department had apparently benefited from a council development grant and now occupied a modest two-floor red-brick annexe squeezed into the narrow space at the back of the netball courts.

It was unlocked.

'Staff have their own keys,' their young guide explained in response to Noakes's admonitory look. 'They'll have been in and out getting stuff for the concert and forgotten to close up afterwards.'

'Of course.'

A great calm had come over Markham. As though some invisible guide was leading him to the appointed destination.

'I wonder, sir, if you'd be good enough to wait outside for us . . . just keep a look-out.'

'No worries.'

* * *

Downstairs, they moved from room to room flicking on lights and passing between craft tables.

All appeared just as it ought. Canvases stacked against walls. Stencils, textiles and silkscreens at this workstation, ceramics and polystyrene blocks at that. What looked like a dressing-up basket overflowed with costumes in a variety of fabrics.

Then it was up the stairs to the first floor, shoes squeaking on vinyl.

There were just two interconnected studios upstairs, both full of mannequins and papier-mâché head masks in various stages of completion.

'Creepy as fuck,' muttered Noakes as they contemplated the unnerving spectacle of what looked like rows of sightless guillotined heads. 'What happened to drawing with crayons? Now it's all Freddy Krueger . . .'

He wandered gingerly towards a small storeroom at the back of the larger studio.

'Oh, there's a full-sized one in here, guv. Pretty life-like with the head an' all—'

The DS suddenly broke off as though he had been karate-chopped. Then he called out hoarsely in quite a different voice, '*Guv, you need to take a look at this.*'

Somehow Markham knew what he was going to find. Had known it from the moment he saw those balloon heads and the long strips of paper pulp wound about them like bandages on a mummy.

Propped against the right-hand wall of the storeroom was a figure clad in a lavishly patterned kimono-style robe and delicate slippers. Atop it was a papier-mâché mask painted to denote a geisha girl, with long, heavily fringed, almond-shaped eyes and a rosebud mouth.

'At first I thought it was a dummy, but . . . he's still warm.'

Markham gestured to the headpiece. 'Lift it off,' he said.

With unsteady hands, Noakes obliged.

Brian Ledwidge's face was shuttered, peaceful, the eyes milkily unfocused.

Almost as though at the end, death had come as a friend.

## 12. CIRCLING THE TARGET

'What the chuff does he mean by landing us with that wanker?' Noakes was virtually purple with outrage. 'An' as for that sodding checklist, well he can stick it where the sun don' shine!'

DCI Sidney's 'gold command meeting' on Friday morning had seen Professor Bill Macfadyen share the fruits of his profiling wisdom with the team.

Markham had not taken to him one bit. Perhaps it was the pointy little beard that he stroked throughout in an orgy of self-regard. With Sidney caressing his own goatee in tandem, their double act had been one of the more nauseating spectacles the DI could remember witnessing in that office.

'It's not as if he really told us anything new,' Kate Burton agreed. 'I mean,' she ticked off the 'key characteristics' identified by Macfadyen, 'resentment of authority figures, conflicted sexuality, subservience to a domineering parent, troubled childhood — they're all standard markers for a serial killer.'

'Yeah, but Sidney *loved* it,' her fellow DS growled. 'Reckon he sees hisself on telly . . . one of them crime investigation documentaries, co-presenting with some breakfast TV dolly bird hanging on his every word.'

Markham chuckled despite himself.

'Well, if it comes down to it, I'll take Sidney over Professor Macfadyen any day. Though they're both pretty irritating.'

'God yes.' Burton nodded with feeling. 'Buttering each other up good-o. And that stuff with the beards . . . *yuk*!'

'Dickheads,' Noakes said succinctly.

'Unfortunately, we're obliged at least to pay lip service to the Professor's insights,' Markham said soberly. 'Brian Ledwidge's murder has raised the stakes.'

His interview with Eileen Ledwidge and her daughter Catriona the previous night had been unbearably poignant, the more so for some indefinable sense that the husband and father had been a stranger whose secret hopes and fears would now remain a mystery forever. Noakes, blessedly, behaved as though the chilly, self-contained clergyman had been the perfect paterfamilias, creating a narrative to which the two women could cling in their grief. 'Your Brian couldn't have helped other folk so well if he hadn't had you to come home to . . . A padre ain't no ordinary Joe . . . needs a team behind him.' It was exactly the right thing to say. Mother and daughter sat up straighter and bore themselves more proudly on hearing those words.

Markham had skated over the circumstances in which Ledwidge had been found. His family could hear the full account at a later date. For now, it sufficed to tell them his body had been found concealed in a building at the school.

Death had occurred by suffocation. 'Plastic bag over the head,' was the pathologist's verdict. Of course, no such bag had been found, but Dimples was positive and the SOCOs had identified microscopic fragments adhering to the papier-mâché mask as well as traces of diethyl ether. 'Relatively painless and no signs of a struggle, so likely he didn't see it coming.'

'Why tog the body out like that?' Noakes asked as they conferred in Markham's office. 'He was taking one hell of a risk messing around with that dressing-up box.'

'He must have been confident the coast was clear,' Doyle observed.

'Plus they were upstairs, so he'd have advance warning of anyone coming in,' added Burton.

'But more even than that.' Markham's expression was unusually tense. 'It seems to have been an ungovernable urge. Obviously Mr Ledwidge was a threat to be eliminated. But unlike Stacey, where the risks of discovery were far greater, he had an opportunity to savour the moment . . . to work though some kind of inner conflict by enacting this ritual . . .' He regarded the team steadily. 'Our man took a chance. The compulsion was that powerful, he couldn't resist.'

'So fixing a bloke up to look like a . . . Chinky princess,' Burton threw her eyes up to heaven at this but held her peace, 'makes him feel good . . . fuck. What kind of psycho are we after?'

'Someone who has been affected by an incident or events in his past life — something that's had a devastating impact on him, Noakesy.'

'Watch it, guv, you're starting to sound like the Prof.' Noakes scratched his chin in some sort of Pavlovian response to Macfadyen and his beard. 'Next thing you'll be telling me chummy didn't get enough cuddles at bedtime or it's something to do with dodgy potty training.'

'I don't like speculative hypothesizing any more than you, Sergeant, but — let's face it — we've got nothing else to go on.'

The DI turned to Burton.

'Did you glean anything from the residents' initial statements, Kate?'

Out came the pocketbook.

'They all turned up at school at more or less the same time, sir. After that, they wandered off to look at displays . . . have a gander at the different departments, that kind of thing.'

'I didn't know it was supposed to be open house.' Markham was startled.

'Well, Mary Atkins wanted to make it like an open evening. Bit of PR for the school, if you get my drift.'

'Mighta known it'd be about that self-promoting cow hogging the limelight.' Noakes was furious. 'So, thanks to her being a glory-hunter, we've got no way of knowing where they all were. *Jesus.*'

'Take it easy, sarge, you'll give yourself a coronary.' Doyle's tone was soothing. The DC turned to Burton. 'Wouldn't they have had kids going round with the visitors . . . y'know, student guides . . . volunteers?'

'Theoretically, yes.' Burton pulled a face. 'Problem was, not all of them turned up . . . So the reps were spread a bit thin, apparently.'

'Prob'ly swigging lager behind the bike sheds.' Noakes had no very high opinion of pupil philanthropy.

'So, we can't pin down suspects' movements?' The DI's voice was leaden.

''Fraid not, boss,' Burton said apologetically. 'They all went off doing their own thing from the sound of it.' She scanned her notes. 'Lucy O'Connor and Martin Henley asked to see the science labs . . . fair enough, I suppose, with them being medics. Julian Hoskinson and Simon Gailey fancied a dekko at drama and art—'

'Hey up,' Noakes had his hunting-dog face on. 'Remember what Eileen Ledwidge said about Hoskinson going into meltdown an' slashing mannequins in the charity shop . . . That studio set-up would be right up his street with all them dummies an' masks an' things.'

'They were able to go into the drama theatre on the main site, but the art block was locked, sarge,' Burton said. 'They'd have needed a teacher to let them in.'

'It was unlocked when we got to it, Kate,' Markham said.

She blinked. 'Oh, right . . . maybe one of the teachers forgot.'

'Or maybe Nutty Boy nicked some keys.'

'Did anyone see Gailey or Hoskinson hanging round the art annexe, Kate?'

'Not that I'm aware of, boss. Apparently, they were happy enough looking at the theatre gizmos . . . the lighting box and sound systems. Mat Sullivan offered to take them over to the annexe, but Gailey said not to bother as he had enough on his plate.'

'Where were Penny Callaghan and Mary Atkins?'

'Conducting tours of the school . . . kind of everywhere at once.'

'You mean greasing up to anyone they fancied was important,' said Noakes with a sour expression.

'More than likely,' his colleague said helplessly. 'Though they had Dan MacAlinden under their wing for some of the time too.'

'Of course.' Markham was thoughtful. 'There was going to be a tribute to Mrs Bussell and Dawn, wasn't there?'

'That's right, sir. Mat Sullivan said it wasn't too bad actually. Councillor Callaghan kept things fairly dignified . . . Ms Atkins followed her lead, so nothing OTT.'

'Any chance you could get hold of those speeches for me, Kate? Just on the off-chance there's something to give us a handle on the two women.'

'No problem, sir.' A quick scribble. 'The head's PA should be able to help out.'

'What about Hop-Along?'

This time Burton shut her eyes as if in prayer, but since no response was apparently forthcoming from the deity, she clamped down on any PC cavil.

'You mean Mr Coleman?' she said po-faced.

'Yeah . . . an' remember that bit of goss about him being able to *walk*? Nothing to say he couldn't have done it if he took Ledwidge by surprise.'

The DI turned to her enquiringly. 'Kate?'

She looked somewhat flustered. 'Sounds as if people took it in turns to check Coleman was okay, boss. There was a sixth-former who gave him the guided tour. He wanted to see drama and music, so she left him to it . . . Gailey and Hoskinson were within shouting distance, and anyway he's used to looking after himself. It's a power wheelchair he's got, so he can whiz round no trouble most of the time.'

'Did he whiz round to the art block, though?'

'Someone was bound to have noticed if he did, sarge.' Burton rumpled her bob distractedly. 'I mean, even if he walked it . . . with that many people around, someone would've clocked an abandoned wheelchair . . .'

Noakes pursed his lips. 'Could've parked it in one of them soundproofed little music studios . . . If Hoskinson an' the rest of 'em were distracted, easy-peasy . . .'

The DI felt a prickle at the base of his spine as he recalled the role Hope Academy's music rooms had played in a previous investigation. As long as he lived, he would never forget discovering the body of the head's PA in that airless practice cubicle with the Hummel piano standing next to the wall.

'D'you think there's any possibility of narrowing down Coleman's whereabouts, Kate?'

More ferocious scribbling.

'I'll do my best, sir.' A gossamer frown puckered her well-groomed eyebrows. 'But it was a bit easy come, easy go . . . access all areas.' Markham could see she was loath to concede Noakes's point about a glory-hunt, but there was no help for it. 'I think Mary Atkins and Councillor Callaghan *were* doing some sort of damage limitation, on account of Mrs Bussell and Dawn having links with the school and ending up dead . . . kind of saying, "we've got nothing to hide, move along."' She consulted her notes. 'There's an Ofsted inspection due any day now. Last night was their way of putting on a show.'

Like the psycho they were chasing.

Markham got up from his desk and moved across to the window.

Swollen with more snow, the cloudy sky seemed almost to crouch closer to the earth. Beyond the car park, Bromgrove's town centre stretched into the distance, its array of faintly winking Christmas decorations only underscoring the bleakness of the perspective. For the hundredth time that week, the DI wished passionately that he had a view of Hollingrove Park and its ethereal winterscape.

He swung round to face the team.

'Look,' he said, 'Marian Bussell and Dawn MacAlinden are somehow the key to all of this. Their murders were *personal* . . . keenly desired and planned.' He pinched the bridge of his aquiline nose in a characteristic gesture of concentration. 'Those that followed were different. Kenneth Dowell confronted the killer and may have tried blackmail, so he had to die—'

'Pegging Dowell out though, guv . . . whoever did *that* got his rocks off making it look like some kind of sicko movie.'

'True, Noakes. With Dowell, it wasn't just necessity . . . the killer staged a tableau for some reason.' The DI's gaze was remote, as though by a supreme exercise of will, he could enter the mind of a killer. 'With Stacey, it was more utilitarian. She knew something and he couldn't trust her to keep her mouth shut, so he pounced after the memorial service.'

'Same with Ledwidge, sir,' Doyle took up the baton eagerly. 'He guessed something . . . put two and two together . . . challenged the killer . . . came over all pastoral and tried to make him hand himself in.'

'Yes, like Stacey, he was a threat that had to be eliminated. But, as with Mr Dowell, the killer found himself with room to be . . . *inventive*.'

Kate Burton's expression made Markham feel glad she hadn't witnessed the grotesque desecration of Brian Ledwidge's corpse, arriving with Doyle only as his sheeted remains were being stretchered off the premises.

'There's got to be some . . . well, some sexual hang-up, sir,' Doyle ventured. 'If the killer couldn't resist putting Ledwidge in a woman's costume . . .'

'Oh aye.' Noakes was laconic. 'Professor Cracker thinks we should be looking for a cross-dressing wooftah.'

Burton didn't miss a beat. 'He did say it might point to sexual fetishism with homosexual indicators.'

'Same difference.'

This time it was Markham who closed his eyes. Unleashing George Noakes on Bromgrove's 'alternative' communities really didn't bear thinking about.

'Trouble is none of 'em really fits the bill,' Noakes observed regretfully. 'Apart from Julian Hoskinson . . . but it's not like he digs fancy dress . . . a bit AC/DC, but no one's said owt about drag.' The air of magnanimity with which this was uttered had to be heard to be believed. Noakes clearly felt he had scaled the summits of political correctness in making such a concession.

Burton smiled weakly. 'Well, the consensus at Ducky seems to be that there's nothing particularly flamboyant about him.'

''Sides from him wearing a bangle.' Noakes wasn't prepared to abandon his fondly cherished prejudices just yet.

'Have another word, Kate. And check out a few LGBT dating websites . . . Chris Carstairs might be able to help on this. See what you can find out about that incident in the charity shop . . . maybe Gailey can shed some light.'

'He's old-school, sir,' said Doyle. 'I tried pumping him about Hoskinson last night, but he wasn't having any. Coleman neither. They sort of closed ranks.'

'*Fuck it!*' Noakes was so vehement, they all jumped. 'This is a pigging serial an' we've got *five* of their friends stiffening in the morgue . . . They can stuff the "after you, Claude" bullshit.'

'Admirably put, Sergeant.' Markham's tone was dry, but he came out strongly for his wingman. 'This isn't a time for false delicacy or sparing feelings. I want to put pressure on all of them.'

'Including Eileen Ledwidge, sir?'

'Yes but go easy, Kate. Check in with family liaison first . . . kid gloves.'

'Got it, boss.' She pretty nearly clicked her heels, Markham noted with amusement.

'What about tomorrow morning, sir?' Doyle had no intention of being left out of things.

'What about it, Constable?'

'The LGBT demo.' The big gangling DC looked embarrassed. 'The DCI wants a stakeout.'

Noakes snorted with derision. 'That was for his new best friend . . . Trying to impress Macfadyen by giving it *Miami Vice* an' all that.'

'I'd forgotten,' the DI said flatly. 'But you're right, Doyle, we need to be there.'

Another puff and snort, as though Noakes was a train ready to steam away.

Before the locomotive could get properly fired up, Markham said hastily, 'Mat Sullivan mentioned there were tensions at Hope around LGBT issues . . . Marian Bussell and Dawn MacAlinden got drawn into it all.'

'That's right, sir.' Now Burton was busily riffling through a folder while Noakes and Doyle exchanged dire glances over her shiny chestnut head. 'Sullivan said there was lots of toxic stuff swirling around . . . parents and locals getting into a state over transgender issues. Mrs Bussell was very hot on individual rights and kids getting to make decisions about their own sexuality . . .'

Markham recalled Julian Hoskinson's resentment at the ex-teacher's desire to turn him into a cause.

Burton continued, 'Dan MacAlinden said Dawn was on the same page as far as LGBT rights were concerned, but she was worried kids were getting rushed into decisions about transitioning before they were ready . . . decided not to make waves about it . . . got back in her box after Lucy O'Connor and Kenneth Dowell more or less told her to shut up.'

Kenneth Dowell, like his neighbour Marian Bussell, had been on the liberal side of the argument. If the killer was indeed sexually conflicted, Markham wondered, why had such progressive types had to die? And then there were the Ledwidges. What was it Hoskinson had said? 'Good people but deep down not keen on queers.' Was the ritual costuming of Ledwidge a defiant two-fingered salute to religious fundamentalists?

He felt a wild urge to be out of the station. To be *doing* something. The other three watched him expectantly. 'Noakes, you're with me. We'll take Dan MacAlinden and Mary Atkins.'

Burton's face had fallen, but she brightened when the DI said, 'You'll be our diplomat, Kate.'

*That's one word for it*, Noakes thought smugly.

'See where you get with the sexual angle.' Markham rolled his shoulders, somehow losing none of his dégagé elegance in the process. Observing how Kate Burton's eyes rested hungrily on the DI's impressive musculature, enhanced rather than concealed by his immaculately cut pin stripe, Noakes amused himself with various uncharitable reflections on the subject of her fiancé Colin Pugh. A right little no-mark but fluent in tree-hugger BS. He figured Burton must've gone for him on the rebound, once she saw there was no hope of anything with the DI.

'You and Doyle might want to probe into the mystery of the headscarfed female too,' Markham was issuing instructions. 'Get a facial composite out of Coslett. And see if it rings a bell with anyone on Chapel Street or Bromgrove Old Road . . . the newsagents or one of the local shops. Take the make-up compact along for good measure . . . one of the locals *must* have noticed something.'

'You reckon she's mixed up in it somehow then, boss?'

The DI wore an expression of brooding intensity. 'Someone was flitting in and out of the close like a ghost, Constable, and I want to know *who*.'

'As in the prowler?'

'Yes . . . and maybe the poison-pen writer as well.'

'Given what Professor Macfadyen said about fetishes and the way Mr Ledwidge was . . . dressed up . . . could it be a bloke in drag?' Burton was hesitant. 'Doing it as some kind of sexually motivated ritual?'

'Or mebbe he jus' wanted to disguise hisself.' Noakes was scornful. 'Don' mean it was owt kinky . . . I mean,' he scowled portentously, 'can you honestly see *any* of that lot going all *Mrs Doubtfire* . . . ?'

The DI raised his eyebrows.

'I didn't know you were a Robin Williams fan, Sergeant,' he said while Burton and Doyle boggled at this unlikeliest of film pundits.

'Saw it with our Nat an' the missus, didn't I?' came the defiant response, throwing down the gauntlet to anyone who dared challenge the cinematic preferences of Muriel Noakes. 'An' 'sides, this Mrs Headscarf looked dead convincing . . . dead *posh* . . . so we'd be barking up the wrong tree with them wrinklies.'

'They're not all "wrinklies".' Burton's air quotes left no doubt that she disliked ageism as much as any of the other 'isms' against which she was habitually making a stand.

'Well, can you honestly see any of 'em for that kind of caper . . . *can you*?'

Burton's face offered eloquent testimony to the fact that, in her eyes too, it was undoubtedly a stretch.

'Check out all the angles, Kate,' the DI added quietly. 'Dare to think the unthinkable.'

'"Think the unthinkable" eh, guv?' Noakes repeated once they were alone in Markham's office. 'You don' want to be feeding Burton lines like that . . . She'll only go all squirrelly on you . . .'

'Talking of "squirrelly", Noakes, the desk sergeant tells me Sidney's pet psychic is downstairs wanting a word. Might as well fit her in en route to our interviews.'

'Do we *have* to?' Noakes's underlip shot out in a pout that boded ill for whoever turned out to be waiting downstairs.

'Better get it over with.' Craftily, Markham added, 'No point alienating the DCI unnecessarily . . . I get the feeling he's just one step away from foisting Bretherton on us.'

The prospect of Blethering Bretherton was enough to ensure his DS's ready compliance.

'Right,' he slouched towards the door, pudgy hands attempting, without success, to currycomb his hair and ill-fitting suit into a semblance of respectability as though he feared Superintendent Bretherton might materialize like an evil genie at any moment. 'But if she starts any of that Ouija board crap, you c'n count me out.'

* * *

In the event, there was no dabbling with the spirits or any other of the more outré manifestations so deplored by Noakes.

'Mystic Meg' turned out to be Mrs Judith Shaw, a diminutive, plump lady clad in sensible twinset and pearls who looked the two men in the eye and greeted them with a firm handshake. Her surprisingly trendy silver crop and statement spectacles suggested a woman who was comfortable in her own skin — a far cry from the howling neurotic of popular caricature.

'I know you're under great pressure, gentlemen,' she said in the gravelly voice of a smoker, 'and I don't want to keep you from far more important tasks.'

'Not at all,' Markham replied with grave courtesy, secretly amused at how they had been wrongfooted. 'It's good of you to have come in.'

Her eyes twinkled as though she suspected their discomfiture at the absence of any cabalistic accessories, but then she became serious. 'I don't claim to see ghosts every day or anything like that. Sometimes I have intuitions that mean I've been able to help people through difficult times, but I wouldn't dream of intruding on the bereaved.' She looked troubled.

'There's no need for you to justify yourself to us, Mrs Shaw. We're pretty much up against it right now, so any information you have to offer would be welcome.'

'I don't know if the woman I've seen has any connection to your investigation—'

'*Woman*?' Noakes leaned forward intently.

'Well, teenager . . . a schoolgirl really.'

'How do you know she's a schoolgirl, Mrs Shaw?'

'The uniform she had on . . . Hope Academy. But it's the old-style one they had up until about ten years ago . . .

frightful sludge-brown skirt, yellow shirt and pullover. She's wearing the school badge . . . I can tell it's Hope because of the bird on the front.'

'A phoenix,' Noakes said complacently.

'Yes, that's right . . . sunburst with a phoenix.'

'What does this girl look like, Mrs Shaw?'

'Delicate-featured . . . long, fair hair . . . almost white. Slim and graceful . . . something elfin about her. Never comes close enough for me to see her expression, but I have the feeling she's terribly unhappy.'

'Does she ever speak?'

'No, she just stands there . . .' An involuntary shiver passed through the woman. 'Each time, she's holding a heart . . . like you see on Valentine's cards . . . only it's dripping blood.'

Markham had a sudden unwelcome image of the religious medals that had been such a feature of his Catholic upbringing. His mother's favourite had depicted the Madonna thrusting a sanguineous heart towards the beholder. To the confused young boy, it had smacked more of the abattoir than any celestial region.

He forced himself to concentrate on the visitor. 'Anything else, Mrs Shaw?'

The woman bit her lip.

'Please don't worry about looking foolish,' he coaxed. 'I can assure you, we're very interested in what you have to say.'

'Well, despite the heart and the blood I've always felt she was quite benign. But the time before last . . . she was wearing some kind of painted headdress . . . like something out of a Chinese opera.'

DI and DS looked at each other. The details of Brian Ledwidge's grotesque apparel were known only to the team.

'I can see this means something to you,' she said diffidently. 'I don't wish to barge in . . . but it disturbed me . . . There was the sense of so much *rage*, unlike before. Her hands were clenched and she was sort of hissing.'

'Could you make anything out?'

'Just a name, over and over . . . I didn't hear it distinctly, but I think it began with an S.' Her tone regretful, she added, 'It was over in seconds. I didn't have time to take it in.'

'Did you see anything else . . . Was this girl in a house or outside?'

'That's the strange thing . . .'

As if what she had already described wasn't sufficiently bizarre.

'The final time she appeared, it looked like she was in hospital.'

'*A hospital?*' Noakes echoed belligerently. 'How'd you make that out then?'

'Well, it seemed as though she was standing in some sort of operating theatre. There was a surgical table and those bright overhead lights . . . machinery and monitors round the walls, and metal instruments laid out on a counter . . .' She flushed. 'Look, I know it sounds bonkers . . . a schoolgirl popping up in *Casualty* or something equally unlikely . . . but I just felt I *had* to tell you.' She drew herself up with dignity. 'I've always had this gift, but never used it commercially . . . wouldn't think of exploiting anyone's grief. Sometimes it's a real burden, I can tell you.'

'Don' suppose you c'n see into the future?' Noakes said gruffly. 'No offence, mind.'

Quite a turnaround from his previous view of her as being more or less on a par with those charlatans who worked seaside piers.

'None taken, Sergeant. I only wish I could see that far ahead. I *do* have premonitions sometimes, but nothing in this case . . . just a terrible feeling of my own body being compressed, as if there's a huge weight bearing down on me so I can't breathe.' She smiled at them sadly. 'Though it's easier now I've spoken to you . . . I'm lighter somehow . . .'

* * *

'Glad *she* feels chuffing better,' grumbled Noakes as they headed out of the station. 'Nowt like shovelling the shit our way.'

'Language, Sergeant.' But the reproof was automatic.

'Sorry, guv.' The DS didn't sound particularly repentant. 'But all that about Valentine's cards an' elflings . . . I mean, *what's she on*!'

'Come on, Noakesy. She knew details we haven't released to anyone outside the investigation.'

'Yeah. S'pose.'

'Remember that photo album in Dan MacAlinden's. The one with Dawn and her best friend . . . The girl whose name began with an S.'

'Summat to do with schooldays, then?'

'I think so.' Markham concertinaed his tall form into the passenger seat of Noakes's Fiesta. 'I want to see that photograph album of Dan MacAlinden's.'

'The one he had out when we went round?'

'Yes.' Markham sounded preoccupied. 'I want a closer look at Dawn's best friend.'

'The one she was "joined at the hip with"?'

'Correct.'

'You reckon it all comes back to Hope then, guv?'

'Something tells me that's where we'll find the answer, Noakesy.' He spoke with a renewed air of purpose. 'Once we've spoken to Mr MacAlinden, I want another word with Mary Atkins.'

The air was thick with the DS's dismay.

'Look, I know she's not your cup of tea.' *Massive understatement*, he added mentally. 'But I want to press her on the subject of Marian Bussell . . . Everything leads back to Hope.'

'Righto, guv.'

And with that, the car picked up speed, white-clad streets and houses flashing past as if in a dream.

# 13. REVELATION

'So as things stand, none of 'em looks good for it an' all we've got is Mrs Wotsit seeing this scrawny kid messing about with body parts like summat out of a transplant op — *bugger*! The council needs to do summat about these potholes . . . freaking lethal in this weather . . . We should've taken *your* car, guv . . . more powerful.'

Markham could have responded that he'd be fearing for his gears with Noakes at the wheel but preserved a discreet silence.

Happily, his DS's thoughts soon turned once more to the investigation.

'Mind, you have to hand it to the old bat . . . She *did* seem to have some kinda connection with — what do they call it? — *the Other Side*. She was bang on the money about what Ledwidge was wearing when we found him . . . *spooky*!'

'Also, that "scrawny kid" she described sounded uncannily like the girl in those photographs Mr MacAlinden showed us—'

'Oh yeah . . . the little blonde lass . . . He said she an' Dawn were joined at the hip or summat like that.' The DS frowned as he manoeuvred the Fiesta round some road works. 'D'you think she's the key to it all then, guv, this blonde bird?'

'Something tells me she is, Noakes.'

'She'd be middle-aged now . . . same age as Dawn. But there's no one in the close fits that description . . . unless she's the one creeping round disguised in a headscarf . . . on some kind of loony mission . . . *Hey*,' he thumped the wheel, 'mebbe she's escaped from the Newman. Mebbe they *all* had a hand in getting her put in there an' now she's picking 'em off one by one.'

'Sounds a bit *And Then There Were None*.'

'Eh?'

'Rather too Agatha Christie.'

'Well, don' forget last year, guv . . . I'm jus' saying . . .'

'Fair point . . . those stories about patient abuse that we unearthed at the Newman sounded like horror fiction to start with.'

And there was no denying that the prospect of pinning these murders on a mentally disturbed escapee would suit the DCI down to the ground.

Mollified, the DS grunted his approval of Markham's verdict. Then he tried another tack.

'P'raps this kid from the photo album had summat bad happen to her . . . an' one of 'em in the close wants payback . . . cos they're related to her or summat like that.'

'Hmmm. That sounds more credible . . . But what's the connection with our first two victims? I mean, we've got a retired teacher and a nurse who was this youngster's schoolmate . . . how did *they* hurt or damage her so badly that someone decides to take revenge on them decades later?' The DI shifted in his seat, fruitlessly trying for a more comfortable position. 'And how does our killer's modus operandi link back to whatever happened . . . this traumatic event or whatever it is? Then there's the *staging* of the deaths of the two women and Kenneth Dowell . . . and that bizarre ritual with Brian Ledwidge's body . . . where does that fit in? What does it all *mean*?'

Noakes just shook his head sadly at the degeneracy of human nature.

They drove on in silence for a time, then the DS said, 'Them two women were decent sorts. Don' see either of 'em setting out to hurt a kid.'

Markham sighed deeply. 'Well, someone hated them enough to plan that sadistic murder . . . someone they *knew*.'

'What if summat *did* go on with this teenager . . . are we saying it happened at Hope?'

'I assume so . . . The way that badge was left with the bodies at number seven makes me think the school has a particular significance for the killer.'

'D'you reckon Atkins knows owt about it?' Merely mentioning the assistant head's name brought a scowl to Noakes's face.

'I have a feeling she may have pieced *something* together,' Markham said wearily. 'Perhaps that hate mail she received gave her an inkling. But she's in denial . . . desperately wants it to be some random crazy.'

'Singing from Sidney's hymn sheet, then.'

'Which is why I'm going to front her up with the details of how we found Brian Ledwidge's body.'

'Shock tactics?'

'Precisely.'

'Good idea. Might work . . . She's jus' like Helen Kavanagh — d'you remember?'

Markham recalled the school's former deputy head only too well. Her capacity for self-deception had caused the team no end of problems during the notorious Ashley Dean investigation.

'If Ms Atkins imagines there's a chance of ending up like Mr Ledwidge, then her survival instinct ought to kick in,' he said trenchantly.

Noakes looked pleased at the prospect of giving The Caring One a good scare, double clutching with a gusto that made the DI wince.

* * *

Dan MacAlinden welcomed the two men with a degree of animation that spoke more clearly than any words of how hungry he was for company.

At least family liaison had played their part, so he already knew about Brian Ledwidge. Bizarrely, the fact that a clergyman was the latest victim seemed to bring him comfort. 'Like he thinks his Dawn an' the Rev are in heaven together, singing an' chatting to God or whatever they do up there,' as Noakes said afterwards. 'You'd think it was some kind of Saga holiday he was talking about.' Markham was simply grateful that MacAlinden was able to derive solace from whatever source, no matter how nebulous.

'They won't let me have her back for a while yet,' the widower told them. 'But she's in safe hands with Mr Ledwidge.' Gently, Markham dispatched Noakes to make tea and engaged the man in easy chat, leading him round by degrees towards the subject of Dawn's schooldays.

On Noakes's return, MacAlinden needed no prompting to produce the treasured album. 'You didn't know Dawn, so I guess this helps make her more real. I showed it to Mr Ledwidge when he called round that last time.'

Personally, the DI would have given anything to be able to transpose the image of the cheery schoolgirl with her Pippi Longstocking-style plaits onto the ghastly memory of that shrivelled mummy found at number seven. But the dead face lurked like some kind of diabolic photographic negative behind every picture and he knew he would never be able to banish it.

With his almost telepathic sensitivity towards the guvnor, Noakes stepped in to cover Markham's silence. 'Looks like she were happy at school, your lass,' he said. Then, almost as an afterthought, 'Her friend looks a bit down in the dumps, though . . . kind of mardy.'

'I got to thinking about her after you were here last time . . . Dawn said she didn't keep up with her after O levels.' He pursed his lips reminiscently. 'There was some kind of bust-up . . . she got too intense . . . clingy, was what Dawn said . . . I could see it made her uncomfortable talking about it.'

'More'n likely they fell out over some lad,' Noakes suggested.

'No.' The other looked ruminative. 'I don't think it was that . . . Sounded like her friend got a bit . . . well, *possessive* . . . so Dawn broke it off.'

Something in their expressions must have alerted him.

'D'you think this has got something to do with what happened . . . why Dawn and Marian were killed?' The mild-mannered widower looked agitated. '*Some playground spat*?'

'We've got no reason to think so, Mr MacAlinden,' Markham said firmly. 'But sometimes a victim's past . . . their schooldays, childhood even, can give us a new angle . . . put the investigation on a fresh track.'

The two spots of colour that had appeared on Dan MacAlinden's cheekbones gradually subsided as the DI, now well in command of his emotions, diverted the man's attention to more pictures and other topics.

When all the time it was the girl with the changeling looks who claimed his thoughts.

* * *

'Nice one, guv,' Noakes said after they had left the flat. 'Looked like he was gonna flip when he thought Dawn's murder had summat to do with her bestie.'

They were back at the undercroft now.

'What's the betting it *did* though, Noakes?'

The DS made a sucking noise through his teeth, as though to express profound scepticism.

'MacAlinden's right though, ain't he, guv? I mean, *a teenage squabble* . . . Don' see how that could end up in murder.'

'Think about what he said. This girl was too intense . . . too clingy and possessive, so Dawn had to break it off.'

The other stared at him. 'You saying they were *lezzies*, guv?'

'I'm saying we could be looking at a schoolgirl crush that got out of hand . . . on one side at least.'

Noakes whistled. 'Mebbe if Dawn was gay, then she an' Mrs B could've been . . . well . . . you know . . . *at it* after all.'

'I doubt very much they were "at it",' Markham replied with heavy forbearance. 'Nothing points to them being in a sexual relationship, and I'd say Dawn was happily married.'

'Lemme get this right, guv.' The DS screwed up his features, looking for all the world as though he fancied himself CID's savviest agony uncle. 'Dawn wasn't up for any of that . . . but this other girl *was* and went doolally when she got the ole heave-ho.' Markham flinched as he imagined the effect of such euphemisms on Kate Burton, before reflecting that these days her shoulders were broad enough to cope.

'Yes, I'm wondering if there wasn't some sort of emotional rupture that could have scarred a vulnerable teenager.'

'But where does Mrs B fit in?' Noakes sounded genuinely bewildered. 'Did she put her oar in . . . keep 'em apart or summat?' Grizzled head on one side, he added, 'Feels a bit *thin,* boss — even if the whole heartbreak hotel story fits with what Mrs Thing said about seeing this girl dripping blood an' the rest.'

'Agreed.' Markham was thoughtful, his eyes remote. He was suddenly aware of how bitterly cold it was. If they waited here in the car park much longer, they must surely become rooted to the spot.

'There was something about those pictures,' he mused. 'That girl's features seemed . . . well, *familiar* . . . I could swear I've seen her, or someone very like her, quite recently.'

'Oh yeah?' Noakes stamped his feet to get the circulation moving. 'Where?'

'That's just it . . . I can't nail it down . . . But I know I've seen that face, Noakesy, I just *know* it.'

The DI came to a decision. 'Let's head to Hope. See if we can refresh Ms Atkins' memory.'

'I can't wait to see how she reacts when we tell her 'bout Ledwidge's panto get-up,' his sergeant said happily.

* * *

In the event, the assistant head's horror was everything Noakes had hoped for, though at a look from Markham, he refrained from any embellishment of the basic facts.

They were sitting in the well-appointed, comfortable office that had once belonged to Helen Kavanagh, whose memory was lamented by nobody. The DS couldn't help reflecting that Atkins had bagged a much cosier berth than Mat Sullivan — a perk of her *caring* responsibilities, no doubt. There was something about the room's chintzy frills and flounces that reminded him of the rape victim suite back at the station. At least the tea was good and she didn't stint on the biscuits — they'd missed out on those at Dan MacAlinden's and it *was* getting on for elevenses.

Mary Atkins, however, had little appetite for the chocolate bourbons, looking as if they had turned to sawdust in her mouth. The ringing shouts of children in the background, happily rampaging at their break, offered an eerie soundtrack to the detective's stark account of their discovery the previous night.

'I know how important the school's reputation is to you, Ms Atkins,' Markham said kindly. 'And I can imagine how careful you must have to be when it comes to disclosing information, what with safeguarding and confidentiality being such a minefield.' He paused to let this sink in. 'But five innocent people are dead . . . We need to apprehend whoever is doing this.' In other words, time to ditch your scruples and come onside.

The woman just stared at them slack-jawed, her usual bombast and platitudes gone.

'Look, luv,' Noakes waded in. 'Your mate Mat told us you know everything about everything . . . finger on the pulse an' all that. He said if anyone c'n help with background stuff, it's you.' Might as well give Sullivan a leg up the promotion ladder. Perhaps he could even wangle a decent office out of it.

Something about Noakes's avuncular bonhomie (and flattery) unblocked Atkins' tongue. But her next words were totally unexpected.

'I think it's someone who transitioned,' she said.

Noakes froze, a biscuit halfway to his mouth, before regaining his sangfroid. 'As in, had the op, luv?'

Mutely, she nodded.

'Was it a lad or a lass?'

Her voice sounded almost rusty as she replied, 'A female student.'

'Er, right.' The DS cleared his throat. Didn't want the guvnor regretting he didn't have Kate Burton there to handle the sensitive stuff. 'So she . . . went an' had the hormones . . . ?' He gestured awkwardly to his torso. 'Got her bits an' bobs chopped off . . . ?'

If the context hadn't been so serious, Noakes's attempt to signal his nonchalance would have been funny, since it was clear he hadn't the foggiest what was involved in the process.

'Well, radical surgery like that comes further down the line, Sergeant.' At least Noakes's ignorance was helpful inasmuch as it resulted in Atkins finding her voice. She just couldn't resist the opportunity to impart her knowledge. 'It starts with counselling about being in the wrong body, with chest binders and other interventions before they move on to the physical treatment . . . puberty suppressants and cross-sex hormones.'

Noakes was looking distinctly queasy, but he gamely ploughed on. 'Thass a good thing, right? Cos they might not be sure about it . . .' Desperately, he tried to remember some of the psychology Burton regularly inflicted on them. 'They might be autistic or summat . . . Or it could jus' be a phase . . . Mebbe they don' like the way they look . . . Or mebbe they get upset when some lad knocks 'em back.' It was touching to watch Noakes, red-faced and way out of his comfort zone, endeavouring to show he wasn't transphobic. 'Could even be they've read summat on the internet makes them think it's a good idea . . . Or p'raps they're just gay . . .'

Before the DS could get on to the subject of hysterical rectomies, thereby undoing whatever progress he was making in the assistant head's good opinion, Markham interjected,

'And, of course, there could be any number of background issues . . . sexual abuse, for example.'

He did not see the deeply compassionate look Noakes shot him, unaware that the other had long since intuited those demons from his boss's troubled childhood.

'That's quite true, Inspector.' A shadow crossed the woman's face. 'It's such a momentous decision to change gender . . . And I don't need to tell you there've been major concerns about young people being rushed into setting out on that path . . .'

'Did something like that happen at Hope?' Markham prompted gently. 'Was a pupil encouraged by someone on your staff to believe she was really a boy . . . maybe even *pushed* towards having surgery?'

The assistant head took a shaky breath. 'Look, Inspector . . . I wasn't here at the time . . . But I believe there *was* a case like that.' In a flat monotone, she recited, 'There were behaviour issues . . . intense one-on-one friendships with girls that invariably ended in tears. The girl in question had difficulty accepting their romantic interest in boys.' Nervously, Mary Atkins plucked at her lanyard before continuing, 'She became obsessed with the idea that she was different, ugly . . . and out of that came the idea that she was in the wrong body — a classic case of body dysphoria.'

'And the teacher behind it?' Markham was gentle but inexorable. 'Was it Marian Bussell?'

'As I understand it — and, look, we're talking about years ago — there were quite a few teachers caught up in the . . . well, the excitement round children's rights. It sort of came out of their awareness of the way minority groups had been treated as second-class citizens . . . tapped into that sense of injustice and all the new psychology springing up around sexual difference.'

'But the teachers weren't trans activists as we would understand the term?'

'Oh no, nothing like that. They were just well-meaning people like Marian who made it their hobby horse. Quite naive most of them.'

Markham recalled the story of Marian Bussell's cousin — the one she had lost to suicide — but merely gestured to Atkins to continue.

'I believe Marian became close to this girl . . . counselled her and that kind of thing.' Impatiently, she burst out, 'Of course, nowadays there'd be other professionals involved . . . no question of well-meaning teachers going it alone. But at the time . . .' Mary Atkins looked wretched. 'I don't know how it all ended, but I *do* know the then-head was uneasy — the parents had complained — and he put a stop to it when she was in the sixth form.'

'Did she complete her schooling . . . go on to university?'

'Oh yes, she was very bright. Read English at Leeds.'

'But she still went ahead an' got the makeover . . . changed into a man?' Noakes wanted to be clear about this part.

'I heard on the grapevine she followed that route then later regretted it and wanted to change back. But something went wrong with that . . . and afterwards, she more or less went under the radar.'

But she's back, thought Markham. *She's back.*

'We need a name for this student, Ms Atkins.'

The assistant head had recovered her self-possession.

'Martine Simisola Knowlson.'

'Simisola?' Noakes looked bewildered. 'What's that all about?'

'A Yoruba name. The family had African connections . . . but she must've quite liked it. Called herself Simi.' Mary Atkins hesitated. 'I would imagine she goes by a different name these days.'

'You don't know if she resumed contact with Marian Bussell at any point?'

'I doubt it . . . If it's true that she wanted to detransition, then she may well have blamed Marian for what happened . . . I suspect Marian later came to view the whole transgender debate differently, but by then it was too late.'

'Why didn't you tell us about this, Ms Atkins? You must have realized it could be significant.'

'But that's just it.' More twisting of the lanyard. 'It only dawned on me gradually . . . I got some ranty correspondence but put it down to bigoted parents who objected to our curriculum being so progressive.'

*That's one word for it*, thought Noakes dourly.

'I didn't even know about Martine — Simi — until I went looking in student records. The files are pretty rudimentary going that far back so I had to ask around and, to be honest, people were reluctant to talk about it.' She pulled a face. 'Particularly given all the hostility we're facing at the moment with our pastoral initiatives . . . I mean, it doesn't help to be reminded how we got it so badly wrong back in the day.' She looked at the two men, as though imploring them to understand. 'And anyway, it seemed so far-fetched . . . Plus Councillor Callaghan said it was almost certainly an ex-mental patient with no connection to the school.'

The detectives exchanged looks, mentally consigning that interfering functionary to the furthermost circle of hell.

'I'm sorry.' There was a new humility about the woman that made her almost likeable.

'What about Dawn MacAlinden?' Noakes wasn't letting her off the hook just yet.

'Well, that was another reason why I didn't think there could be any connection with . . . ancient history. Dawn was just a schoolgirl at the time . . . no involvement in all the drama surrounding Martine.'

'You referred to "intense friendships with girls that ended in tears".' Markham watched her closely. 'So Martine's relationships with female classmates were clearly volatile . . . Had she been spurned or rejected by Dawn, it would have intensified her feelings of inadequacy and self-hatred.'

Atkins' hamster cheeks visibly paled. 'You mean, she seethed about something like that all those years and then killed Dawn for it?'

'Yes,' the DI said simply.

'But Dawn had no part in pushing her to change sex. In some ways, I felt she was on the other side of the argument from Marian. She was worried about the huge numbers of girls wanting to be boys and the way hormone blockers were being handed out willy-nilly . . . said people were ignoring things like normal adolescent angst . . .'

'Who can say what happens in a disordered mind, Ms Atkins? Hatred of the woman Martine held responsible for ruining her life could have fused with deep resentment of that teenage classmate who refused to accept her for who she was . . . Somehow they became interchangeable.'

'But that's monstrous.' Her hands were shaking. '*Monstrous*.'

'Not really, luv.' Noakes's voice was kind. 'When you think how muddled kids are at that age . . . all over the place really while they sort themselves out.' It was the father in him speaking. Privately, he could only thank his lucky stars their Nat knew what was what. No messing about with any of this wrong-body hoo-ha. 'Like the guvnor says, who knows what happened in this lass's brain . . . Summat screwy, that's for sure.'

'But waiting all those years for revenge . . . I mean, she must have *stalked* them . . .' The assistant teacher sounded tremulous. 'Are you positive about this, Inspector?'

'It's a scenario that I think explains some of the . . . features in these murders.'

Not least the freaking kimono thingy and Mikado mask Ledwidge was wearing.

'You didn't keep any of those abusive letters you received?' Markham asked.

'No, I got rid . . . didn't want them around.'

'Perfectly understandable,' Markham murmured, inwardly cursing the loss of evidence.

'We've beefed up security on site,' she said desperately.

*Not before time*, Noakes's expression seemed to say.

'Do you think she — he might come back here?'

'I'd say it's unlikely but,' a thought struck him, 'the LGBT demo will be taking place outside school tomorrow, won't it?'

'They won't be allowed onto our campus, but yes. The demo is scheduled to come past the cemetery and then along Beaconsfield Road at the bottom of the school drive.'

'Angry parents and suchlike?'

'Protestors from both sides most likely.' Clearly about as welcome to the beleaguered assistant head as a cold cup of sick.

'Try not to fret, luv. I mean, look at the weather . . . mebbe some of 'em'll get cold feet.' Enchanted with his pun, Noakes repeated, 'yeah, cold feet . . . Or p'raps they'll slope off an' do some Crimbo shopping an' leave your lot in peace.'

She didn't look particularly reassured by either of these helpful hypotheses.

'Course there's free speech an' all that . . . They've got a right to protest, after all.' The DS was keen to demonstrate his understanding of democratic processes, though the way he sniffed as he made this observation suggested he might not be a card-carrying libertarian.

'There will be a police presence, Ms Atkins,' Markham was swift to interpose. 'Plain clothes as well as uniformed . . . But in the meantime, I'd ask you to keep the personnel on site to a minimum and take no unnecessary risks.'

* * *

'*She's* not gonna sleep a wink tonight,' Noakes observed comfortably as they left the school after exchanging some stilted pleasantries. 'Imagining this Martine one coming for her.'

They had reached the car.

'Look, guv, are we deffo going with this?' Noakes dropped his keys and then dove into the snow for them with a flurry of expletives. 'I mean, we can't jus' come out an' start asking folks if they're a tranny!'

Markham waited till they were seated in the car and he felt some faint warmth suffusing his toes before replying, 'Transsexual please, Noakes. And no, that's not likely to achieve anything.' Except a slew of complaints to Sidney.

'Back to base,' he said knuckling his eyes wearily. 'Who knows, Kate and Doyle may have something for us . . .'

*We need a break in this case*, he thought. *And we need it* now.

The car passed by Bromgrove South Municipal Cemetery on the other side of the school drive, its snowbound sleepers oblivious of the wickedness that flourished all around them . . .

Noakes was huffing and puffing over the steering wheel, as though in contrapuntal dialogue with his wheezing Fiesta.

Markham felt a great wave of affection for his lumbering number two.

'How are you and the lady wife fixed for tonight?' he enquired. 'Got any plans, or do you fancy taking pot luck with me and Olivia?'

'Nowt special, guv,' came the reply. Noakes knew that any previous arrangement would be readily jettisoned for the chance to dine with *Gilbert*.

'Excellent. That's settled then . . . Let's say eight-ish.'

Olivia would kill him for the short notice, but the DI needed Noakes close at hand. And with it being Friday night, churlish not to include Muriel.

When he saw the pleasure stealing over his subordinate's face, he concluded that some minor personal discomfort would be worth it.

* * *

Back at the incident room, they found Burton and Doyle. The latter looked somewhat glassy-eyed, hailing their arrival with a relief that suggested he'd had about as much as he could take of his colleague's diagrams and bar charts.

'Nothing stands out from the carol concert speeches, sir,' Burton said earnestly. 'Nothing controversial . . . just a string of clichés.'

That figured.

'Well, Kate, I think we may finally be getting somewhere.'

Without preamble, the DI brought them up to date on developments.

By the time he had finished, the young DC's eyes were out on stalks.

'Bloody hell, boss . . . But no one here fits the bill. And anyway,' his response was an echo of Mary Atkins', 'that means they must've been building up to it for years. How could anyone manage to live like that? It'd send you nuts . . .'

'Thass the whole point,' Noakes said with a superior expression. 'Them being a nutcase.'

Burton said thoughtfully, 'Slow-burn for the longest time . . . and then *whoosh*!'

Gazing wistfully at her trusty *Diagnostic and Statistical Manual of Mental Disorders*, she longed to start brandishing the psychological precedents for such a personality. But neither Doyle nor Noakes wanted to encourage her in this, so instead she asked, 'Could we be looking for a relative of this Martine . . . a family member affected by what happened . . . looking for revenge?'

'Yeah, *I* said it could be a rellie,' Noakes said loftily. 'What with none of 'em here being a tranny — *sorry*,' with magnificent condescension to Burton, he corrected himself, '*transsexualist*.'

Markham wasn't sure he didn't prefer the old unreconstructed Noakes as opposed to this 'woke' impersonator. From the expression on her face, he guessed Burton felt the same. Doyle merely grinned with lazy tolerance.

Hastily, the DI said, 'Any luck with Coslett and the locals, Kate?'

Out came the pocketbook and scary glasses.

'A cashier at Bestway Cash and Carry was pretty sure she'd seen a woman in a headscarf going into the close, though she didn't get a really good look . . . slight and silver-haired, wearing a Puffa jacket. The scarf looked like it was expensive . . . Liberty or Hermès . . .'

She riffled through the pages and unfolded something paperclipped to the back. 'We got an e-fit courtesy of Coslett.'

They passed it round.

'Looks like that Camilla Parker Bowles,' Noakes snorted, 'the one who married Prince Charles.'

'She's the Duchess of Cornwall these days, sarge.'

'Whatever . . . same horsey features.'

'This face isn't so much horsey as refined . . . good bone structure.' Markham seemed very struck by it. 'There's a resemblance to the girl in Mr MacAlinden's album.' And the one the psychic had described.

'She our prowler then, guv, this Sloaney character?'

'Feels very much like it, Noakes.'

'Looks a bit upmarket to be skulking out in the snow spying on folk,' Doyle ventured.

It was true. Markham looked back at the e-fit. It was the eyes. No hint of madness in them. No hint of the rage that had been stoked for decades.

'What about the make-up compact — ring any bells?'

'Oh yes, now that *was* interesting.' More riffling. 'There was a lady at the antiques centre — you know, that nice place behind the tearooms — used to be an old church, then they relocated it brick by brick . . . well, *she* thought it might've come from their stock.'

'*Really*?' Markham's heart skipped a beat.

Burton hated to deflate him. 'Problem being, it's an old-fashioned set-up . . . paper receipts, old-fashioned log-book with a record of purchases, but nothing to identify who bought what . . .'

'What about credit card sales?' Doyle could hardly credit the benightedness.

'Oh, they've got the card machine alright, but if someone paid in cash — and apparently most of their customers prefer it — then they just note down the item in the ledger and do a receipt for the amount.'

Noakes was fed up of hearing about this retro blast-from-the-past.

'So did any of 'em at Antwacky Central remember selling this thing or what?'

'One of the assistants thought she might've made the sale.'

'*Might've*?'

‘Well, the description in the book was in her handwriting and it matched the compact . . . cloisonné, 1920s Art Deco . . . flapper girl . . . cost a hundred and seventy-five pounds . . . a cash sale.’

‘Did she remember the customer?’ Markham’s tone was eager.

‘Middle-aged woman, she said . . . very Home Counties . . . asked if they had anything in the Egyptian style.’

‘So we’re looking for some bird with a thing for King Tut,’ Noakes said with heavy sarcasm.

Burton checked her notes. ‘She was after something with Isis on it, actually . . .’

The deity with both male and female features.

‘Interested in African tribal art too.’

The Yoruba connection.

‘Anything else on the residents, Kate?’

‘Nothing coming out of the woodwork, sir.’ Despite the attempt at crisp efficiency, her voice was downbeat. ‘I’ve been trying to get hold of Councillor Callaghan all day, but the town hall’s giving me the run-around.’

‘Anything new from Dimples or forensics?’

A dispirited shake of the head. Attending the PM on Stacey Macmillan the previous evening had been awful, though seeing her distress Davidson had eased back on the dark humour which was his stock-in-trade on such occasions. Doyle had been uncharacteristically subdued afterwards, as though the sight of that bubbly little woman on the slab was guaranteed to haunt him for days. Neither of them was in a hurry to volunteer for Brian Ledwidge.

‘Once we’ve got someone in the frame, maybe they’ll be able to pinpoint a viable DNA profile . . . At the moment, it’s the usual stuff about cross-contamination and multiple transfers.’

‘Like a freaking stuck record.’ Noakes was sympathetic.

‘The climbing equipment used on Dowell came from Halfords in town, but the e-fit didn’t jog anyone’s memory.’

The DI surveyed his disconsolate team.

'Any chance the DCI's magic woman could have another try at contacting Martine?'

Three pairs of eyes were riveted on Doyle who blushed to the roots of his carroty hair.

'You mean *have a séance*?' Noakes sniggered. 'I c'n see us now . . . sitting in CID with candles an' a crystal ball . . . an' Sidney's fortune teller croaking, "Is anybody there?" We'd never live it down, son.'

Doyle mumbled something inaudible. Markham suspected Noakes's raillery on the subject was by no means exhausted but cut him off at the pass.

'Mrs Shaw was very different from what I was expecting, Constable. She had some interesting insights and I may well consult her again.' That should squelch his number two. 'In the meantime,' looking at their wan faces, 'I suggest we sleep on it.'

Doyle's dejection lifted.

'You mean we're finished for the day, sir?'

'Well, I imagine you're not raring to rendezvous with Professor Macfadyen or the DCI,' Markham said drily. 'And there's the LGBT march tomorrow, which means an early start.' He dredged up an encouraging smile. 'I suggest you hunker down here for now . . . sift through the witness statements, have a brainstorm.' And avoid Sidney. 'There'll be another press conference either tomorrow or Sunday, so before you clock off why not prepare a summary of,' here his tone became ironic, 'progress to date.'

'I'll make a brew,' Doyle said with alacrity, casting a wary glance at Burton who was clearly itching to get stuck into her beloved spreadsheets.

The DI raised an eyebrow at Noakes. 'A quick word, Sergeant . . .'

Outside, it was bitterly cold with something almost metallic in the air.

'You look done in, guv. Are you sure about me an' the missus coming round for our tea?'

'Absolutely, Noakes. If we don't make an effort, our other halves will desert us for better quarters.'

The DS laughed dutifully, relieved that the guvnor was cracking one of his weirdy jokes. It meant he wasn't beaten yet.

* * *

Olivia rose wonderfully to the challenge of preparing a dinner for four from scratch, cheerfully decanting a family-size Waitrose macaroni cheese from its foil container into an oven tray. 'I'm going to pretend it's home-made, so don't let me down, Gil.'

'Perish the thought.' As an afterthought, 'Any chips with that? You know what Noakesy's like.'

'There's some triple-cooked in the freezer,' she replied, 'and Cartmel sticky toffee pudding. I'll do a salad too and you can rustle up a cheeseboard . . . hopefully that'll distract Muriel from George's gallant attempts to eat himself into an early grave!'

Markham chuckled. 'I'll be sure to keep her well plied with Merlot . . . that ought to help.'

'Oh, she'll be so busy drooling over you that the rest of us won't get a look-in,' his lover said with some asperity.

Markham slid an arm round her waist. 'Thanks for this, dearest. I know Muriel isn't the easiest.'

'She can't stand me, Gil. But,' with her head mischievously on one side, 'I will just have to follow Oscar Wilde's advice: "Always forgive your enemies; nothing annoys them so much."'

A burst of laughter concluded the exchange.

* * *

In the event, their evening passed smoothly enough. Muriel Noakes kept her claws sheathed and even threw out the odd compliment to Olivia, admittedly of the double-edged variety but surprising for all that. 'With your figure, you can get away with anything,' was one such gem, accompanied by a complacent glance at the knitted tangerine two-piece brought out to dazzle Noakes's charming boss.

She'll be bitching about make-do-and-mend hippies with those cats at the Women's Guild, her hostess thought wrathfully as Muriel looked up at Markham through heavily mascaraed eyelashes like some monstrous reincarnation of Barbara Cartland. But then, seeing how Noakes basked in his wife's dodgy affectations, glowing with misplaced pride at her dubious allure, Olivia bit down on any waspish sallies.

They were enjoying the cheeseboard when Muriel said, 'I didn't realize Margery Bastin's former solicitor is one of your suspects, Gilbert.'

'Who might that be, Muriel?'

'Simon Gailey.' She gave a coquettish simper, as though piquing him on a rival's charms. '*Such a sweetheart*. And *so* knowledgeable about all kinds of subjects. Cynthia Alderman says they never had such a good talk as he gave to their women's group in Medway last year. What that man doesn't know about vintage jewellery . . . He could give the *Antiques Roadshow* a run for their money.'

Markham was suddenly very still. 'I didn't know Mr Gailey's interests were so wide-ranging.'

'Oh yes. And *so* distinguished-looking . . . those silver wings of hair and cheekbones to die for . . . like one of those silent movie stars.'

She babbled on. But it was as though a veil had fallen between them and he could not hear the rest for the clamour in his brain.

*Simisola.*

*Simi.*

*Simon Gailey.*

'Guv.' Noakes was looking at him in consternation, alarmed by his boss's pallor.

'It's alright, George.' Markham stood up. 'We need to get back to the station right now.' He bowed slightly. 'You'll have to excuse me, ladies. Duty calls.'

'I'll get your coat.'

Out in the hallway, Olivia leaned into him.

'What is it, Gil?'

*'I know, Liv. I know who the killer is!'*

## 14. BEYOND ANYONE'S REACH

'*Nah, guv.*' Noakes was obdurate. 'Not Gailey. I mean . . . if you'd said Julian — sorry, *Jules* — Hoskinson, I might buy it . . . But you're barking up the wrong tree. Gailey's kosher . . . respectable solicitor . . . plays dominoes with the vicar, for God's sake.'

'Mah-jong.'

'Same difference. Anyway, we've all seen him . . . good-looking bloke for his age an' nice with it . . . everyone likes him . . . used to visit Marian Bussell an' all. *Nah.*' The DS wasn't having it. 'No way Sidney'll wear this . . . not to mention Professor Fanakerpan.'

Markham had hurriedly convened a council of war in CID. The outer office was deserted, a trail of half-eaten mince pies and assorted sweet treats providing clear evidence that their fellow officers had started the weekend early. Everywhere was hushed and still. Only a cleaner, dull-eyed and incurious, moved from desk to desk emptying bins and wiping surfaces.

'What makes you think it's Gailey, sir?' Burton asked cautiously.

'Something one of my neighbours said this evening about Gailey giving a talk to the local women's group about vintage jewellery.'

Instinctively, the DI knew not to mention that the Noakeses had been dining at The Sweepstakes. Hearing that her fellow DS had such privileged access would only hurt Kate Burton. Noakes, quick on the uptake, understood and said nothing.

'So he knows about antiques, boss,' Doyle too was unconvinced. 'But that's not unusual, is it? Retired . . . money to burn . . . er, cultured.' He didn't dare look at Noakes whose lips were forming the word *poofy*.

'It was the way my . . . friend . . . spoke about him.'

Markham was finding it difficult to articulate how things had suddenly crystallized in his mind.

'She was talking about his matinée idol looks — almost as though he was Rudolph Valentino — said he was like a silent movie star. And I remembered looking at Gailey during the memorial service . . . thinking there was something classical, almost Grecian, about his profile . . . those wings of silver hair swept back from the temples . . . It hit me suddenly that he was the spit of that fey-looking girl in Dan MacAlinden's photograph album.'

*Rudolph Valentino. Grecian profile. Silver wings. Christ, the guvnor couldn't be having a mid-life crisis, could he? The way he was talking, it sounded like he was thinking of batting for the other side. And where did that leave Olivia . . .*

'Easy, Noakesy.' Markham could read him like a book. 'This DI's not for turning. Nothing like that.'

Beetroot-red, Noakes muttered, 'I didn't mean ter imply . . . It's jus' . . .'

'I know, I know.' His sudden panegyric about Gailey's charisma had taken them by surprise.

Noakes had found his second wind. 'Okay, so Gailey's got a touch of the Fred Astaire about him . . . don' make him a murderer,' he said stubbornly.

'I think Gailey is a transgender male, Noakes . . . one who passionately wishes he could revert to his former state.'

Complete silence for several minutes.

'But *why*, guv?' Noakes was genuinely trying to understand. 'Why'd he — she — want to cross over in the first place?'

'It's likely we'll never know, Sergeant.' The DI's face darkened momentarily. 'Perhaps she was sexually abused as a child. Or maybe for a time she just felt she'd been born into the wrong body . . . wanted for whatever reason to become a different person . . . take on a different identity.'

Noakes swallowed hard.

'D'you reckon she went the full monty then, guv?' He looked embarrassedly at Kate Burton whose composure was impenetrable. 'Got a set of the full tackle?'

'Mary Atkins said Martine opted to seek surgical treatment . . . so it sounds like the full female-to-male transition did pan out. It just didn't make him happy.'

'An' then . . . he wanted to . . . cross back?' Noakes ruffled his hair wildly, so that it stood up in all directions, the wayward tufts ample testament to his confusion.

'I think he wanted to reverse it, yes. But he couldn't wave a magic wand—'

'Or maybe he was afraid detransitioning would be even more harrowing than the first lot of surgery.' Burton was starting to come round to the theory.

'What a frigging mess.' Despite himself, Noakes was sympathetic. 'Imagine living like that . . . not knowing if you're animal, vegetable or mineral . . .'

It was an odd way of putting it, but the DS was now so far out of his comfort zone as to be practically on another planet, therefore allowances needed to be made.

Doyle pressed, 'But what about the alibis. Weren't Gailey's solid?'

'Weak for Mrs Bussell and Ms MacAlinden.' With Burton it was a case of virtually instant recall. 'Over at the Ledwidges playing cards or whatever, but that finished around three and then he was just watching telly.'

'What about the others, Kate?'

Ms Spreadsheet happily obliged. 'For Dowell, he was supposedly tucked up in bed — so worth zilch. With Stacey, there was a window of opportunity before the residents headed off down Chapel Street . . . Could've done Ledwidge too . . . with the end-of-term chaos at Hope, people were floating about no questions asked.'

'Didn't you say Gailey went round drama and music with Hoskinson, sarge?' Doyle's expression was intent as he wrestled with the coordinates.

'The concert started at half eight.' Concentration puckered Burton's brow. 'Before that, there was the open-evening arrangement with visitors pretty much free to roam. And folk from the close joined in . . . looking at different departments, touring classrooms, admiring kids' work, that kind of thing.' She traced concentric circles on Markham's desk with her fingertips, reasoning it through. 'Now, we know Ledwidge arrived early—'

'To meet the killer.'

'That's right, sarge . . . The killer knew Ledwidge had suddenly recognized him at Eileen's tea party and sent a text suggesting they met up at Hope . . . When Ledwidge got that text, he raced straight off to the school . . . If the killer had somehow blagged his way in, he could have done the business, waited until the open evening got underway and then blended in with everyone else . . . When Gailey popped up in drama and music, people most likely assumed he'd been there all along or wandered over from another part of the building . . . No one'd realize he'd been hidden away in the art block all that time . . .'

Doyle frowned. 'You could say the same for the rest of them, though . . . I mean, no one's sure who arrived when cos that receptionist didn't bother with the signing-in book and just swiped folk through.'

*Dopey bint*, thought Noakes.

Burton sighed. 'Yes . . . None of the residents' faces meant anything to her and we drew a blank with the student volunteers. So there's nothing to say one of the others couldn't have pulled it off . . . met Ledwidge, killed him and then melted back into the crowd.'

'I don't think it was any of the others.' Markham's voice was quietly certain. 'Jeff Coleman would have attracted too much attention—'

'Yeah, too bleeding risky him having a Lazarus moment an' legging it to the art block,' Noakes agreed.

'Whoever made that appointment with Ledwidge had the confidence — the chutzpah — to count on being able to smooth-talk his way into the school.'

*Such a sweetheart.* Muriel Noakes's words echoed in Markham's ears.

'I don't see Julian Hoskinson having the presence of mind for that, but Gailey is suave.' There was something infectious about the DI's enthusiasm. 'I believe he wangled his way inside somehow, then slipped into the art block, laid his hands on a set of keys . . . or, most likely, found the annexe unlocked and sneaked inside before texting Ledwidge to say where he was.'

'What about the doc or lover boy . . . What's to say *they* didn't think of it?' Noakes's tone conveyed the impression that where Martin Henley was concerned, anything was possible.

'But where's the motive, Noakesy? And anyway, even supposing they wanted Ledwidge dead, medics are always afraid of being bothered when they're "in civvies".' In much the same way he dreaded being collared when off-duty.

'Yeah.' Noakes chuckled. 'Like when some poor sod on the plane hears "Is there a doctor on board?"'

Burton saw the logic. 'A sort of Good Samaritan complex . . . You're worried a patient's going to pop up from somewhere . . . or there'll be a medical emergency out of the blue when you just want to keep your head down and mind your own business.'

'Exactly. Medical professionals are too *get-at-able* . . . patients and ex-patients potentially lurking round every corner. It's one reason why so many of them develop a God complex.' Markham suspected Martin Henley possessed this quality in abundance. 'Whereas a middle-aged retired solicitor need have no fears on that score.'

Noakes conceded the point. 'Stands to reason . . . if them two wanted to top Ledwidge, they'd be more likely to do it in the loony bin . . . then frame one of the fruit an' nuts for it.'

Doyle stole a sly look at Burton, but she bore the political incorrectness with stoical resignation. One day the diversity squad would catch up with her colleague, but until then . . .

'There's another thing,' she said. 'I just don't see them for the ritual stuff . . . the positioning of the two women and dressing Ledwidge up like that . . .'

'Cos they're medical?' Noakes sounded combative. 'There's serial killers who were doctors and nurses, you know.'

'Right, sarge. But that pair . . . they're just too chilly and self-contained . . . almost antiseptic . . .'

'Yeah, the kind who'd go for something clean and tidy . . . poisoning or an overdose,' Doyle concurred.

'And neither of them fits Dan MacAlinden's photograph of Dawn's friend,' Markham pointed out. The girl whose name began with an S. Now, like Burton earlier, he was restlessly tracing patterns on his desk. 'It bothered me when I saw that picture. It reminded me of someone. Of course it was Simon Gailey . . . fine-boned . . . silver-haired . . . oh, I don't know, the facial structure and something about the eyes.' All thanks to Muriel Noakes, he thought. 'And then there was the make-up compact. It's the kind of thing I can imagine *Gailey* picking out but not the others . . .'

'You'll need more'n that for Sidney, guv.' It rather tickled Noakes's fancy to imagine Markham broaching the subject of Gailey's taste in jewellery with the DCI. The fur would fly alright!

'Yes, everything's circumstantial, Noakesy. But taken together . . .'

'There's the name too,' Burton put in helpfully. '*Simi* . . . sounds like a contraction of Simon.'

'What about *Martine*, then?' Noakes was keen to show nothing got past him. 'You could say that's a girl version of *Martin* . . . As in Martin Henley.'

Burton gave him a cool look.

'*I'm jus' saying*!'

'D'you have a copy of that photo Mr MacAlinden showed you, sir?'

'No.' Markham's shoulders sagged. 'He was in such a fragile state emotionally . . . and at that point I hadn't made the connection.'

'If you think she's a dead ringer for Gailey, that's good enough for us, sir.' Doyle nodded vigorous assent.

The DI was touched by their faith in him. He hoped to God he could justify it.

'Mrs Shaw's . . . the psychic's description of the girl she saw matches the photograph—'

'An' she said summat about her being in an operating theatre, remember, guv? With a surgical table an' bright lights an' metal instruments.' Noakes was working himself up into quite a lather. 'That'd fit with having the op to go from girl to boy.'

'Indeed it would, Sergeant. And the bleeding heart that the figure was holding could stand for mutilation of the body as well as the heartbreak of rejection.'

'Yeah, cos she came onto Dawn who didn't want to know.'

'And like Dan MacAlinden, Mrs Shaw mentioned a name beginning with S.'

'The idea of its being *Gailey* . . .' Doyle mused. 'I mean, he was *friends* with them. And what he did to the first three . . .' The DC wrenched open his shirt's top button as if he was suddenly too hot. 'Sorry, sir, but I don't care if he made a mistake about transitioning and all that. He's a frigging monster.'

'What d'you reckon put Stacey onto him then, guv?' Noakes looked to Markham as the man with all the answers.

'Who can say?' Markham was sombre. 'I remember you commenting that she looked as though she had a hot date when she was talking to us after the memorial service . . . and she'd been eyeing Gailey up inside the church. I should have realized she had come across something about *him* . . . something that titillated and intrigued her.'

'Maybe it was cross-dressing,' Doyle volunteered. 'Maybe she got a closer look at the woman in the headscarf or saw Gailey browsing women's things . . . pegged him for a transvestite or thought he was kinky,' the DC's glance slid away from Noakes. 'Y'know, into an alternative lifestyle . . . like Eddie Izzard or Grayson Perry.' The expression on his grizzled colleague's face suggested the youngster would be cross-examined on these exotic personalities at some point in the pub.

'Could've thought he was the poison pen.' The possibilities were opening up for Noakes. 'P'raps she saw him putting something through a letterbox or caught him out.'

Burton was enthused now. 'Remember what Hoskinson said about him and Gailey being kindred spirits. He said they'd bonded. Maybe Stacey noticed something. Maybe she saw Gailey at Lili's or in some kind of compromising position . . .'

'Whatever it was Stacey fancied she knew, Gailey was afraid she'd shoot her mouth off and the trail would lead back to him,' Markham said.

'What about Dowell, guv?'

'You said he looked "gobsmacked", Noakesy — that day in the church hall when we were interviewing residents, after we found the women's bodies at number seven . . . like he'd "seen a ghost".'

The DS looked highly gratified at his words having made such an impression. 'Yeah, I remember now. He didn't want to hang about with the rest . . . kept staring round like a zombie. D'you think he had some sort of eureka moment like Ledwidge, then?'

'I think it's possible.' The DI held himself very still, taut with the effort of remembering. 'Dan MacAlinden said Dawn got back into her box after Mr Dowell slapped her down in the LGBT debate. It was obviously a subject that came up from time to time amongst the residents . . . sounded as though emotions ran high. Maybe looking back, Dowell was struck by something Gailey said or how he looked — something he hadn't noticed at the time but remembered after the double murder at number seven.'

'Like what?'

'That's the million-dollar question, isn't it . . . ?' Markham exhaled wearily.

'What if he recognized Gailey from somewhere?'

'Go on, Kate.'

'Dowell's specialism was body dysmorphic disorder — BDD. He was about ten years older than Gailey, so might've come across him as a trainee psychologist or early on when Gailey was having pre-op therapy as Martine.'

'An' it took him all that time to realize he *knew* the bloke?' Noakes was incredulous. 'They were *neighbours*, for chuff's sake. Don' tell me he only worked it out after we found Bussell an' MacAlinden stuffed under that bed!'

'Actually, Sergeant, I think that's quite feasible,' the DI said patiently. 'I didn't see it myself until that photograph and some chance remarks triggered something in my brain.'

'Yeah, but Dowell an' him jogged on together in the same housing estate, guv . . . lived side by side for yonks. What kind of dipstick wouldn't clock that Gailey was someone he'd *treated*!'

'Gailey reinvented himself, Noakes. And did so very convincingly. A confirmed bachelor, but nothing effeminate about him . . . nothing that jarred or struck a false note . . . at least not until things began to unravel.'

'But he didn't stand out as being particularly agitated when it all came out about the murders, boss,' Doyle said. 'Leastways no more than any of the others.'

'Dowell was an experienced psychologist, Constable. He might have picked up on signs that were invisible to an ordinary observer . . . something he *sensed* or some giveaway in the way Gailey behaved.'

'Mother of God. Why didn't he come to us instead of tackling Gailey on his own!'

'Perhaps it was that God complex we were talking about earlier,' the DI said sadly. 'You see, Noakes, I think Mr Dowell — like Brian Ledwidge — may have had an inflated idea of his own "bedside manner".'

'Eh?'

'Both men saw themselves as *healers*, Sergeant, belonging to a higher order of beings, if you like. It would have flattered their egos to imagine they could coax Gailey down from the ledge . . . make him show contrition . . . turn himself in.'

'He was a freaking *serial killer*, guv — a total *nutter*! Which bit of that didn't they get!'

'You said it yourself, sarge,' Doyle riposted. 'On one level, he was their neighbour . . . a *friend* . . . someone they'd known a long time.'

'Which meant they underestimated the pathology.' This was Burton.

'Plus there was the intellectual conceit,' Markham added.

'How d'you mean?'

'Well, remember what Stacey told us about Mr Dowell liking to put people down — "didn't suffer fools, never backed away from a good old ding-dong". I got the impression he could be supercilious . . . dismissive.'

'Oh right, I'm with you. Yeah, sounded like he was up hisself alright. So he woulda seen it like some kind of test . . . to make Gailey blub an' say he was sorry?'

'Exactly. He would have been fascinated by it as a case-study as well,' Markham said slowly. 'Most likely he wanted to hear the full story.'

'Stacey said Dowell *respected* Gailey.'

'That's right, Noakes. Which makes me suspect he saw himself as being up against a worthy opponent in terms of intellect.'

'What a fuckwit.' Which, Markham supposed, was one way of looking at it.

'There was the Rohypnol too, so his defences would have been lowered.' Burton shivered as though mentally transported back to those desolate playing fields.

'I doubt we'll ever know the full truth, but I think Mr Dowell saw the rendezvous as a trial of strength.' And emerged the loser.

'D'you remember when we first went to see the Ledwidges, guv? We thought summat was bothering the Rev . . . making him twitchy.'

'Yes, that's right. He was uncomfortable.'

'Mebbe he was on to Gailey — had his suspicions — an' then when he saw him at the tea-party thingy with the rest of 'em, it clicked . . .' Noakes was hitting his stride. 'His missus said he did a shot-in-the-back face like he'd seen a ghost, so she thought he was having a funny turn.'

'Correct.'

'Mr Ledwidge had come straight from visiting Dan MacAlinden,' Markham said. 'He was likely shown the photograph album . . . would have had those pictures of the young Dawn and her friend in his mind . . . then something — a turn of the head, a gesture, a look, a trick of the light catching his hair — *something* alerted him to Gailey's real identity.' The DI breathed more rapidly. 'That's how it went, I'm *sure* of it. With Mr Dowell and Stacey their suspicions were somehow aroused by Gailey's behaviour, but in Brian Ledwidge's case it was that photograph of the two schoolgirls . . . two teenagers who were once best friends.'

'I still can't get my head round Gailey living alongside them all that time and no one having a clue.' Doyle jiggled restlessly in his seat, perturbed. 'I mean, Bussell was his *teacher* at Hope . . . and he used to be best friends with Dawn MacAlinden.'

'Marian Bussell was an elderly lady and Dawn her middle-aged friend. I doubt *I'd* recognize people from school after all that time,' Markham pointed out.

'And don't forget, Gailey was a transgender male,' Burton added, 'no matter how much he might have wanted it otherwise.' She looked earnestly round at her colleagues. 'We know from Mary Atkins that he wanted to detransition . . . but it hadn't worked out and Gailey was stuck with secondary sex characteristics, so he got on with living as a male. He was a million miles removed from pathetic little Martine Knowlson and successful to boot . . . a retired solicitor interested in antiques. What could be more respectable and reassuring?'

'Let's face it,' the DI declared, 'none of *us* cottoned on to who he really was. And we're trained to notice details. On the surface, Gailey comes over as intelligent, urbane, highly civilized—'

'"In touch with his feminine side" alright,' Noakes couldn't resist interjecting.

'Quite, Sergeant, and therefore attractive and unthreatening to women.'

'When in reality . . .' Burton shivered again.

'Yes, Kate. He is exceptionally dangerous.'

'How could he have *waited* so long?' Doyle's restlessness was back.

'I imagine he derived considerable satisfaction from the fact that he was — what do they call it? — *hiding in plain sight* . . . He would have enjoyed the feeling of superiority it gave him as well as *savouring* the prospect of the two women's reactions when they found out who he really was.' Markham paused. 'In the meantime, the prowling and hate mail afforded him a sort of safety valve.'

'How did he expect to get away with it?' Burton murmured.

'He very nearly did, Kate. It was his bad luck that things spiralled out of control with the other residents . . . and that Dawn's widower kept that book of mementoes.'

'Yeah, Martine Knowlson was dead an' buried.' Markham flinched at the unfortunate phrase but Noakes bulldozed on. 'No paper trail — he knew how to take care of that side with being a lawyer — an' as for what happened at Hope . . . well, it was all ancient history. That no-mark Atkins only fessed up cos she got freaked out.'

*Hubris*, thought Markham. Gailey had overshot himself thinking that he had all the residents in his pocket . . . in their different ways, Dowell, Stacey and Ledwidge had proved combustible as gunpowder.

The hum of the vacuum cleaner in the outer office had long since ceased.

Markham's room was feeling even chillier than when the team had arrived, the harsh strip lighting turning them into pallid spectres.

'What happens now?' Burton spoke for them all.

Markham rose and walked to his window. Outside, the lights of the town centre cast their lurid phosphorescent glow while a distant throb testified to festive high jinks being in full swing. There was something almost fiendish about the metropolitan fleshpots at this time of year. Irrationally he thought, it will be peaceful in St Chad's cemetery on the other side — pure and pristine and perfect.

He was starting to feel light-headed. Better bring this meeting to a close.

'Gailey will keep for tonight,' he said. 'Discreet surveillance on him first thing tomorrow morning.' He thought for a moment. 'I have a feeling he'll be at the LGBT demo.'

'Won't he be more likely to lie low, sir?'

'I don't know what it is, Kate. I just feel he won't be able to stay away.' Drawn like a moth to a flame.

As he said this, in his mind's eye, the DI saw Sidney chastising him for reliance on his 'dangerous flair'.

Noakes must have been visited by a similar intuition. 'What'll you tell the DCI, guv?'

'Nothing for now. We'll cross that bridge when we come to it.'

Sidney's likely reaction to the news that their prime suspect was a respected local solicitor was something he didn't care to imagine.

'D'you reckon he's got any idea we're on to him?'

'I think he might be ready—'

'To throw in the towel?' Doyle burst out eagerly.

'I was going to say, he might want to go out on his own terms.'

'What, like do summat crazy at the demo?' Noakes was startled.

'Possibly.' Markham cast a last look at the cityscape with its infernal penumbra then moved back to his desk. 'He knows we're focusing on the school . . . knows we'll have followed in Ledwidge's footsteps and seen the photograph . . . knows the net's closing.' His voice very quiet, he pronounced what felt curiously like an epitaph. 'Maybe on the brink of the abyss, it's flashes of childhood and bursts of youth, and all he can think of is that untroubled time when he was *whole*.'

Noakes was always wary when the guvnor waxed poetic. Better bring him back to earth pronto. 'So he wants to die cos he thinks that way he'll go back to being whole? An' he figures on taking out a few of the bastards who screwed him over . . . as in them LGBT headbangers . . . ?'

Doyle grinned at the expression on Kate Burton's face as she heard this description of the demonstrators. Looked like something had gone down the wrong the way, he told Noakes afterwards.

'I think it's *possible*, Noakes, so we'll be there watching.'

'Why not just arrest him? What if he lashes out or starts summat?'

'We haven't got enough to make a case. Even with his transgender background, I doubt we'd get it past the CPS . . .' Markham held his palms upwards. 'Okay, so he knew Marian and Dawn back in the day, *so what* . . . ? If he had a fraught history with the two of them, *what of it*? Photographs, hate mail — *phooey* . . . pure coincidence . . .' He held each of their eyes in turn. 'If he's planning a grand gesture of some sort, we may catch him in the act . . . get a confession.'

'That's a big freaking if.'

'We've got to chance it. Right,' the DI was brisk now, 'I'll drop you home, Noakesy.' Unmentioned was the fact that Olivia would have sorted a taxi for Muriel. He turned to Burton and Doyle. 'Did you two drive?'

They nodded in unison.

'Safe journey. I'll see you at seven sharp for the briefing.'

With that, they dispersed and CID returned to darkness.

* * *

In the event, Noakes found the LGBT demo a distinct anti-climax — nothing but earnest commie types with red noses, swaddled in university scarves and banging on through their megaphones about 'minority rights', while various sections of the community glowered at them from a safe distance. Clearly expecting something like the Notting Hill Carnival — frivolous headgear, furbelows, war paint and lots of bare midriffs — he was visibly disappointed.

'No sign of Gailey,' he hissed at Markham during yet another interminable speech by Councillor Penny Callaghan, pink-cheeked and clearly in her element. 'Where's the fuss an' feathers?'

The DI was visibly deflated but replied gallantly enough, 'It's the depths of winter, Noakesy. They're thinking thermals not flimsies and body paint.'

Markham felt as though he had ice water in the pit of his stomach to match the freezing conditions.

Gailey was a no-show.

Could he have gotten it all horribly wrong? Was Sidney right about him being seduced by his own cleverness?

'Let's head back to the incident room,' he said, trying to conceal his dejection from the team.

'I'll go round by the cemetery, sir.' Kate Burton was visibly reluctant to call it a day. 'Maybe he's in there somewhere with the stragglers.'

With that, they split up, Burton heading for Bromgrove South Municipal Cemetery while Markham and the other two trudged despondently back towards New College Close.

Halfway along the route, Markham turned to Doyle. 'Check in with the uniforms outside the close, Constable. I want an update.' The DC duly lagged behind a few steps, fumbling with his radio.

Minutes later, Doyle ran to catch up with them. 'Nothing doing, boss . . . no movement. Just some Mrs Mop, but other than that nada.'

*Mrs Mop.*

'Get back to them, Doyle,' Markham barked. 'I want a description of the woman.'

'What, you mean *the cleaner*?'

'*Yes*!' Markham's expression was dangerous, his eyes emitting sparks.

'Just some woman, guv,' the DC panted after a brief crackling exchange. 'Nothing special. She came outside for a smoke and then went towards the car park . . . bird in a . . .' Suddenly, he stopped.

'In a *headscarf*?' Markham interposed grimly.

'Yes . . . oh *fuck*.' Realization had dawned.

Noakes was already turning round, heading back the way they had come.

'He's dressed as a woman,' was all the DS said as they retraced their steps. 'Thass why we didn't see him.'

'Where will he go, boss?' Doyle was agitated.

'I think we can guess the answer to that, Constable.' Markham looked so haggard that he was almost unrecognizable as CID's resident pin-up. 'Gailey was at the demo watching us . . . and now he's got Kate.'

Noakes's pace quickened perceptibly. It was the climax of the Newman Hospital investigation all over again. Only when it looked like Kate Burton was a goner had her cantankerous counterpart realized how much he rated her. Like some freaking Jiminy Cricket, he couldn't dislodge her from off his shoulder, but he knew that, where the guvnor was concerned, they thought as one.

'She'll be alright, boss' was all he said. 'I've allus said she's the next Cressida Prick — *sorry, Dick*. No scuzzy screwball's gonna stop her getting them pips!'

* * *

Like the DI, Burton enjoyed exploring graveyards and cemeteries.

The bleak contours of Bromgrove South Municipal Cemetery were softened — somehow blurred — by a counterpane of snow, so downy and picturesque it was almost a consolation to think of the town's deceased tucked up carefully under the rows of headstones and monuments . . . at least so long as she didn't remember the roll-call of murder victims who lay there too.

Now she dawdled, enjoying the solitariness . . . the sense of having the place to herself.

There were no stragglers from the demo to be seen and it felt satisfying, like she was the only person on earth.

Her lips quirked.

Apart from the snowwoman.

Stout and uncompromising, it stood just in front of the strange little Norman folly over by the children's memorial garden.

She wandered across for a closer look.

It had a pointy carrot nose and pebbles for the eyes and mouth. As she took in the bright-red jaunty patterned headscarf and shawl, she realized someone had gone to unusual trouble.

She found she couldn't tear her eyes away from the headscarf . . .

The next moment, Burton's world exploded as her face slammed into the snowwoman's torso. She felt blood trickling from her nose and for a moment couldn't breathe, as though her head was enveloped in a suffocating pall.

And then she was yanked backwards by strong arms like steel girders and found herself looking into a face that somehow was and yet wasn't familiar.

Simon Gailey.

His face was so distorted by a snarl that she wondered how anyone could ever have thought him handsome. And the eyes . . . the eyes were those of a man in hell.

'If it isn't Inspector Gilbert Markham's little lackey.' The words were uttered in a crooning, sibilant whisper, so unlike the solicitor's light baritone that she felt her skin crawl. 'The one in the Chairman Mao trouser suits.' His breath was hot on her neck. 'The one scared to dress like a woman. The one in love with her boss but frightened to tell him.' Even in that moment of extreme peril, Burton felt a scorching wave of shame ripple through her like the aftershock from a volcano. She would never forget this psychopath who spoke her secret aloud in a snowbound graveyard.

'Mr Gailey . . . *Martine* . . .' Somehow she got the words out through cracked, chilblained lips. 'There's nowhere left to go . . . It's over.'

The strong arm lay across her throat in a choke hold.

This is how it must have been for Stacey Macmillan, she thought . . . neck stretched back, then crushing pain followed by merciful oblivion.

'I don't want to die,' she whispered.

And suddenly she wanted life with a passion.

The words of an old school poem came into her mind.

*She neither hears nor sees;*
*Rolled round in earth's diurnal course,*
*With rocks, and stones, and trees.*

She wasn't ready for that. Wasn't ready to be forgotten. Wasn't ready to leave the gang. Not yet.

And then she heard the much-loved voice.

'Let her go, Gailey.'

DI Gilbert Markham had come round the other side of the folly with Noakes and Doyle. Her fellow DS made a discreet thumbs-up, piggy eyes fixed on her face as though he would memorize its features.

Markham took a step closer. 'Let her go,' he said very calmly. Then, 'It's been a heavy burden, hasn't it . . . ? Time to lay it down and set yourself free.'

Something clicked in Gailey's throat as though he was trying to speak past some obstruction.

'*Beyond and above you all.*'

There was the flash of a knife. Noakes leaped forward and Burton felt the hot gush of blood. The DS enveloped her in a tight bear hug that showed no sign of slackening.

Meanwhile, the snowwoman watched impassively as crimson stained the white.

* * *

Two days before Christmas Eve, the team and Olivia sat in the backroom of their favourite hostelry, The Grapes.

'Denise needs ter do summat about that godawful carpet in the lounge. Them swirly patterns are enough to give punters a migraine.'

'It'll be a brave man who gives her suggestions about interior decoration, George,' Olivia laughed, eying the bosomy blonde landlady who had just plonked menus in front of them. 'I know Gil's her blue-eyed boy,' she added, in a sly allusion to Denise's shameless favouritism when it came to Markham and his team, 'but I don't see her giving up her fleur-de-lis for anyone.'

Kate Burton sat quietly, sipping her gin and tonic, and enjoying the banter.

Their oak booth was dark and warm and cosy, while the quaintly nautical brasses and copperware had the familiarity of old friends.

'Supper tonight is on the DCI,' Markham announced, only the corners of his mouth giving the lie to his air of solemnity. 'By way of thanks for our sterling efforts in wrapping up the New College Close investigation before Christmas.'

'Thought we'd be saddled with Professor Fanakerpan,' Noakes mumbled.

'Regrettably Professor Macfadyen has another appointment and is unable to join us.'

'I've gotta say it, guv.' A premonitory belch. 'He was a big fat waste of space.'

'Well, we certainly took the wind out of his sails by the end, Noakesy.'

'Yeah. He deffo wasn't expecting it to turn out like that . . . Sidney neither.' The DS lapped up his beer contentedly. 'Wonder how they'll spin the boy-girl thing, though . . . They won't want "tranny town" headlines or owt like that.'

'Oh, if Councillor Callaghan has anything to do with matters, I'm sure by New Year it'll be yesterday's news.'

'A good thing too.' Kate Burton surprised them with her vehemence. 'I felt sorry for Gailey — Martine Knowlson — forced to live a lie . . . her whole life ruined.'

'Don't waste your sympathy, luv. He were in two minds about topping you. An' I reckon only the thought of a lifetime banged up in the loony bin made him cut *his* throat 'stead of yours . . . If we hadn't rocked up . . .' Noakes left the sentence unfinished but shook his head portentously.

Gently, Olivia laid her hand on top of Kate's.

'All that matters is you live to fight another day.'

Their food had arrived and a cheerful bustle banished gloomy thoughts.

* * *

Afterwards, as Olivia and Markham walked home together hand in hand, she turned to her lover. 'George said Simon Gailey whispered something to Kate right at the end before he died, Gil . . . but he was too far away to hear.'

'The trauma means she's blocked it all out.'

Markham had heard those final curses, carried to him on the still air of the cemetery. But he would never breathe a word. And if George Noakes knew, he certainly wasn't telling.

**THE END**

## ALSO BY CATHERINE MOLONEY

## THE DI GILBERT MARKHAM SERIES

Book 1: CRIME IN THE CHOIR
Book 2: CRIME IN THE SCHOOL
Book 3: CRIME IN THE CONVENT
Book 4: CRIME IN THE HOSPITAL
Book 5: CRIME IN THE BALLET
Book 6: CRIME IN THE GALLERY
Book 7: CRIME IN THE HEAT
Book 8: CRIME AT HOME

**FREE KINDLE BOOKS**

Please join our mailing list for free Kindle books and new releases, including crime thrillers, mysteries, romance and more.

www.joffebooks.com

Follow us on Facebook, Twitter and Instagram

@joffebooks

Thank you for reading this book. If you enjoyed it please leave feedback on Amazon or Goodreads, and if there is anything we missed or you have a question about then please get in touch. The author and publishing team appreciate your feedback and time reading this book.

We're very grateful to eagle-eyed readers who take the time to contact us. Please send any errors you find to corrections@joffebooks.com

Printed in Great Britain
by Amazon

61312818R00137